"I'M AN IMPATIENT MAN, BUT I WANT YOU. HOWEVER LONG THAT TAKES IS HOW LONG I WAIT."

Sam looked at her with a mysterious half-smile that left her breathless.

"I thought you would call." Helga moved slowly over to the couch and sat down at the opposite end, kicking off her shoes and tucking her feet under her. "I was so sure you would that sometimes I didn't answer the phone."

She hugged her arms in front of her fuzzy blue sweater in a gesture entirely foreign to her. She was bursting with desire for him. She thought vaguely of the many women who passed through his life, of his political future. None of those things seemed real. All that mattered was Sam—and her decision to take matters into her own hands. . . .

A CANDLELIGHT ECSTASY SUPREME

POLITICS
OF
PASSION

Samantha Hughes

A CANDLELIGHT ECSTASY SUPREME

Published by
Dell Publishing Co., Inc.
1 Dag Hammarskjold Plaza
New York, New York 10017

ISBN: 0–440–16991–7

Printed in the United States of America
First printing—December 1983

To Our Readers:

Candlelight Ecstasy is delighted to announce the start of a brand-new series—Ecstasy Supremes! Now you can enjoy a romance series unlike all the others—longer and more exciting, filled with more passion, adventure, and intrigue—the stories you've been waiting for.

In months to come we look forward to presenting books by many of your favorite authors and the very finest work from new authors of romantic fiction as well. As always, we are striving to present the unique, absorbing love stories that you enjoy most—the very best love has to offer.

Breathtaking and unforgettable, Ecstasy Supremes will follow in the great romantic tradition you've come to expect *only* from Candlelight Ecstasy.

Your suggestions and comments are always welcome. Please let us hear from you.

Sincerely,

The Editors
Candlelight Romances
1 Dag Hammarskjold Plaza
New York, New York 10017

CHAPTER ONE

The long black limousine that glided along the banks of the Potomac River seemed impervious to the crunch of traffic that streamed into the nation's capital. Behind the glass partition that separated her from Senator Mitchell's uniformed chauffeur, Helga Tarr glanced nervously at the delicate gold watch on her pale wrist. Frowning, she leaned her sleek blond head toward the smoky-gray windows of the limousine. Utterly private, encased, entombed—she could see out but *they,* whoever *they* were, could not see in. Somehow that sort of privacy sent an eerie chill up her spine. No doubt the windows were bulletproof as well.

She should have been able to settle in a bit, to enjoy the plush beige interior of the senator's car, which had met her at the airport. But alone in the spacious backseat with its telephone, television, and bar, the silence struck her as ghastly almost, too unreal. She shook her blond head emphatically. Now *ghastly* was a word she never used. She was not given to melodrama or extremes either in her words or in her behavior. But it was ghastly and unreal to be slithering through bumper-to-bumper traffic without hearing a sound. It was not the silence of snow nor the silence of a starry night on the shores of one of the lakes in her home state of Minnesota. It was a new sensation, a silence that made her wary rather than peaceful.

She closed her eyes briefly and her long blond lashes brushed lightly against her high, finely chiseled cheekbones. The paleness of her skin accentuated the impression of sophisticated fragility.

9

Even in repose she possessed an elegance that, had it not been for the exquisite molding of the delicate bones, would perhaps have seemed haughty. As usual her expression remained placid; only an occasional flicker in her pale blue eyes suggested the remotest possibility that she might not be as poised and composed as she seemed. On the surface she seemed quite content and at home in such a hushed, luxurious atmosphere, and anyone seeing the classical simplicity of her navy suit, which she wore with a white silk blouse, would have been inclined to take her for an important dignitary.

The beginning of a new life . . . today was. A new life beginning today. Her eyes flew open and a flicker of annoyance crossed her face for an instant as the litany played and replayed itself inside her head. As if she needed to remind herself that the decision to come to Washington was something of a momentous step for her . . . and she had dreaded it so. And now she was here.

She forced her mind onto professional duties. She was all too keenly aware that her job was her anchor, the one known quantity in a morass of unknowns. Again a frown disturbed her composure and she crossed and uncrossed her long slender legs, annoyed with herself for not being able just to let go, to relish the splendid October sunshine that was so different from the dark snowy morning she had left back home.

No, of course there was no reason to be nervous, no reason at all to feel rushed and harried. She ran her tongue slowly around the outside of her full rosy lips and commanded herself to regain her composure. She was, after all, used to impromptu changes and unexpected contingencies. At the prestigious Minneapolis law firm of Matthews, Matthews, and Stubbs she was valued for her poise, for her unwavering ability to deal serenely and efficiently with any and all crises. She knew perfectly well that her cool, ash-blond sophisticated Scandanavian appearance, the dark tailored clothes she always wore, the fine but understated gold knot earrings and the antique pendant, all contributed to her overall impression: one of absolute control and dignity. She was quite cognizant of the fact that it wasn't only her extraordinary skill as a legal secretary that had prompted Willard Matthews and his partner Kenyon Stubbs to ask her to act as Washington liaison for an impending case with the Northern Railway. She was capable of holding down the fort not simply because of her professional acumen. She was able to hold people off, to gain time and control situations merely by her appearance, by her aloofness. She knew that some people called her an iceberg and that was all right too. She also knew they were wrong.

But today, just when the detachment that people ascribed to her would come in handy, she felt fragmented, untethered, like a craft adrift outside the safe confines of its familiar harbor.

Kenyon Stubbs's last-minute decision not to take the early morning flight to Washington had shaken her. Or perhaps it had been the sound of her name being announced over the public address system at Minneapolis Airport. *Helga Tarr . . . Paging Helga Tarr . . . Will Mrs. Helga Tarr please report to Northwest Airlines immediately.* She had actually blushed. Really, it was ridiculous and she was just thankful there had been no one there to observe her flustered reaction. Imagine a thoroughly independent, intelligent, thirty-three-year-old widow blushing at the sound of her own name.

Helga expelled a loud breath from between her pursed lips and noted with a wry smile that the chauffeur was oblivious to anything she might do. Well, of course she was nervous. She chided herself as she clasped and unclasped her pale hands with their long, tapering fingers and perfect oval-shaped nails. This was her first limousine, her first paging, her first . . .

Her customary serenity was replaced with the flush of excitement. The pale blue eyes, always intelligent, with a questioning, curious steadiness, were lively, their hue deepened by the excitement. Yes, she was excited and afraid to name it that. Better to name it fear, apprehension, nerves . . . anything but excitement.

She had left Minnesota. Not for the first time, but for the first time in many years. The sound of her own name echoing through the air terminal had made it all excruciatingly real for her. She was leaving Minnesota, had left. Yes, of course she would be returning when the case was settled, but that was beside the point. The point, she knew, was that she had finally opted for a change in her life, even if it was only a temporary change, a change more or less dictated by her job.

She glanced at her watch again even though her inner clock told her precisely what time it was. It was a hypocritical habit she disliked in herself. She knew she used the gesture when she was at a loss—usually in uneasy conversations or when she needed an extra moment to arrive at a decision or the right phrase to soothe some distraught client. Yes, the gesture was a habit—a fidgety, superficial habit that reminded her somehow that she was thirty-three years old and that she was beginning to give off the faint, fluttering, cool fragility of a spinster. Aunt Helga.

In a family of five older brothers it sometimes seemed to her that she stood out like a polar island, adrift. She was Aunt Helga to so many nieces and nephews that at some point during the past ten years even her parents had begun referring to her with the dreaded prefix. Aunt Helga. And lately she had begun to feel the dignified cloak of confinement slipping around her and had actually begun thinking of herself in much the same way. The beloved aunt, single and alone . . . despite having once been married.

Most people assumed she had never been married. Not Kenyon Stubbs, of course, or anyone at the office for that matter. But most of the newer clients had by now relegated her to the position of trusted secretary, devoted to the firm, devoted to her three bosses and their families. Even those who had known John Tarr when he had first been taken into the firm as a junior partner had by now probably forgotten the tragic automobile accident that took his life when he was only twenty-eight years old. And surely they had forgotten his wife . . . Helga, a smiling, reticent student in her final year at the university. The poised, competent, stately

12

woman at M M & S bore little resemblence to that wide-eyed blond girl.

The memories held no pain. Despite what her friends in Minneapolis thought, she had not returned to her parents' farm as an escape. She and John had always planned on living in the country, they preferred it. After his death she had merely followed *their* plan, except for going on to law school—something John had encouraged her to do. That had been impossible financially and even emotionally it had seemed too much to ask. When Willard Matthews, the senior partner at Matthews, Matthews, and Stubbs, had offered her a secretarial job, she had seized the opportunity.

The senator's limousine paused at a traffic light and Helga leaned forward to catch her first glimpse of the White House. Its green, velvety lawn was dotted with crimson and gold and several uniformed men were gathering the scuttling leaves into huge piles. The day was mild. She had been surprised at how warm it was and had immediately shed her sheepskin-lined trench coat. The navy suit was more than enough. By afternoon no doubt she would want to shed her jacket as well.

Unable to tolerate the confinement a moment longer, Helga leaned over to roll down the window and sniff the heady October breeze that rustled the leaves and sent them spinning out along Pennsylvania Avenue. How strange that the air seemed almost tropical . . . or in any case what her memory of "tropical" was. There had been two trips with John . . . a honeymoon to St. Thomas and an earlier trip that no one knew of—a secret rendezvous in Fort Lauderdale before she and John were married.

A soft smile crossed her face at the sweetness of the memory. She had been only nineteen. John, at twenty-four, had been the older man, just graduated from law school at the top of his class. They were engaged, but still her family would have been shocked at the idea of their quiet, studious daughter spending a long weekend with her fiancé. No one had ever guessed and in all the intervening years Helga had cherished those five secret hideaway days above all else . . . It was oddly consoling to know that her love for John had been so sure, so deep and committed that even at nineteen she had been willing to put convention aside, to trust and to find joy as it was offered. How many times since his death had she thanked God that she had taken those five days? In retrospect she understood more fully than most that each day was precious, that time may be nothing more than an illusion, and that happiness must be seized.

Something stirred inside her and she rolled the window back up and moved to the center of the backseat. Technically she was not expected at the office until tomorrow. Willard had specified that she was to take the day off, get settled and play the tourist. He had insisted that even with Kenyon's change in plan there was no need for Helga to work on her first day in town.

Helga ran her hand through her thick blond hair, which fell just below her forthright chin in a perfectly straight cut. She'd worn it in just such a utilitarian cut since John had pointed out to her that anyone with her high cheekbones and classic strong jawline would be a fool to waste their time on curls. How many women, he had asked, could afford such neglect and still look beautiful? Helga smiled, remembering. The haircut suited her. It suited her not to feel obligated to changing styles, and as far as she was concerned this was her haircut . . . This was *it* for the rest of her life. She had been fortunate to find the right style on her own and doubly fortunate to have her opinion affirmed by a man whose integrity in all matters had been something of an inspiration to her.

How odd that she was thinking of John so strongly today when for the past few years, in the very places they had spent so much time together, she was often free of all the memories.

When the chauffeur stopped at the next intersection, Helga tapped lightly on the glass partition.

"You know, I think I'll just hop out along here." Her voice was low and wispy. A good "phone voice" she had been told.

14

"You have my friend's address. If you could just drop my luggage off and tell Mrs. Sell I'll be along in an hour or so?"

"Right." The chauffeur smiled and before Helga could protest he jumped out of the car and held the door open for her.

She smiled graciously. Anyone seeing the tall, slender woman emerging from the limousine would have thought her accustomed to such luxury.

"You know where you're going?" the chauffeur asked. "You have a map and all?"

Helga nodded and patted her leather handbag. "I've come prepared. Michelin green guides, Chamber of Commerce maps . . . I have them all. And thank you for all your help. Please, tell Senator Mitchell how much I appreciate this. I'm sure Mr. Stubbs will be phoning him the minute he arrives."

Now what? The minute the limousine disappeared around the corner Helga was seized by the same unfamiliar feelings of confusion and bewilderment. Marilyn would be expecting her. She really should have gone ahead in the car. Good heavens, she had never felt such indecision in her life.

She stood at the corner of Pennsylvania Avenue and Twenty-third Street and studied one of the small maps that she had tucked into her neat, orderly handbag. Willard had said she should enjoy herself, but all she could think of was sliding into a desk chair and losing herself in the legal jargon that she found so comforting.

Ridiculous, she told herself as she turned down Twenty-third Street and headed for Massachusetts Avenue. She should be eager to seek out all of the cultural opportunities—the Smithsonian, the National Museum of American Art. The city offered limitless possibilities, yet all she could think of was familiarizing herself with what would be her new office for the next six months. How was it possible that back home on the farm she had felt such hunger, such anticipation for the long hours she would spend at the National Air and Space Museum, the Hirshhorn Museum and Sculpture Garden? For weeks prior to her departure she had poured over guidebooks, injesting the most minute details as if she were preparing for an examination. She had made a long list of particular paintings she would visit, of private homes that exhibited notable architectural details. She knew, for instance, that a certain stucco-covered manor house on Cathedral Avenue was built in 1800 by an uncle of Francis Scott Key, who spent a great deal of time there before writing "The Star-Spangled Banner." Her mind was bursting with details and obscure facts. She had, over the course of several months, become a veritable scholar on the nation's capital. Yet finding herself there on this sparkling, ideal October morning, she could think of one thing only.

Work. The safety provided by the typewriter and the telephone. The security offered by immersing herself in the needs of others. As her sensible navy heels clicked against the sidewalk, she found herself wondering to her dismay if Kenyon had made the ten-o'clock flight or if he was coming on the one o'clock.

She had left her parents' farm while it was still dark. She thought of her father crunching through the snow to feed the cows, just as he had done every morning of his adult life. Inside her mother and sister-in-law, with customary Scandanavian reticence, had moved soundlessly around the kitchen as if this day were no different from any other. Even the children, Helga's nieces and nephews, had seemed nonplussed by the luggage stacked in the corner of the kitchen.

But beneath the surface? Helga paused to stare at a large edifice with a bronze plaque identifying it as the Turkish Embassy. Beneath the surface, inside her mother's mind and her father's, the emotions ran deep. She knew they had worried about her after John's death, knew that as much as they loved having her back at home, they also recognized that it would be far better for her to begin to reach out, to move out into society. They kept their thoughts to themselves, as did everyone in her family.

As I do, she thought as she moved on down the street. But

16

solitude was essential to her. She had gravitated toward it for as long as she could remember, and despite what people said she had not retreated into isolation after John's death. She had always preferred a good book to a large cocktail party, a concert to a dance. She needed to jog through the icy woods before climbing into her car and driving into the city. John had understood that. Perhaps more than anyone he had recognized that it wasn't shyness or lack of confidence that made her retreat into a quiet study at large gatherings. Nor did she dislike people. On the contrary, her tastes in people were broad and unexpected. She might find herself as easily and deeply in conversation with a salesgirl or a janitor as with one of the enterprising young attorneys who passed through her life. She was drawn to people not because of who they were or what they did, but because of a response within herself, a click that would sometimes open her up quite without warning.

Marilyn Sell was one of those people who affected her that way. Helga smiled, thinking of her loud, boisterous friend. What an unlikely match they made. But from the instant they had met during their freshman year at the University of Minnesota, they had been as close as the best of sisters. She and Marilyn had roomed together until Marilyn had dropped out of school. For the past ten years Marilyn had besieged Helga with glowing letters of her life in Washington, urging Helga to abandon her icy Minnesota existence.

Well, she must, despite the crazy, confused nervousness she felt, be ready for a change. Her decision to stay with Marilyn and her family had definitely sealed her social fate for the next several months. Marilyn was nothing if not a social butterfly and even though her husband, Neal, held a modestly important job at the Justice Department, Marilyn had somehow managed to become a magnet for Washington society.

Helga tilted her face up to the sun and smiled, thinking of Marilyn, her gabby good nature, her obsession with food both as a cook and as a consumer. Who else but Marilyn would drop

17

out of college at the end of her junior year to fly to Paris and study cooking at the Cordon Bleu? No, her decision to stay with the Sells clearly indicated that solitude was not part of the Washington Plan!

Her stomach gave a sudden lurch at the idea of being thrust out into society. Perhaps it had been too long. Only briefly in all of her thirty-three years had she totally emerged from her shadowy existence, and that was during her marriage to John. Before John, as the only female in a family of five strapping agriculturally minded brothers, Helga had all but mastered the art of silence, hiding her ambition to become an attorney, knowing that such ambitions from a girl would be considered pretentious, not to mention unrealistic. But as conversation in her family was minimal, and since she had earned enough money to attend the university on her own, no one questioned her motives. It was assumed she would become a teacher. It was taken for granted that anyone as singularly quiet and unobtrusive as Helga could not possibly harbor any grand ambitions.

She stopped abruptly as she came upon the famous Buffalo Bridge at the corner of Q Street and Twenty-third. With its stone balustrade and solid masonry it was, just as the guidebooks had told her, reminiscent of a Roman aqueduct. She chuckled softly to herself as she sought out the massive buffalo that guarded the approach to the bridge. Willard would be proud of her for following his advice to do a bit of sight-seeing.

But only *a bit* of sight-seeing. By the time she had crossed the bridge and discovered Marilyn's Georgetown street, she was once again impatient to be ensconced in her new office.

The federal-style mansions that lined the block were exactly as she had imagined them—elegant brick edifices surrounded by tall sycamores whose leaves were just beginning to fall. She spotted Marilyn's house immediately. It was different from the rest, a four-story town house, restrained and aristocratic with a touch of French flavor reminiscent of the pictures she had seen of the houses in St. Germain on the fashionable Left Bank of

Paris. The deep red brick was offset by working green shutters at every window. The sense of privacy was enhanced by an ironwork gate that led to a small brick-paved courtyard still lush and verdant with blooming roses. The house had been in Marilyn's family for years, and though she had seen pictures of it, nothing had prepared her for the truly elegant grandeur. Only a bike rack peering out behind a fat magnolia tree identified the estate as a twentieth-century home.

"You're here!" Helga had no sooner placed her index finger on the door bell than the wide green door flew open and Marilyn, her dark hair frizzed within an inch of its life, came flying outside to embrace her.

"Let me look." Marilyn wiped her floury hands on her smudged oversized chef's apron and stood back to gaze at Helga. "You haven't gained an ounce." She flounced her frizzed head and placed her hands firmly on her ample hips.

Helga laughed and her smooth sophistication gave way to an expression so radiant and genuine that her face seemed utterly transformed. "You're baking. I might have known. I hope it's nothing that will fall."

"Cookies, pies, cakes." Marilyn put her arm through Helga's and led her straight through the elegant marble foyer into the huge kitchen redolent with sweet, seductive aromas.

"You're going to fatten me up?" Helga's blue eyes twinkled as she looked at her small, stout friend.

"I fatten everyone up." Marilyn laughed. "Mostly myself. Thank heavens the children are all thin. Neal's thin . . . they take after him. I just keep stuffing him year after year and he just stays skinny as ever. The perfect marriage. What would I have done if I'd married a man who was always watching his weight? I'd be divorced or busy having affairs. As it is I'm too busy cooking."

Helga laughed and shook her head. It was always this way with Marilyn. No matter how infrequently they saw each other, they just seemed to pick up a conversation as if it had been in progress. They simply jumped in with each other, each feeling completely at home and at ease.

"Now listen." Marilyn dashed to the large restaurant stove to check the oven. "People in Washington think I'm in my late twenties . . ."

"You expect me to lie about my age?" Helga teased. "Why not just say I was an *older* friend at school?"

"Oh, we're going to have fun!" Marilyn turned to her with a flushed face. "Helga, this is the best thing that could have happened to you. I didn't think a bomb could rout you out of the polar place. You don't look a day older than you did when . . . When did I see you last?"

"Five years ago." Helga picked up a spatula and helped remove some delectable puffy cookies from a hot cookie sheet.

"I couldn't believe it when some chauffeur rang the bell and said he had your luggage."

"I'm sorry," Helga apologized. "I had a sudden urge to walk and Senator Mitchell sent his car to pick up Kenyon Stubbs . . . Kenyon wasn't on the flight so he got me. I should have called but . . ."

"Don't apologize." Marilyn put her spatula aside and looked pointedly at Helga. "Now . . . you're not here as a guest. We have to understand that from the start. You don't have to phone home if you're going to be late for dinner or if you're going to stay out all night."

Marilyn gave her a wicked look that brought a sudden rush of color to Helga's cheeks.

"Blushing!" Marilyn exploded. "You can still actually blush? Oh, they're going to love you in this town, Helga. An honest-to-God intelligent woman who's not a namby-pamby and still blushes? My dear, you'll have them panting!"

Once again Helga was reduced to laughter. "What else can I do? Shall I help with the rest of this batter?"

"You'll mess your suit . . . Sure! Here's one of my fancy aprons." Marilyn tossed Helga a clean white apron and rushed on. "Like I said the guest house is yours." She gestured wildly to three high arched windows at the far side of the kitchen. Outside another garden was still miraculously blooming with great orange marigolds. A narrow brick walk led to a small stone ivy-covered structure.

"It's beautiful." Helga walked over to the window and stared out. The little stone guest house, a former ice house and root cellar, was just as Marilyn had described it—quaint and lovely and completely removed from the main house.

"Now I know you, Helga." Marilyn joined her at the window and stood with one leg thrust out to the side. "You'll feel obligated to do all sorts of things . . . baby-sit, read to the children, mend the linen . . . God knows what! But you mustn't. I don't want you playing Aunt Helga around me! You must come and go exactly as you please and my feelings won't be hurt if I don't see you for days at a time. I know you must have your privacy. Promise?"

Helga put her arm around Marilyn and hugged her. An unexpected lump formed in her throat, but she could not swallow it. She had the strangest sensation that something was slipping away, as if she had been outfitted in layers and layers of clothes that were magically floating off of her body, leaving her free . . . but at the same time terribly exposed.

"It's been a long time." Marilyn's voice was sympathetic.

"I've been thinking so much of John today." Helga felt tears spring to her eyes. "It's not as if I've been in mourning all these years but today . . ."

"You're starting a new life," Marilyn offered softly.

"I'm just here for a time." Helga shook her head. "Just until the case is tied up . . ."

"Some people say if you have a perfect marriage it's easier to go on. I'm not sure that's true." Marilyn perched on a stool. "John was an incredible man . . . as you know. The two of you were alike in so many ways. I'd say if you were the most quiet person I've ever known John was the second."

21

Helga smiled softly as Marilyn went on. It was good to talk about John. Her family and most of her friends in Minnesota were so careful about mentioning him, as if Helga would shatter at the sound of his name when the truth was she enjoyed talking about him.

"Anyway, I don't subscribe to the theory that just because you've really loved someone it's easier to find someone else. Nothing is easy in love, or very little, and so much depends on timing."

Marilyn paused and considered Helga a moment. "However, I would have to say you've done your damnedest *not* to meet anyone. Are there any men in your life at all?"

"You're so subtle." Helga's mouth twitched in amusement.

"Well?" Marilyn leaned forward eagerly.

"Of course there are men." Helga replied enigmatically.

"Anyway, I know the answer." Marilyn bounded back across the kitchen and resumed her baking. "The answer is you probably *allow* an occasional male to escort you to some string quartet or some hideous chamber music concert where the atmosphere is about as romantic as a dentist's office. There's no one special, right?"

Helga nodded. "I have no objections, you know it's just . . ."

"Just that—" Marilyn broke off with a shocked expression. "You must be horny as hell!"

"You're impossible!" Helga jumped off the stool, grabbed a dish towel, and threw it at her friend. If she wanted a decorous, circumspect companion she'd come to the wrong place.

"I know." Marilyn looked pleased as she popped another cookie sheet into the oven and set the timer. "Well, you're in the right town—one of the few towns in the country where men outnumber women."

"I'm here to work," Helga reminded her wryly.

"As long as you come to my dinner party next week. That's the only obligation you have."

"I promise." Helga began removing the dirty dishes from the marble-top island in the center of the kitchen.

"No, no, no," Marilyn restrained her. "I have a housekeeper, Libbie Marsdale, you'll meet her. Did I tell you I'd started a business? That's what all this cooking's about."

Helga shook her head in disbelief. Nothing Marilyn did should surprise her but somehow everything always did.

"I'm partners with another woman." Marilyn unlocked the back door and motioned for Helga to follow her. "Lauren Richards, you'll meet her too. We distribute all of our wonderful recipes through a little gourmet shop at Watergate. We're making a bundle!"

"That's wonderful!" Helga enthused. "Maybe you can use my old Swedish Yule bread recipe."

"Not on your life!" Marilyn laughed. "You're a whiz at the piano but stay outa the kitchen!"

Helga went out into the back garden as Marilyn ran back inside to answer the phone. The contrast between the chaotic fullness of Marilyn's life and the meticulous order of her own existence was incredible. Yet she loved the stark cold winters in her native state, loved the extremes of the seasons and the special silence of long snowy nights. She ran her hand over the upturned curly face of a lemony marigold and touched her fingers to her nose to enjoy its fragrance as she moved to the door of the stone cottage. Marilyn's voice faded as she opened the door and moved inside.

The cottage was one large room, rustic, with heavy wood beams, but well-appointed with a large oriental rug in deep crimson tones. There were delicate lace curtains at the windows, a large fireplace with a raised hearth and a place for storing wood underneath. There were two large couches, nicely worn, one in a deep beige velvet, the other in a colorful French provincial print of blue and red. As she sank down into one of the couches she closed her eyes.

The silence that surrounded her was of a different sort than the silence of the snow, but it was silence nonetheless. Even with the door open she couldn't hear Marilyn chattering away in the kitchen. Only an occasional twitter of a bird broke the quiet. Yes, the silence seemed *old* to her and filled with history as if the stone cottage held many secrets.

Silly, she told herself as she stood up to acquaint herself with other details. There was a nice round oak table and four chairs, a small pullman-type kitchen that she knew without looking would be fully equipped to do any cooking she would be doing, which meant tea in the morning, an occasional soft-boiled egg, and perhaps some popcorn. She would have to tell Marilyn that she had completely mastered one culinary feat: popcorn. It had been years since she had had to throw away the pot because of charred hulls.

On one side of the rectangular room was a loft with a king-size bed covered with a beautiful old quilt in shades of violet and blue. Helga stared at the bed and the same bewilderment she had experienced in the limousine again swept over her. Her bed at home was narrow and plain. It occurred to her now that her life was the same.

"Lunch!" Marilyn burst in just as she was climbing back down the ladder. "Can you have lunch with me? I'm taking you to the most fabulous—"

Marilyn broke off, reading the answer in Helga's face. "You're going to say you have to work."

"I do." Helga glanced nervously at her watch. Such a despicable habit and what better time to begin breaking herself of it?

"I don't *have* to," she admitted ruefully. "But I would feel better. I would love lunch one day. It would be wasted on me today. I feel like I have to keep on the move somehow."

"I understand." Marilyn bobbed her head. "My feelings aren't hurt. But you can't say no to the man I want to introduce you to. His name is Jacques Moreau and he's with the French embassy. He's perfect . . . not too French, very very intelligent,

24

he loves music, likes to ski, and for a Frenchman he's a man of few words."

"Okay." Helga laughed.

"You mean it?" Marilyn was incredulous.

"I'm open to new adventures." Helga felt her stomach tighten as she ran a comb through her blond hair, checked her watch again, and headed for the door.

But she wasn't open and she knew it. Walking along the narrow cobblestone streets of Georgetown on her way to the M M & S offices, she was aware of a great emptiness in her life. With a chill it occurred to her that had she never left Minnesota, she might never have noticed it; she might have noticed it when it was too late.

She was dissatisfied. Not with her job or her preferences for quiet and music and books, but with the tight, overly organized woman she had become. And it wasn't that she envied Marilyn her house and her children, her husband and now her vastly successful business. No, she was truly happy for Marilyn. But some part of herself, of Helga Tarr, was missing. There was something she had lost.

It would be easy to say she had lost a beloved husband, a man who had valued her and encouraged her as her own family had not. But she was not a self-indulgent woman. In theory, she did not believe in suffering and grief. Marilyn was right about the men in her life. They were there of course, but neatly confined, ordered as precisely as the row of sharp yellow pencils in the top middle drawer of her desk back in Minneapolis.

The temporary M M & S law office was on the third floor of a modest brownstone just off DuPont Circle, within easy walking distance of Marilyn's Georgetown residence. The moment Helga opened the door and saw the back of Willard Matthews's white head she felt more like her old self.

"I told you to stay away." Willard, a grandfatherly, rather

nineteenth-century gentlemen in his mid-sixties greeted her with a peck on the cheek.

"There were two depositions I didn't have time to retype before I left the office yesterday." Helga glanced around the shabby surroundings trying to decide which desk would be hers. Willard had warned her that the temporary quarters would bear little resemblance to the sumptuous Minneapolis offices.

"I told you it was primitive." Willard chuckled.

"You were right." Helga slipped off her jacket and threw him a smile. The outer office consisted of bare wood floors, two dusty desks with rickety swivel chairs, and a coat rack that teetered when she approached it.

"I meant it about taking the day off." Willard regarded her with a kindly smile.

"I know. I took as much time as I needed. I'm all settled in." Helga slid behind the larger of the two desks.

"I think you'll be better off in here." Willard gestured to one of two doors that opened off the outer office. "Kenyon and I will be flying back and forth. Our paths won't cross that often and we can share the other office. You'll want to hire an assistant. Tate Brown has some suggestions, but I'll leave the final choice up to you. Tate! Come meet our angel."

Helga forced an uneasy smile. Of course Willard meant no harm by calling her an angel, but every time he used the term, especially in front of other people, something in her tightened. Angels were too perfect, above earthly pleasures, beautiful, perhaps, but untouchable. Was that how people thought of her? Well, she thought wryly, it was better than being thought of as a robot. She was still one step ahead of the computers. And at least no one in the office had started calling her Aunt Helga!

"I'm the angel." Helga extended her hand to the dark-haired man who entered the cubbyhole office that was to be hers.

"And I'm Tate Brown." He clasped Helga's hand firmly and his dark eyes searched her face more intently than she would have liked. "Willard said you were beautiful."

Helga met his searching eyes coolly. "Willard is prejudiced."

"I'm not." Willard appeared at Tate's side.

"He also says he couldn't do without you and now I understand why."

Helga stood behind her desk with her fingers resting lightly on the large green blotter. She smiled politely at Tate's flirtatious innuendos. This same repartee had taken place dozens of times. Willard always flattered her and the men, usually other ambitious young attorneys always responded by echoing his sentiments. Usually she felt a bit sorry for the young men. If they were at all sensitive, Willard's flattery embarrassed them as much as it did her. But something in Tate Brown's brazen dark eyes annoyed her. He was handsome, sleek, and probably only an inch or two taller than she. His navy pinstripe suit was expensive, perfectly tailored, and his shoes were so new they squeaked. She sensed he was the sort of man who made an art of saying the right thing.

"Are you working on the case?" Helga inquired with customary serenity. Her mind was ticking off the details. There was an air of importance about Tate Brown. She would need him as an ally.

"Not officially." Tate folded his arms and leaned against the doorway. "I've known Kenyon since law school and I'm interested in any cases relating to mass transit. Just trying to make myself useful."

He threw Willard a winning smile then moved forward to hand Helga a list of names.

"That's very nice of you." Helga accepted the list without smiling and sat down behind the desk.

"Willard and I were just going to lunch. Won't you join us?" Tate eyed her closely as if he had just detected the reservations she had about him.

"I just got here." Helga met his eyes evenly.

"You won't talk her into it." Willard laughed. "She's got an iron will, Tate."

"I see that." Tate smiled as he turned away. "Some other time."

"Yes," Helga called after them, "some other time. I'd like that."

The Washington Game. She knew the town was a network of intrigue. The most important deals were made in the subtlest of ways and one never knew where the winning card might come from. It was important not to alienate anyone. Usually her reserve was enough to keep her safe from any personality clashes. People ended up liking her for her honesty, for her efficiency if not for her warmth. But she perceived instantly that Tate Brown was a man who liked to push his luck. He needed one-hundred-percent approval, and unless he got it he might not be as helpful in winning the Northern Railway battle as he might be.

A humorous glint came into Helga's blue eyes as she inserted a piece of paper into the typewriter. Here she was less than five hours in town and she was already creating intrigue and complexity where none existed. Tate Brown happened to be a very handsome man and maybe that was what made her uneasy. In any case she was here to work. Her commitment to winning an equitable settlement in the Northern Railway case went beyond that of a job. She, too, was a champion of mass transportation. Willard and Kenyon knew that if the Northern case was not settled by the May 1 deadline and the unions who were disputing their contracts went out on strike, it would cripple the entire Northwest. Willard hadn't really been surprised to see her pop into the office today. He knew her well enough after nearly ten years to know that she would not rest until she had ordered her launching pad and set her front lines to begin the attack.

For the next four hours Helga was so deeply engrossed in her work that she did not even hear Kenyon Stubbs, the youngest partner in the law firm, enter the office. By four she had retyped the depositions and with the help of Tate's list set up appointments on the following morning to interview someone to act as her assistant for the next six months. She was about to open up an entirely new kettle of fish by phoning the lobbyists who would be most effective in Congress when Kenyon stuck his blond head in her office and ordered her to leave for the day.

"I didn't know you were here." Helga smiled at the sharp-featured man who looked more like a tennis champion than one of the country's toughest young attorneys.

"I knew you were," Kenyon said with his usual sternness. "I would have been shocked if you hadn't been. Listen, the long hours will come later. Take it easy while you can, Helga."

"I suppose." Helga shrugged. She was already getting nervous about leaving, about the thoughts that might besiege her the moment her mind wasn't focused on work.

"Absolutely." Kenyon smiled tightly. His attitude, unlike Willard's, verged on arrogance. Still she respected his ability as a lawyer. It was unusual for Kenyon to exchange more than a few words with her. Perhaps in his mind she had already gone beyond angel to computer. Most of the time she was certain he didn't even see her.

"Did you have a good flight?" Helga asked as she gathered up her papers.

"Yes. And you?"

"Oh, yes. I had a fine flight."

"Good." Kenyon smiled again and disappeared.

She sat for a moment staring out into the late-afternoon hazy sunshine. Then rather abruptly she stood up, ran a comb through her hair, and slung her jacket over her shoulder. By the time she stepped out onto the street she was smiling. She would walk along the river, walk and walk with no destination. An exhilarating sense of freedom swept over her. It was good to be here. It really was!

She was just digging in her handbag for her map when a cab pulled up and Tate Brown got out. He caught sight of her immediately.

"They kicked me out." Helga smiled.

"If word gets out about you," Tate observed, "every office in town is going to be making you offers."

"I doubt it." Helga was still smiling. "I don't know what to do with so much sun."

"Have a drink with me," Tate suggested.

"Honestly"—Helga's expression was sincere—"I will sometime. We should. Please understand, I can't now. I just feel the need to . . . meander."

"What about tonight?" Tate inquired quickly as if he had not heard her reply. "There's a big party at the Phillips. It should be the perfect introduction to Washington nightlife."

"Really, thank you." Helga frowned slightly. "I just can't tonight. Don't hold it against me."

Tate nodded reluctantly. Of course he held it against her. She could tell that rejection did not sit well with him.

Power trips, she thought as she walked on down the street. What she felt from Tate wasn't so much interest in her as some need in himself. She couldn't imagine spending an evening with him and she was damned if she'd play a social game just to be nice. She would earn his respect professionally, not over a gin and tonic.

She frowned at her straight-laced attitude. Was she really being a humorless prude? Maybe she should go along, spend hours with people who didn't really interest her. Somehow she couldn't do it.

But even the unfortunate encounter with Tate Brown did not dull the pleasure of the hot afternoon sun beating down on her back. Once the Potomac came into view she stuffed the map back into her handbag and just walked. Couples were lying on the grass as if it were summer, and a few young men had removed their shirts to take full advantage of the remaining rays of sun. There was a sense of heady exhilaration, of a frolicking abandon that accompanies an unexpectedly beautiful day.

She walked with a slight smile on her lips, her arms swinging easily at her sides. The day was a blessing. She felt it almost as an omen and she didn't even believe in such things as omens.

Perhaps it was the exhaustion from the flight that made her body all warm and tingly. She sank down onto the grass and finally she stretched out, rubbing her cheek against the cool blades, breathing in the rich loamy aroma of the earth. The moment was so dreamlike it seemed entirely appropriate to roll onto her back, close her eyes, and drift, smiling softly with her arms crossed primly across her breasts and her legs crossed at the ankles.

Her body was released, she was sinking into the earth, and the thought amused her so that her lips twitched slightly and her smiled broadened. She was at that delicious point just before sleep where the body feels itself nourished, replenished. In that state she floated, sometimes hearing the shouts of those around her, sometimes not.

An uninhibited low sigh escaped as Helga rolled onto her side, tucked one arm under her head for a pillow, and slowly opened her eyes.

"Have a good snooze?" A man's voice, low, with a faint Southernish accent, penetrated the sleepy haze that seemed to engulf her like a puffy cloud.

"Oh, yes," she answered the voice groggily, not knowing or caring where it came from.

A low chuckled followed and a moment later Helga met a pair of smiling hazel eyes. Without thinking, she smiled at the stranger then closed her eyes again, savoring the residue of languid fluidity that filled her body.

For a few moments she listened to the laughter of children, the hearty cries of adolescents involved in a game of something-or-other. Then she opened her eyes again, more fully this time, and stared into the hazel eyes, which were still smiling in her direction.

A warm, syrupy sensation oozed over her and in spite of herself she smiled a second time. The stranger was seated parallel to her, about three feet away. Though he was sitting with his long arms wrapped around his legs, she could tell he was a large man, probably well over six feet tall. He was dressed in a business suit, a brown plaid that struck her fancy, for it was both conservative and jaunty at the same time. His tie was a colorful red and blue stripe with a thinner brown stripe, something she would never have chosen but somehow it was perfect. The red in the tie suited his smile, which was open and almost boyish. His hair was a wavy sandy mop as if people were always tousling it as they would a child's. The face was handsome, sharp-featured, and, she'd be willing to wager, Irish. It was several moments before she realized she was staring at him with a silly lopsided grin on her face.

When she looked away he laughed. "You were really out."

"I know." The same lopsided grin formed as she pulled herself to a sitting position and ran her hands through her hair.

"I don't blame you," he said. "Best naps I ever have are in public. I tell you . . . once I went through a period of insomnia . . . Ever have that?"

Helga nodded.

"Well I have attacks every now and again but this one time was the worst. It went on for four months. Got so I was afraid to go to bed at night. I tried everything . . . warm beer, hot baths, even pills wouldn't work cause they'd just zonk me out and about an hour later my lids'd fly open and I'd be wide awake for the rest of the night. Then I discovered that I could sleep at movies and concerts. The more I wanted to see the movie or hear the music, the better I'd sleep. It also seemed to help if I paid a lot for the ticket. If my seats were in the balcony somehow I wouldn't rest as well."

An infectious laugh escaped from Helga. "Sorry," she apologized but her eyes were still twinkling.

He grinned and his eyes crinkled as he looked at her. They sat smiling at each other for several moments before Helga looked off across the river.

"I didn't mean to laugh at your insomnia," she said. "I guess mine wasn't as severe as yours. A cup of Ovaltine always put me out."

"Yours was *nothing*," he told her and she glanced back at him with a quick smile.

"This is the best time of day," he said after a minute. "I mean, unless you've had a rotten day. Or even if you've had a rotten day . . . If you can pull yourself away and just curl up on the grass."

"It's hard to curl up in the snow," Helga replied almost to herself.

"Sure is," he chuckled. "I'm from Texas. We don't worry much about that."

"Well, we worry about it where I'm from." Helga tucked her legs off to one side.

"There's a bird, an oriole, that comes here every afternoon about this time."

"How do you know it's the same bird?" Helga swung around to face him. He was absolutely serious.

"Because she's used to me." He shifted his large frame, stretching his long legs out in front and leaning back on his elbow. "I've known her since she built her nest in that magnolia over there . . . since last April. She's so tame now the click of my camera doesn't even scare her off."

Helga stared at his profile. From the side his appearance was anything but boyish. It was a rugged face, large, almost heroic, with a strong jaw. Something tugged and twirled in her stomach and she caught her breath. She wished he would stay that way, staring out into the river, so she could continue to look at him. She felt compelled to study his prominent, finely shaped nose, the broad high cheekbones and heavy brows. There was an air of importance about him, of power, although his easygoing manner was almost the antithesis of the hard-edged pomposity of so many notables.

33

"Birds get to know people same as any other creatures," he observed, still staring out at the Potomac.

"I suppose that's true." Helga felt a ripple of pleasure at the sound of his voice.

"It's partly a question of habit and partly it's trust, but first comes the habit, the ritual. I find it comforting to meet a bird every afternoon around five thirty." There was a note of humor in his voice, but his eyes were serious when he turned back to Helga.

"I go for walks. Long walks," Helga told him. "Back home . . . Minnesota, that is, I walk or jog, depending on how energetic I am that day, for twenty minutes in the morning before work, an indefinite amount of time in the evening, and sometimes I even go out again before I go to bed."

"That's nice." He nodded his approval. "You walk in the woods or along streets?"

"In the woods." Helga smiled, thinking of the sixty acres of tall pines that was only a portion of her parents' farm.

"You can't have too much space," he said pensively.

"My folks have over a hundred acres," Helga said.

"I'm from Texas." He grinned.

"And you have thousands of acres." Helga laughed, finishing his train of thought.

"No, ma'am. I'm a poor boy. My folks come from a small town outside Galveston. What they have is a big yard . . . or maybe I should say what they own is a big yard. What they *have*, you're absolutely right, is space. Texas space. Ever been to the Salmon River Mountains in Idaho? That's up near you."

"Relatively near." Helga's heart quickened as he shifted his tall, lean body closer. The move was an easy one, like everything about him it was self-assured and without self-consciousness. But the effect of his proximity had a dizzying effect on her. The tugging in her stomach, which at first had been pleasant and gentle, exploded into fiery, undulating waves. Beneath her white silk blouse her breasts tingled; she was keenly aware of the tender skin on her inner arms, the back of her neck was prickling, her entire body was so sensitized, so galvanized by his presence that for an instant she could not remember the thread of their conversation.

"Relatively near," she repeated in a faint voice. She could feel his eyes on her. She waited for something in her to tighten, for all of her usual defenses to spring to her rescue. But the liquid fires continued to surge until they finally concentrated in one small area, burning and demanding. She didn't even know his name. He hadn't asked, she hadn't even offered. Yet she felt she knew him. Without warning the word love exploded inside her head, raging there just as other fires continued to burn and seethe below. How could she love him?

Because he made her smile? Because she had not smiled or laughed this much in years? Because he was content to talk, to talk of deep, enduring things? If he had said my name is Tom, I work for the Justice Department or the Pentagon, how much would she really have known about him? But she knew he waited here for a bird every afternoon! She knew his heart. She knew he was curious about her . . . not what her job was, or where she lived, or whether or not she had children as a way of defining her. He would rather know *where* she walked!

She was so totally immersed in the moment, in the presence of this tall Texan stranger, that it did not even occur to her how bizarre her feelings were, how uncharacteristic. His presence absorbed her, obliterating everything else.

"But Minnesota," she began softly, "is actually some distance from Idaho. North Dakota comes next and then a long stretch of Montana. I camped there once . . . on the shores of Lake McDonald . . . in Montana, that is."

There was an electrifying tension between them now, something so taut that it seemed to Helga the least movement, the least breath would be dangerous. She knew, without looking at him, that he was equally cognizant of the highly charged air. His voice had taken on a husky quality. In the silence that preceded his reply the sound of his even breathing was like an insidious seduction.

"Coldest water I ever felt," he said lowly. "Lake McDonald, that is."

"Yes." Helga did not dare glance at him.

"Did you go swimming in Lake McDonald?" he inquired after a moment.

Helga nodded, then as a way of combating the dizziness, or perhaps because she felt driven to reveal a part of herself that was usually protected she added, ". . . with my husband. I went with my husband over ten years ago."

She paused to catch her breath and cast a brief glance in his direction. "My husband was killed many years ago."

"I'm sorry." He turned to her finally and she met his eyes without wavering and held them. They stared at each other unabashedly as the rosy hue on the horizon faded to violet. Finally he looked away.

"I guess she's not coming today." He twisted his large torso and looked off in another direction.

"Maybe I frightened her away." Helga felt the color spring to her cheeks. Good Lord, she had just told a complete stranger about John. There were people in her life whom she had known for years who didn't even know she had been married.

"I doubt if you'd frighten her." He turned back to her, smiling. "You're not a scary person, you know."

Helga laughed unexpectedly. "I know."

"You play the piano?" Before she knew what was happening he had covered her hand, which was resting palm down on the grass, with his.

"Yes." Her voice was barely audible. She felt the heat of his body throbbing in his hand. She looked at him curiously but he was staring at his own hand as it covered hers. For an instant she felt the panic rising in her throat. The absurdity of what was happening was almost catching up with her, and in her mind she saw herself leaping to her feet and running off.

36

"Do you play Schubert?" His expression was quizzical.

"I do." She forced herself to look at him, knowing full well what she would read in his eyes.

He lifted her hand slowly, held it between his hands a moment, then shifted it back and forth as if he were weighing it. All the while his eyes roamed her face with a friendly curiosity that somehow stilled her panic even as it quickened the rhythm of her heart.

"I bet you're good too." He smiled softly and despite herself she felt complimented, as if he had already heard her play.

"I'm fair," she admitted. With her hand sandwiched between his he exerted a gentle pressure. A warm shiver ran down her spine. It was if they were making love. Yet at the same time, despite her awareness of her unusual behavior, everything that was happening seemed perfectly natural.

"My guess is if you say you're fair you're far more. How long did you study?"

Helga smiled. The unpredictability of his conversation was what made the whole thing plausible. "Twelve years . . ."

"You see!" He grinned. "You've got to be good. You're the kind of person who doesn't do things halfway."

Helga slid her hand from between his and looked bemused. "All that you do, do with your might . . ."

". . . Things done by halves," he recited, paused, and regarded her expectantly.

". . . are never done right," she finished the rhyme.

"Things done by halves are never done right," he mused softly.

"I probably should—".

"Imagine a city without parks," he interrupted her solemnly, and there was a new intensity in his voice. "Imagine a world without trees and grass, without space for nothing at all. There is value in space, in forests where no one even walks . . . or only a few. Don't you agree?"

"Yes." Helga felt herself once again mesmerized by him.

"Of course people have to have jobs, of course people have to eat, but people have to know it is still possible to get away."

"That's why I live in the country. Some people need more . . . more silence, more wilderness than others." Helga reached for her jacket reluctantly. "But everyone needs it, you're right, and not just the people who can afford it."

"Absolutely!" He roared his agreement and sprang to his knees. "And it's always a fight to keep that undeveloped land, national parks, wetlands. Well, I'll fight 'em, damn it!"

He puffed out his cheeks and shook his head, then he looked at Helga with a sheepish grin. "Sorry. I got carried away."

Helga smiled. Thank God, she thought. His passionate outburst had at least given her palpitating heart a chance to recover. But those erotic sensations were replaced by something equally intriguing and bewitching. His passion for the wilderness, the commitment she sensed he had for a balance between ecology and social necessity had further captivated her. He had an exuberant, off-the-cuff, raw way of expressing himself that she liked. And the soft Texas drawl—she liked that too. Nothing he said or did seemed in the least premeditated, yet she could see that he was sensitive to her, to what might offend or frighten her. When he studied her it was his genuine curiosity that she saw. She knew she intrigued him too.

"Twelve years . . ." Without warning he picked up her hand again, setting off a series of violent erotic sensations.

"I had my first piano lesson when I was barely five," Helga withdrew her hand gently but the warm quivering in the pit of her stomach would not stop. "My grandmother left us her old player piano when she died. The kind with player rolls?"

He leaned forward, enthusiastically devouring her every word.

"My folks are very utilitarian people, not exactly the sort of family to lavish dance and music lessons on their children. As far as they were concerned, having a piano which could produce ready-made music was far preferable to an ordinary piano. But I soon became bored with the same old piano rolls and somehow

. . . I started badgering for lessons. I was such a quiet, obedient child . . . I think they were astonished that I would make such a request. I've never really understood why they agreed; money was always short and my five brothers were always outgrowing their shoes—"

Helga broke off with a shy smile. "I'm talking a lot."

"I like the part about your brothers outgrowing their shoes." He nodded sagely. "Didn't you outgrow yours?" He glanced down at her navy blue heels, then grinned at her.

"Funny," mused Helga as she stared at the tips of her shoes, "I only remember my folks talking about my brothers' shoes."

When she looked back at him he was staring hard at her as if he were trying to see the five-year-old child whose long, skinny legs had dangled over the piano bench. Noticing for the first time the tiny gold flecks in his hazel eyes, she felt another warm wave of desire begin to gain momentum. She drew in a deep breath, both thrilled and incredulous that such a thing could be happening . . . to her, to Helga Tarr.

CHAPTER TWO

Without warning he sprang to his feet and shoved wildly at his jacket sleeve, emitting a loud groan of consternation that caused everyone around them to turn and stare.

"Damn!" His face flushed and he smacked his lips in annoyance with himself as Helga continued to stare up at him.

He was tall, much taller than she had guessed. She stood up quickly. The top of her head came scarcely to his underarm. He was probably six feet six or maybe even more.

"I'm late," he puffed as if he had already been running to his destination. "I'm late . . . sorry, sorry!"

"It's all right." Helga reached out instinctively as if she could help him. His total frenzy was in complete contrast to the easygoing relaxed man she had been talking to.

"I'm just trying to figure out . . ." He glanced at his watch again, jerked his tie into place and looked at Helga with a bewildered expression. "Can I call you?"

"Start walking," she said. "I'll come along a ways. You're late."

"Yeah!" He grinned appreciatively and began striding across the grass as he dug frantically in his pockets.

Helga hurried along beside him, struggling to hide her amusement. Right before her eyes he had changed from a charming, drawling Texan to a nervous, distracted giant. He reminded her of the White Rabbit in *Alice in Wonderland,* apologizing and muttering to himself as he turned his pockets inside out in search of something.

Finally he produced a card and shoved it into the pocket of her jacket. "I really am sorry. I'm taking you out of your way but . . ."

"It's okay." Helga could not wipe the smile off her face. "It's really okay," she soothed. "Would you like to know my name?"

He halted his rapid gait to stare at her with the same fascinated look he had bestowed on her during their conversation.

"This is pretty strange, isn't it?" His eyes were calm again.

"Helga Tarr." Helga began to walk in the direction he had established.

"Helga." He repeated her name slowly. She had never heard it pronounced by a Texan. "Helga." He nodded with a pleased expression.

"Do you have a name?" Helga glanced up at him.

"Sam." He clasped her hand and shook it as they walked.

"It suits you." Helga felt as if she were skimming over the grass.

"McCalahan," he added. "Does that suit me too?"

"I thought you were Irish." Helga's face was radiant as she looked up at him.

"I'm sorry I have to rush off like this." Sam looked annoyed again.

"Don't apologize." Helga's euphoria knew no bounds. She was practically running to keep up with him and her voice was breathless.

"You really are beautiful, you know that?" Sam threw her a baffled look.

"I'm staying with a friend." Helga felt some urgency to communicate essential information. She could not shake the feeling that she was floating along beside him, flying above the grass in some magical state. She needed to ground herself in reality. She fumbled for the card he had shoved in her pocket as she continued.

"I don't know the phone number," she said. "My friend's name is Marilyn Sell."

"Oh, good!" Sam exclaimed before giving another distracted glance at his watch.

"Marilyn Sell." Helga's heart was thudding wildly as they approached the curb and he began waving frantically for a cab.

"Damn cabs!" he cursed softly and shook his head. It seemed almost as if he had forgotten she was there but then he turned to her. "I'll call you."

Helga nodded. "Marilyn Sell," she repeated for the third time.

"I won't forget. I know who Marilyn Sell is. Runs a food shop." His eyes caressed her and for an instant he swayed closer as if he wanted to take her in his arms.

Helga backed up, waving as a cab drew up. "I hope you make it in time!" she cried.

By the time Helga let herself into the stone cottage her heart was still thundering, her mind was whirling, and her body felt about ready to burst with pent-up energy. She couldn't even think about what was happening because every time she tried to order the events her body flushed with the instant recall of how it had felt to sit next to him.

Sam McCalahan. She repeated his name over and over as she made herself a cup of tea and sat in the dark sipping it. Sam McCalahan. The name had a familiar ring, but maybe that was just her imagination because so much of what had passed between them had seemed so familiar. Several times she tried to censor herself, tried to pull in the reins and perceive what had happened in less-vivid colors. But she could not in all honesty tell herself that what had happened was simply a casual meeting. She would be doing herself a disservice if she did not recognize the experience for what it was: an extraordinary happening, a chance encounter, something of a miracle.

She thought of Tate Brown's calculated smile and how he had wanted to take her out without any genuine interest in who she

42

was. Sam had hung on every word; she had felt his fascination in the depths of her being. No, she shouldn't be too hard on Tate. What had taken place between her and Sam was rare.

But what if he didn't call?

She switched on the floor lamp next to the couch, kicked off her shoes, and swung her legs up over the arm. He would call. She was absolutely sure he had been as affected as she. He was a man of integrity. Yes, of power, vigor, and integrity. A big man. A tall Texan who, she guessed, could be quite boisterous. But a kind man, a gentle man with a keen sense of humor and a teasing nature.

She flung her arms over her head and searched her mind for all of the things he was. Thank heavens she was alone so she could take these moments to luxuriate in fanciful thoughts of him.

When he had stood up she had nearly gasped at the magnificence of his towering form. What if he was married?

She bolted to an upright position with a stricken expression, then she collapsed back onto the couch with a dreamy smile. No, he wasn't married. She was too good a judge of character to fall into that trap. And he was too honest, too forthright and candid not to have said something about a wife if there had been one.

Then perhaps he had been married. Perhaps there were children somewhere. She smiled to herself, wondering how many children and if they looked like him and if he had parted from his ex-wife on good terms. She'd be willing to bet he had. She knew he was a fabulous father, could just see him heaving a football to his son or walking throught the woods with his daughter. All of his children's friends would gravitate to him and he would tease them as he had teased her.

Only maybe he didn't have children. It was possible that he was a bachelor. Did that mean he was heavily involved with another woman?

On and on her mind shifted Sam McCalahan about, putting him in different roles, giving him three children, giving him

43

none, giving him a law degree and taking it back and making him a professor at George Washington University. It didn't matter what her mind did with him, merely thinking of him gave her pleasure. He and everything about him was like a song she could not get out of her head.

When the phone rang she leaped across the room to answer it.

"I'm not bothering you, am I?" It was Marilyn.

"No, no, no," Helga stammered.

"You all right?" Marilyn inquired solicitously.

"Yes," Helga replied too quickly.

"You sound strange," Marilyn persisted.

"Jet lag," Helga insisted.

"Oh." Marilyn sounded glum. After a pause she continued in a coaxing voice. "I was hoping you'd join Neal and me at a nice gathering. Your style too with a harpsicord recital. It's at my favorite gallery. But maybe another time."

"I'd love to." Helga felt ebullient. She could not imagine spending the evening alone, replaying her earlier encounter.

"Can you be ready in twenty minutes?"

Five minutes later Helga stepped out of the steaming shower cabinet and toweled herself dry in the violet-carpeted bathroom. The excitement would not subside. By now she had anticipated the cool hand of reason would have rescued her from the throes of palpitating fantasy. She could not wipe the image of the tall Texan out of her mind. She saw him running to catch planes, saw him riding on the open range, saw him striding toward her, and against her will she found herself entertaining thoughts of what it would be like to be encircled by those strong arms of his.

She stared at her reflection in the steamy bathroom mirror and was surprised to see that her appearance had not altered drastically. Her tall, lean body was well-endowed with full breasts, and she was acutely aware of them as she walked naked into the other room to sort through her clothes, which Marilyn's housekeeper had placed in the large French armoire.

44

She gazed at her meager wardrobe for several moments before chosing a black knit sweater dress with a wide cowl neck. She placed her navy shoes in the bottom of the armoire and slipped on a pair of identical black pumps, humming lightly to herself as she returned to the bathroom to dry her damp hair.

The figure she cut as she walked through the garden to the back door of the main house was dark and elegant. Her blond hair gleamed in the moonlight and her gait, which was always subdued and graceful, was buoyant.

Inside Marilyn's three children, the youngest of whom was four, filled her in on the relevant details of their young lives. By the time Marilyn and Neal joined them in the kitchen Helga was well-acquainted with and thoroughly enchanted by the three children.

"They're great," she lauded as Neal helped her into the backseat of the car.

"They're pretty good." Marilyn turned around in her seat to accept the compliment. ". . . if I do say so myself. You know, I wasn't too keen on mother stuff. Neal had to talk me into the first one." She turned to her bespectacled husband and patted his sleeve fondly. "Nobody had to talk anybody into Tommy but then I had to talk Neal into the third, Betsy."

"And nobody"—Neal laughed—"is going to do any more talking."

"You're so enviably thin." Marilyn hugged Helga when they got out of the car. "Oh, I almost forgot . . . you had a call."

Helga caught her breath. "Why didn't you tell me?"

"I am." Marilyn slipped her arm through Helga's and guided her toward a rather staid nineteenth-century brownstone. "It was your boss. Mr. Stubbs. You needn't come in till noon tomorrow because he'd like you to stay late for a press conference."

Helga nodded and a wave of depression swept over her. It was ridiculous for her to be so hyped up. It might be days before he phoned . . . if he phoned at all. Just because he was the first man who had really intrigued her since John didn't mean she had to behave like a ditzy adolescent.

By the time the two women reached the front door, Neal had joined them and they entered together. The harpsicord recital was already under way and the familiar strains of a Bach invention filled the air. For the first time Helga realized that they had just entered the Phillips Gallery. Unwittingly she had ended up at the same affair to which Tate Brown had invited her earlier.

She shook off a twinge of guilt and managed to enjoy the remainder of the recital. When the audience began to drift out of the recital hall into the adjoining rooms where the vast Phillips art collection was exhibited, she wandered over to the harpsicord and studied it.

"Helga!" Marilyn was motioning to her from the foyer. No doubt she was worrying that Helga felt ill at ease. Helga joined the group and was introduced around. She exchanged a few words with several new acquaintances but soon found herself wandering off alone to enjoy some of the paintings.

Duncan Phillips had elected to display his collection in a homey atmosphere. He had arranged the works according to his own artistic tastes in comfortable surroundings so that one could go from room to room and settle in a chair to contemplate the many masterpieces. It suited Helga perfectly, for despite the large gathering she felt free to view the collection.

"Are you okay?" The only problem was that Marilyn could not accept the fact that she was having a fabulous time just wandering around by herself.

"I couldn't be having a better time," Helga enthused as she turned away from a shadowy painting of two little nineteenth-century girls in starched party dresses.

"You can come to the gallery anytime." Marilyn looked doubtful. "Don't you want a glass of wine? They've laid out a lovely buffet downstairs."

Helga chuckled. "I haven't eaten a thing all day."

"How can you not eat?" Marilyn groaned her dismay.

"Sometimes I forget." Helga turned back to the William Merrit Chase painting. Her body was dominated by an undulating current of desire, which spread without warning. She had forgotten all about food, all about everything.

"I wish I could forget to eat." Marilyn interrupted her reverie.

"I'm really fine here just looking at paintings," Helga told her. "I loved meeting your friends but . . . Well, I find I have to take meeting people in small doses. More than three or four new acquaintances at one time and I start feeling . . . glutted."

Marilyn shook her head incredulously. "You're worse than when we were in college."

"I'm not worse." Helga smiled. "I just don't feel as insecure as I did then. I used to feel obligated to pretend I was as socially oriented as everyone else. But I did like your friends. Especially the O'Briens. Sally and Michael, right?"

Marilyn scrutinized her. "You're sure you're okay?

Helga nodded. Several other guests had drifted into the room to view the paintings. For an instant she was tempted to mention Sam, to see if Marilyn, who knew everyone in Washington, could shed any light on him. She felt an almost obsessive need to speak his name aloud to someone.

"To prove I'm okay"—she shook her blond head decisively—"I'm going to go downstairs with you and have a glass of wine. It will probably put me on my ear and I may do something outlandish and embarrass you but . . ."

Marilyn chuckled. "The day *you* embarrass me? Now I feel like I've interrupted you . . ."

"You have!" Helga laughed and started toward the door.

Downstairs the gathering had swelled and people were standing back to back laughing and talking, squeezing past one person to reach another. Marilyn introduced her to several more people, a senator from somewhere and a reporter for *The Washington Post* whose name she immediately filed away for the future. Neal managed to secure a glass of white wine for her, but she soon

47

gave up all hope of ever reaching the table where the light supper was spread.

Her tolerance for so many people amazed her, and despite her fatigue she felt pleased with herself. Maybe Marilyn had been right all these years. Maybe she had simply needed a change of scenery. For the first time in her life it was not completely unpleasant to feel the buzz of so many loquacious bodies pressing in on her. Still, she was more content to observe than to exert herself in conversation. She was happy just standing off to one side admiring the colorful fashions of both the men and the women, studying faces and attitudes and allowing herself to take in the full array of Washington dignitaries.

By the time she noticed Tate Brown threading his way toward her it was too late to lose herself in the crowd.

"I had no idea I was going to land here." She ducked her head toward his ear to offer an explanation. "I really had planned on spending the evening recuperating . . . adjusting to the culture shock of being transplanted."

Tate nodded. He seemed to bear her no grudge. "It's a rather noisy crowd." He smiled as he gestured.

"Sardines," Helga observed wryly.

"A drink?" Tate shifted from one foot to the other as he regarded her.

"If I have another I may collapse in a corner." Helga shook her head, then regretted it immediately. How tactless to reject him three times in one day.

"Just a touch." She leaned forward so he could hear. "If you can steer me out of this corner into a more peaceful space."

She felt his hand slip into hers as he led the way weaving in and out, his head ducked down and his face set like a small quarterback headed for the goalposts. Amazingly they broke through the crowd and found a deserted corner next to the front door.

"That wasn't easy." Tate laughed.

"Perhaps we should do without the wine," she suggested.

48

Tate waved her off. "I'll be right back."

Helga watched him elbow his way through the crowd with her glass. The same crowd, she thought, would part for Sam McCalahan. How silly! She chided herself silently though she recognized a grain of truth in her observation. Even in the midst of his White Rabbit frenzy about being late Sam McCalahan had exuded a powerful authority striding across the lawn. And the power, Helga mused, was not strictly the result of his heroic proportions. No, there was a fire in him, something that burned deeply and steadily.

"Here we are." Tate handed her a brimming glass of white wine and clinked his glass of scotch lightly against it. "Here's to the Northern Railway."

"I'll drink to that." Helga's blue eyes were still glowing from thoughts of Sam.

"So tell me about yourself, Helga Tarr. What's it like living out in the woods of Minnesota?" Tate leaned casually against the wall and sipped slowly on his drink.

Suddenly Helga felt completely exhausted. How could a person tell somebody about themselves? The phrase had always inhibited her, but now she found it irritating. Did he really expect she could sum herself up neatly in a tidy little statement?

"The woods are quiet. I like living away from things." Her voice held a coolness she had not intended.

"I've often thought I'd like that." He smiled and glanced sideways to nod at a passing friend.

The hollowness of his reply struck Helga as humorous and she smiled. She would be willing to swear Tate Brown had never thought of retreating to the wilderness. She saw now that his attention was split. She had disappointed rather than offended him with her candid reply. Behind his smiling eyes he was already calculating a way to extricate himself from such a tedious conversation.

Helga checked her smile. Men often reacted to her exactly like this. They were initially intrigued, but more often than not their enthusiasm waned quickly. She thought again of Sam McCalahan and how the words had spilled out of her. But then Sam McCalahan had never asked her to tell him about herself. Probably Tate was already thankful that they had not made a formal date for the evening.

"You went to college with Kenyon?" Helga made a gracious attempt to fill in the uneasy pause.

"Law school," he said.

Helga nodded. "I appreciate the list of names you gave me. I've already made several appointments."

"Anything I can do to help." Tate gave her a perfunctory smile and for a moment she felt sorry for him. He was as uncomfortable as she was, yet here he was stuck with being polite. She was on the point of pleading fatigue when the door to the Phillips Gallery swung open. She had the sense that a great tornado had whipped into the room. The four new arrivals entered at a peak of joviality. One deep baritone dominated their laughter, calling out names and greeting people with robust good nature.

Helga knew without looking that it was him. His hearty laughter cut through the buzz of conversation. People called his name and the foyer, which moments before had been deserted, was swarming as people rushed forward to greet him, slap his broad back, and pump his hand.

"Look who's here!" Tate's face lit up in genuine enthusiasm at the sight of the tall Texan. "The man of the hour." He waved an arm and motioned for Sam to join them.

But Sam had been swallowed up by a group of men, all pumping, slapping, and laughing as if they shared some deep, hilarious secret. *Sam McCalahan.* Finally Helga remembered where she had heard the name. He was a congressman whose outspoken, unorthodox ways had netted him a modest amount of national publicity during his first year in office. She had seen his name from time to time in the paper.

"Sam McCalahan." Tate bobbed his head and there was a hint of boyish hero worship in his face that touched her.

50

"I know." Helga's smile was serene though she could only think of one thing. She wanted to bolt, to vanish as quickly as possible before he saw her. He was with a woman, she had seen the back of her dark head, which was cropped short in something approaching a punk cut.

The hilarious laughter crescendoed. But it wasn't just because he was with a woman. Suddenly she was afraid that the fantasy was about to end, that what she had deemed precious and rare would be relegated to the ordinary. Perhaps she had blown the entire event out of proportion.

"Tate! Hey there fella!" Sam's lusty voice seemed to plough through her as he approached.

He clasped Tate in a bear hug, slapping the smaller man on the back and wrestling him around fondly. The woman at his side called Tate by name and offered her cheek to be kissed. She was quite tall, taller even than Helga, and very thin. Her gray silk dress was of the latest fashion and in excellent taste. Helga found herself staring at the woman and looked away.

Too late, she told herself. Too late. Just make the best of the situation. After whispering a few words to Sam, Tate swung the large Texan around until he was facing Helga. A look of utter bewilderment crossed his ruddy face and his mouth flew open. Their eyes locked in instant recognition.

"Sam and Mindy, I'd like you to meet Helga Tarr. She's in town with Matthews and Stubbs working on the Northern Railway case."

Sam and Mindy. Helga's breath stuck in her throat as she extended her hand first to Mindy and then to Sam. She felt dazed and it was moments before she realized that Tate had concluded his introduction and that Mindy was Mindy Willoughby and not Mindy McCalahan.

But her momentary relief was soon overturned by a surge of doubts. Just because a person had a different last name didn't necessarily mean they weren't married. She tried to concentrate on the conversation. She heard herself commenting how much

51

she liked Washington, and noted a hint of amusement in Sam's face when she added that it was such an exciting town.

"It's like a small town." Sam caught her eye briefly but made no mention of their earlier acquaintance.

"It really is," Mindy piped in. "Everyone knows what everyone else is doing."

"I wouldn't have thought so." Helga's hands felt like ice. "I mean . . . if you've never been here before Washington just seems terribly sophisticated and important."

Sam laughed. "Everyone wants everyone to think it's important. Some of it's important . . . most of it is paperwork, right, Tate?"

Tate laughed. "There is no end to the paper in this town."

"I'm from New York." Mindy turned to Helga with a friendly smile. "When I come to Washington I feel like I've gone back home to Middleboro New Hampshire, population three hundred."

Sam chuckled. "That's because Mindy's a snob."

"That's because"—Mindy smiled up at him—"I don't like people nosing into my business."

"Would you excuse me." Helga managed a cordial smile that included everyone. Better to be disappointed now, straight away than to nourish silly hopes. Good Lord, how she'd gone on and on about him.

She handed her full glass of wine to a passing waiter and went upstairs to one of the deserted rooms where she sank onto an antique red velvet horsehair couch and stared bleekly at her pale hands. And she was disappointed, painfully so. And tired. Yes, it would all look different to her after a good night's sleep.

Well, he had good taste in women, she had to hand him that. Although Mindy Willoughby was a good deal more gregarious than she, they shared a respect and need for privacy. She glanced at her watch and told herself she should try to locate Marilyn and Neal and tell them she was going to leave. But the ache of disappointment would not subside.

When she finally looked up, her eyes were drawn to one of the most famous paintings in the Phillips collection. Renoir's "Luncheon of the Boating Party" was surely one of the happiest, sunniest pictures ever painted. As she studied it, some of the tension that had crept over her after Sam's arrival began to subside. The important thing was that she had been able to feel something, that she was at this point in her life capable of and ready to reach out to another human being. If she had suspected herself of falling into dry, spinsterish patterns, then today had taught her how much more she was capable of. He had awakened something in her and that was good.

"May I join you?" She had not heard him come in. She raised her eyes slowly and nodded.

"I couldn't believe it." He sat down next to her on the hard little couch. "I couldn't believe it was you!"

A bubble of irrepressible excitement began bouncing inside and whatever disappointment she felt vanished. "I almost fainted." She gave him a sidewise glance and was stunned by the hungry look in his eyes.

"Mindy's only a friend." He offered the information pointedly, knowing it would be on her mind.

Helga caught her breath. They were certainly unable to mince words. She accepted the information with an even glance in his direction.

For several moments they sat together, wordlessly staring at the lusty Renoir. The erotic tension between them was almost unbearable, but neither of them seemed able to break it. The words that had flowed earlier felt stifled, stifled in a desire so poignant and overpowering that it obliterated everything else.

She felt the sleeve of his jacket brush against her dress and swallowed hard to contain the passion that swelled inside. She wished he hadn't come. It would have been better to dream of him for a while. Suddenly she felt claustrophobic, as if she needed space as well as time.

"Ever been to Paris?" His inquiry seemed forced.

She shook her head and her breathing accelerated even though she did not look at him.

"They've a lot of Renoirs at the Jeu de Paume," he said after a moment.

"Oh, I've heard of it." Helga glanced at his profile, which was stern as he studied the painting. They were like two awkward adolescents sitting on Grandmother's horsehair couch in a shadowy Victorian parlor.

"It's at the other end of the Tuileries, isn't it?"

"Yes," he answered. "It's an incredible museum."

The conversation was inane. She was too aware of his powerful masculinity. Outside on the grass there had been a playful ease; now what she sensed from him was raw and urgent. But then wasn't that what she sensed from herself as well? And wasn't that what was frightening her?

"How do you know Tate Brown?" Helga asked, hoping to infuse the halting conversation with some life.

"Everyone knows Tate." Sam turned to her but his heart was not in his words and his mind was clearly not on Tate Brown.

"Yes, he does seem to be the sort of man who has his hand on the pulse of activity." Helga felt herself sinking into the heavy seductive promise that his eyes signaled. She crossed her legs in an effort to quell the fiery needles that zigzagged along her inner thighs. Perhaps she had gone too long without really feeling anything for a man. Perhaps she was unprepared now and totally out of control. Perhaps her earlier vision of him had been distorted.

"What are you thinking?" He moved his face closer. She could feel his warm breath against her cheeks and smell the spicy aroma of his after-shave. His face was smooth. He had shaved in the interim and everything about him was fresh and sweet.

But not his eyes. The mischievous glint of humor was gone, and in its place . . . a hungry intensity. The face that was studying her with such ruthless zeal was not, as she had originally thought, a young face. Probably he was in his late thirties, either approaching forty or already there. No, it was his spirit and effervescent energy that gave the impression of youth. No doubt he would continue to captivate people with his youthful vigor for the rest of his life.

She felt mesmerized by the power she read in his rugged face. As she continued to stare, she detected a smattering of gray blending smoothly into his sandy hair. In repose the lines on either side of his mouth were clearly etched.

She saw the distorted image of her own face reflected amidst the golden flecks in his eyes, and at the same time she felt herself sway toward him as if an irresistible force were drawing them together. She closed her eyes and their breaths mingled gently, titillating her into a mindless state of ectasy making her forget the frigid emptiness of so many long winter nights. Time was drawn out like a bead of silver stretched thin and fine on into eternity. She felt his nose rubbing against hers, felt the fullness of his mouth pressing into her, moving warmly and insistently against her until her lips parted.

The kiss exploded suddenly like a rocket launched without warning. The aggressive power she had sensed in him erupted inside her mouth and his tongue shot fiery currents as he sought to know and to gain complete possession of the territory.

Instinctively she reacted against the assault, and with the palms of her hands placed against his chest she pushed, at first gently, but then with greater force.

She felt torn. His plummeting tongue had unleashed a torrent of needs too long denied. She wanted him, wanted to abandon herself to the shattering sensations. She was also shocked, both at herself and at him. This was not the open-faced boyish man who had come to meditate by the Potomac. That man had been gentle, sensitive. The man whose long, fervent thrusts had turned her body into liquid heat was a marauder. He was a man who took what he wanted.

CHAPTER THREE

When she finally managed to wrest herself from his embrace, she was shaking, her cheeks were on fire, and her eyes, usually so placid and cool, were deep with outrage. She was not herself. Things like this did not happen to Helga Tarr!

Here? In a public room, with half of Washington buzzing below them? She could not even begin to articulate her shock. She could only stare at him, her breast heaving, her hands knotted tensely at her sides. And she had thought herself such a good judge of character.

She watched as he removed a handkerchief from his jacket pocket and blotted his forehead. He was moved, flushed, still short of breath. But he was not angry.

"What is it?" His tone was solicitous as he bent toward her.

Every reply stuck in her throat. She glanced at the smiling faces in the Renoir painting, but something deep inside would not stop trembling.

"Helga?"

She turned her back to him and pressed her lips together to stop the tears. Her mind and her emotions were at the center of a violent vortex. He should not have done what he had done. She owed him absolutely no explanation.

"Won't you say something?" He tapped her lightly on the shoulder. There was a gentle coaxing tone in his voice. He was once again the lighthearted, good-natured fellow. But she no longer trusted him.

"Please," he whispered softly. "I thought you wanted to kiss me too."

Helga felt the tears stinging in her eyes and tightened her jaw. She could not even remember the last time she had cried. God, how she resented him!

She whirled on him suddenly, but once again the idea of a direct confrontation made her dizzy and she shook her head as if she could make everything unpleasant vanish. The silence of long winter nights reproached her, and she thought of the safety of her narrow bed on the third floor of her parents' house.

"I can see I was wrong." Sam's voice was filled with concern.

"You were wrong," Helga said in a low, tight voice as she got to her feet. She thrust out her chin as she headed for the door.

"Please wait a moment."

Her spine stiffened as she continued. She placed her hand on the doorknob and turned it. It was locked.

"You didn't think I'd leave the door open, did you?" As he came up behind her, the light teasing tone returned to his voice. "You heard what Mindy said about wagging Washington tongues."

"I can't believe this." Helga shook her head, her hand resting on the doorknob. "You came up here to find me, you locked the door and—"

"And kissed you. Yes."

A faintness swept over her. She did not know whether to be angry or relieved.

"You can turn the lock," Sam said. "I'm not holding you prisoner."

Helga reached for the tiny lock, then hesitated. "You're very unpredictable," she said lowly.

"And you're not sure you like that?"

She turned around slowly and faced him. His face was drawn and serious. He looked like a shamed boy . . . again.

"I'm not sure I do," she answered calmly.

"Shall I apologize?" he asked.

"Do what you want. It seems you do anyway." Helga wondered vaguely why she was still in the room.

"I am sorry," he apologized sincerely. "Admittedly, I'm not a patient man. I'm bullish . . . a bit of an oaf. Do you accept my apology?"

He gave her an imploring look. "I thought about you every minute after we parted by the river. I tried phoning your friend. The housekeeper said you'd come here. I had previous dinner plans . . . I dragged everyone here before they'd even had their coffee."

"I think I should sit down." Helga experienced the same floating sensation she had experienced earlier as she moved back to the horsehair couch. He was confirming everything she had felt, that something rare had taken place between them. But then what about the kiss, the confusion she felt?

"Maybe you should unlock the door," she said sarcastically as he started to join her.

"I might want to kiss you again." He started to grin, thought better of it, and shrugged. "Bad joke."

"You're right." Helga stared at his broad shoulders as he unlocked the door. She was already beginning to thaw toward him.

"I was only being thorough," he said as he swaggered over to sit next to her. "I wanted to be a pragmatist and a gentleman. Gentlemen do not go around kissing ladies in public."

"And they go around locking doors?" Helga fired at him.

"In Washington they do." He grinned.

But it wasn't just a question of a locked door and she knew it. There was something both puzzling and unsettling in the duality she sensed in him.

When she did not respond to his attempt at humor, he frowned. "I wanted to get to know you better so—"

"You locked the door!" Helga interrupted in a burst of anger that surprised her more than it did Sam.

"So I was wrong!" He made a broad gesture with his right

arm. "But you can't fault me entirely on my intentions. I didn't want to be interrupted. Look, we don't really know each other *that* well yet; I'm entitled to a few mistakes, am I not?"

The understatement somehow amused her and she smiled.

"Thank heavens!" he exclaimed and sprawled back against the couch and shoved his long legs forward.

"Tell me the truth." He eyed her mischievously. "You did think of me a few times this evening, didn't you?"

"I did." Helga's stomach did a crazy spin. She could already feel herself careening precariously toward the edge of desire.

"I should probably go now." She fought off the feeling. "I should be tired. I'd say I was but . . . I'm not. At least I don't feel the fatigue. I know it's there though."

"So why worry about it if you don't feel it?" Sam chuckled in amusement.

"Fatigue makes people behave strangely . . . or in ways they don't normally behave."

"Hmmmm." Sam considered this with a twinkle. "Perhaps fatigue *allows* a person to behave the way they really want to behave. Perhaps it lowers the defenses?"

Helga drew in a deep breath. That was precisely what it did and that was precisely why she wanted to leave.

"Just a minute." He took her hand gently to stop her from getting up. "What do you do for Matthews and Stubbs?"

In contrast with Tate Brown's cursory inquiries Sam McCalahan's curiosity colored his handsome face as he studied her.

"I'm a legal secretary," Helga answered.

"Really?" Sam seemed surprised.

"What did you think I was?" She smiled, remembering all the various roles she had cast him in.

"Oh, I don't know. An administrator, the head of some worthy, altruistic cause, the president of beautiful young Scandanavians for Peace."

"Seriously." Helga laughed.

"I am serious." He sat up straight and regarded her. "You

59

seemed like somebody who would be in charge . . . of something."

"Well, I'm more or less in charge of the office here while we're fighting this thing out with the federal courts."

"Well, damn it I back the railroad one hundred percent here! You just let me know if I can do anything!" Sam's voice rose to a low roar, and Helga had the image of him striding into the courtroom and bellowing out his demands for instantaneous settlement.

"What did you think I did?" He wrinkled his face up into a perplexed expression and she had the sensation that he was still thinking about the Northern Railway case.

"I thought you were important," she admitted. "But mostly . . ." she hesitated. Did she really want him to know that the most vivid images she had of him were as a father? Wasn't that just a bit too revealing?

"Tell me!" Her reluctance whetted his appetite, and his eyes grew round with anticipation so that she wanted to tousle his sandy hair.

"I'm not going to tell you." She smiled at him but her voice was firm.

"I believe you." He narrowed his eyes and stared at her. "You're a person with very definite tastes and opinions. I would not like to be in a lengthy debate with you."

Nor I with you, Helga thought, smiling enigmatically.

"I know your friend, Marilyn Sell. Rather I know of her through an acquaintance of mine." His hazel eyes were beginning to emit warm signals once again.

"Part of the small-town-Washington syndrome." Helga cautioned herself to remain calm. The idea of leaving him was as confusing as the idea of staying. She could already feel the passion building between them.

"I've known Marilyn since college." Helga offered the piece of useless information with a flutter of blond lashes.

"You have five brothers, a mother, a father, and what else? Any dogs, cats, or chickens?"

"Fifty chickens and three roosters," Helga told him, and he stroked his chin thoughtfully as if that information were particularly pertinent. "I feed them Mondays, Wednesdays, and Fridays before driving in to work. I get up at four thirty on my feeding days."

"Good Lord!" He looked aghast at her. "You don't look like a woman who feeds chickens."

Helga laughed. "That's a prejudiced remark," she said.

Sam raised his eyes guiltily. "I suppose it is." He held her eyes for a moment, then looked away.

"And what about you? You're a congressman from Texas and what else?"

"One of eight . . . also a big family. Dirt poor but never less than three dogs and several cats in residence. Managed to get a football scholarship to the University of Texas, lost it after the first year because I got bored rolling around in the dirt and getting socked in the gut. So I went to work for a two-bit newspaper in Dallas. It covered expenses at school and taught me how to string a few sentences together. After I graduated from college I got bored again. So I joined the rodeo."

"What?" Helga interrupted with a startled cry.

"I have two scars to prove it." He gave her a suggestive smile and then laughed. "One on my neck and one on my arm! I wasn't much good at the rodeo. Too cumbersome for the bulls if you want to know the truth. Anyhow I did it mainly for the romance. Lota characters out there, Helga. And I liked wandering in the West, playacting. It was my last big bid for the macho life. I soon returned to Pottsville, Texas, population ten thousand, and within a year I was editor of the *Pottsville Star*. I was not exactly William Randolph Hearst, but I did increase the circulation and write a few splashy editorials which interested some folks in Amarillo, which is where I went next. I even had a couple of offers to come up north, up east and work for one of the 'reputable' periodicals. But I knew I'd have more of a chance in Texas where I felt comfortable. And I knew by then that as much as I liked the role of ace reporter and conscience of the community what I really ached for was politics. Politics, you know, is a lot like life in the rodeo. You get bucked off pretty easy sometimes. You can even get yourself gored. But it's the excitement. It's an irrational battle same as the rodeo. There's a lot of brute force in politics, a lot of unseen hands pullin' strings. The truth is I always felt safer on bulls. But then obviously safety has never been a prime concern of mine. Anyhow, I insinuated myself into the political scheme of things in the Amarillo vicinity and managed to get elected to Congress. That is the story of my life in a nutshell. Do you like it?"

Helga's heart gave a lurch as he gazed into her eyes. She liked it, yes. She was fascinated by it. She could have listened to his soft Texan drawl all night long and her face reflected as much.

"You must have a lot of tall tales to tell," she teased lightly to cover the quivering onslaught of eroticism.

"I'm good at tall tales," he countered with a boyish grin.

Someone had once accused her of having an impenetrable countenance, a dignified mask that allowed her to think and feel freely whatever came into her head. But she didn't feel that way now. She felt, and rightly, that every nuance, every emotion was reflected in the glimmer of her eyes. She could almost feel him reading her, peering inside to dark, forbidden places. She had barred not only men, not only women from those places, but herself as well.

Initially when she had cordoned off a small portion of herself, it had been a question of self-survival, and she had done it as she did all things, consciously and rationally. But over the years that small portion of ignored territory had grown. Now, in the face of his scrutiny, she felt herself being opened wide, the light was flooding in, blinding her and setting her off balance.

"We should go back downstairs." She could not hide her ambivalence. "Or rather, I should."

"I should too," Sam agreed quickly but made no effort to move. "We should come back here sometime and look at the pictures."

Helga nodded as she stood up.

"Helga . . . ?" As she reached the door he stood up and grasped her shoulders with his large, bony hands. She turned her head to one side and watched his long, sturdy fingers kneading and massaging her shoulder. His touch was gentle, persuasive, and despite her decision to leave she gave in to the slow, rhythmic stroking. The hair on his hand was sparse, very blond, and there were dozens of tiny freckles. His nails, she saw, were expertly rounded, the cuticle white and even as if these details were especially important to him.

"You need a good rubdown," he murmured against her hair. "How long has it been since you had a good Swedish massage?"

A reply would have broken the magical spell. She moved her head slowly from side to side, easing the muscles of her neck as his hands spread out along the tops of her arms, proding out the tension and at the same time infusing her with a wealth of other sensations.

He moved his hands down her arms, shaking them lightly to release even more tension. A ripe, mellow feeling flowed downward as he slid his hands onto hers and laced his fingers through hers.

"Shall I lock the door, just for a moment?" His voice was softly inviting. "You would like to be kissed?"

A yielding smile parted her lips and she felt something quicken in his body. His hand slid around her waist, drawing her full against him while the other hand reached out and turned the lock on the door.

"There!" She smiled languidly at the finality in his voice. One kiss. She really needed one kiss to send her off into the night.

This time he proceeded with infinite gentleness. With his hands encircling her long slender neck he tilted her head backward, luxuriating in this new perspective. He smiled softly as he traced along the angular planes of her face with his forefinger.

"Does today seem long to you?" There was a dreamy look on his face as he ran his finger around her lips. "I mean does it seem long since we met . . . That we've known each other for longer?"

He read the answer in Helga's wondering eyes as his lips brushed hers. His kiss was tentative and sweet and it aroused in her an even deeper awareness of the magnitude of her desire. He flicked his tongue along her lips and drank long, searching kisses as her arms went around his neck, encouraging and aiding him. There was a sense of expectancy and wonder as they tasted and tested the secret moist places. As they continued their breathing became as one, ragged and intense with burgeoning passion.

His arms tightened around her and she gasped in recognition of his hard, muscular body. The pressure of his steely thighs against her brought her up short, and she pulled away with a dazed expression.

"Is that what you call a kiss?" She threw back her blond head and gave him an exalted smile as she caught her breath.

"Oh, yes!" His face was rapt, brimming with a sort of adoration that made her blush. He reached for her and drew her to him, kissing her lightly on the lips, kissing her and kissing her as his hands swept down the sides of her body.

She was going to soar! They both were. Only they had to stop. Helga kissed him back urgently and her narrow tongue shot into his mouth with an abandon that seemed nothing short of miraculous.

I will stop, she told herself, but his hands, so chaste and prudent as they moved down the length of her torso, were like a narcotic. It was so easy and the power that surged through her was clean, like a strong, good wind.

She twisted her body against his hardness and felt herself pliant and open. She felt herself free!

"Is that what *you* call a kiss?" He held her at arm's length, his face flushed, his eyes admiring and gleaming.

"I don't want this to end," he cradled her against his throbbing chest. "I'll come by the house later. The housekeeper told me you were staying in the stone cottage. I know the house. I'll phone you."

An assignation? The term stuck in her mind and brought her up short. Was that the way things were done here? After a few kisses? All right, so they had been very impassioned kisses. She was not blaming him for that. But wasn't he jumping ahead, making unwarranted assumptions? And there was something experienced in his tone, as if this were standard procedure.

"I'll have to drop Mindy off," he whispered. "She has an early call tomorrow so she's probably ready to leave right now. I don't have any appointments till eleven. What about you?"

Helga ran her tongue over her upper lip. She did not have to strive for control now. Something had frozen up. She glanced at him, but he was preoccupied straightening his tie and reaching for a comb, which he ran through his thick wavy hair.

He was thinking of something else, detached and absorbed in another detail of his life now that this area had been settled. She eyed him with the same detachment she observed in him.

She glanced at her watch. This time out of necessity because she knew she had, for once, lost all track of time. Her inner clock had been stilled. It was after ten.

"Shall I go down first or do you want to?" He smiled at her warmly, sensing none of her reservations.

She gave him a withering glance as she opened the door. "I will. Make sure you allow plenty of time before you follow. Perhaps you could enter from a different door. I think I noticed a back stairway."

She turned to him with a composed, placid expression. "And don't phone because I'm a light sleeper and I don't want to be disturbed my first night in town."

CHAPTER FOUR

Helga ripped a sheet of paper out of her typewriter, smashed it into a ball, and tossed it into the wastepaper basket. She could just barely hear the buzz of voices in the outer office. Tate Brown was here again chatting it up with Kenyon about something. She had yet to figure out exactly what he did, but somehow he managed to stop by the office every other day. Since the evening at the Phillips he had little more than a perfunctory nod for her. She was a fixture now. Neither angel nor robot as far as he was concerned, simply a secretarial fixture.

Why did she care? She inserted another clean sheet and began again. She didn't care about Tate. She cared that he reminded her of Sam McCalahan and that his presence kept the image of the tall Texan far too alive.

She looked out into the rainy afternoon and frowned. The Washington Monument was cloaked in steamy fog. The top of it was not even visible and hadn't been for days. The gloom of the past week had settled in her heart, and she was beginning to wish she had never agreed to this tour of duty in the nation's capital.

The case was not going as well as it might have been. Yesterday the White House had issued a statement recommending a twenty-percent wage increase over a three-year period. That was nothing. They may as well have remained silent on the issue because such a statement was virtually noncommittal. Well, they had always known they would probably have little help from that corner.

Still, it was depressing. The only bright spots in the past ten days came when she was spending time with Marilyn's children, especially Betsy, the youngest. Somehow she'd hit it off just right with the four-year-old. Last weekend, half teasing, she had suggested teaching the little girl to play the piano. Much to her astonishment Betsy had jumped at the opportunity, so for the past several days she had hurried home from work with that obligation to absorb her. Thank God for Betsy, even if the piano lessons brought back the suffocating feelings of . . . Aunt Helga.

Depression. Cloying, morose Scandanavian depression, a retreat into the cool nether regions of her psyche. At times like these she could practically feel her complexion turning gray. Well, she had no one to blame but herself.

Helga glanced at the document to the left of the typewriter and began to type. She never made errors. Today she was full of them and each one increased her irritation with herself. She honestly thought that if it would only stop raining she would take the afternoon off. She was pent up. She needed to move, needed to run and stretch her limbs. Back home she was always active . . . walking for miles, cutting wood, doing a variety of outside chores. Feeding the chickens.

It had not been her mistake; it had been his. He had been presumptuous. She was not a prude!

She botched another whole line on what was supposed to be a *perfect* copy. She did not like to think about Sam McCalahan nor about the woman she had become in his arms. Her mind fled from those thoughts as if she were recalling some loathsome atrocity. She did not want to remember the feelings of power and exaltation coursing through her body.

"Going out for a bite." Kenyon stuck his head in the door. "If Ted Levenson phones you know what to tell him. Also you may want to brief those two men the union sent out."

"I already made an appointment," Helga referred to the large datebook on her cluttered desk. "I'm going to meet them for breakfast tomorrow. Do you want to join us?"

"You handle it." Kenyon ducked back out and Helga stared at the empty doorway.

She stood up suddenly and stretched. The dark green wool-jersey dress clung to her body, accentuating the fluidity of her graceful lines. The man of the hour was how Tate had referred to Sam McCalahan, and now that she had been in Washington awhile she understood what he meant.

Sam McCalahan had modestly identified himself as a congressman from Texas. Well, that was certainly true, but it was also true that Sam McCalahan's name was on everyone's tongue, men and women alike. From what Helga could gather he had cast a spell over the Washington political arena from the moment he had strode into the House of Representatives. At a time when the country was hurting in so many ways, when leadership was often bereft of inspiration, along came a man with a heroic aura. People were comparing him to Kennedy, and once she'd even heard his homespun, yarn-spinning manner likened to Lincoln. She had stifled an abrupt laugh at that.

But then who really knew what had gone on behind closed doors in Lincoln's time? In any case, Sam McCalahan was the man of the hour. In two years he had become the party hard-liner's most popular golf partner, the most sought-after bachelor, and everyone's favorite party guest. Big Sam they called him. Apparently the heavyweight party fathers were just waiting to spring Sam on the unsuspecting nation. At the moment he was mostly a Washington phenomena. Everyone seemed to agree that he needed an issue, something dramatic and compelling with which he could become identified.

Although Helga knew she supported a major amount of the legal workload on the Northern Railway case, she was also well aware of the decisions that Matthews and Stubbs made behind closed doors. Lately she had begun to fall into the Washington propensity for scuttlebutt and intrigue. Big Sam was a vociferous champion of public transportation. She was beginning to wonder if her bosses weren't angling for Sam's involvement in their case.

Super Sam, as she had begun to think of him, the man of the hour. Had she known anything at all about him she would have avoided him like the plague. Or so she told herself.

After several minutes of staring out into the gloomy afternoon she wandered into the outer office and addressed the older white-haired woman at the typewriter.

"Milly, why don't you go for lunch. I'm going to stay in."

"Can I bring you some soup?" Milly removed her glasses and smiled at Helga.

"No, thanks." Helga shook her head and went back inside her office.

It was past seven by the time she got home. Too late for Betsy's piano lesson, too late for anything but a hot shower, a cup of raspberry yogurt, bed, and one of the gory suspense thrillers she'd started reading since her arrival in Washington.

Against her will thoughts of that first day in Washington flitted through her mind. As she approached the denouement of the paperback, she kept losing the thread, had to keep shuffling back through the pages to keep the details straight. Finally she closed the book and stared up at the beamed ceiling. Marilyn wanted to fix her up with the French attaché. She mentioned it every time their paths crossed, which wasn't that frequently since Marilyn's gourmet business was as time-consuming as Helga's work.

But perhaps she should agree. Marilyn knew her as well as anyone, and if anyone could pair her up with an appropriate companion, it would be Marilyn. But she could muster no enthusiasm for the idea though Marilyn kept reminding her she had initially agreed. But that was before Sam McCalahan.

She plumped up the pillows and switched off the bedside light, but she could not put him out of her mind as she had managed to do on other nights. The last image she had of him was with his mouth agape at her bitingly sarcastic exit line. Although it had been a good fifteen or twenty minutes before she left the Phillips Gallery, he had not reappeared, or if he had the crowd had swallowed him up. But that was unlikely. She would have sensed his presence, would have heard his rumbling baritone or seen him towering above the others. Now she imagined him simply sitting back down in front of the Renoir painting, his big hands folded in his lap.

The image was a lonely one. But it was probably farfetched, and it was absurd for her to start feeling sorry for him now, after nearly two weeks of silence.

The phone next to her bed rang several times, stopped, and began again. Despite her effort to remain calm her breathing accelerated. She told herself she didn't feel like answering. The truth was that since last seeing him the phone had rung four or five times, usually around this time, and she had had the same tumultuous reaction. She would not admit the possibility that it was him.

The next morning she awoke to the same deluge, dressed in a crisp pale-blue oxford-cloth shirt, a gray wool skirt, and boots. After bundling up in a belted trench coat with her collar turned up, she headed defiantly out into the stormy day. So what if she was soaked all day at work? If she continued to cab everywhere she would be a basket case in another week.

"Hey! You'll drown!" Marilyn, still in her nightgown, was hanging out the second-story window. "You have a minute?"

"Just," Helga shouted back and dashed to the front door.

"What about dinner tonight?" Marilyn motioned Helga inside and closed the door.

"I don't know what time I'll finish." Helga stood tensely on the doormat.

"I feel awful," Marilyn apologized. "We haven't had a chance to talk. I've been at the store every night till ten or so. I haven't even seen Neal in over a week . . . I see the back of his head on the pillow and that's all."

"Don't feel bad." Helga smiled.

"But tonight I'm sprung. Lauren insisted. The only thing is, Neal has to fly to Atlanta to act as executor in his uncle's will. It'd just be the two of us."

"Can it be a late dinner? I never know what time I'll get out of there."

"Chez Bosc is open till midnight. Call me as you're leaving the office and we'll meet there. It's more or less on your way."

Helga ducked back out into the rain and sloshed briskly toward the office. Marilyn looked exhausted. Too much work. And how good could it be only to see the back of her husband's head for a week? It would be good just to sit and chat. Maybe she would even mention Sam.

Her stomach tightened at the thought, and even though she knew she would benefit from unburdening herself, she suspected she probably wouldn't. It had been the same after John's death. People had worried that she was keeping too much inside, not sharing her grief. But she had known what was best for her. Time had healed her. It was inevitable that time healed with or without words.

What if Sam McCalahan had been trying to phone her? What if she bumped into him, or worse, what if he became involved in the Northern case?

Helga was practically to her office building when she remembered that she wasn't supposed to be in the office this morning. She was supposed to be at a business breakfast at the Mayflower Hotel.

"Damn!" The expletive exploded out of her and several people turned to stare at the tall, stately blonde who, even in the midst of a downpour, managed to look dry and poised.

"Taxi!" Helga waved furiously. She felt anything but poised. She pulled off her tan pigskin gloves, shoved up the sleeve of her trench coat, and looked at her watch, knowing perfectly well that she was going to be late. And the men from 602, Mr. Coley and Mr. Lamreci, were terribly shy and uncertain. This was their first trip to Washington, their jobs and livelihoods were in question, they had probably never stayed in a hotel as large and grand as the Mayflower before, and *she* was keeping them waiting!

She continued to wave one arm as the traffic streamed past. Finally a cab screeched to a halt and someone in the backseat rolled down the window.

"Mrs. Tarr . . ."

Helga caught her breath. "Damn!" The word, used rarely by her, escaped for the second time in several minutes.

"Is that anyway to greet a gentleman who's offering you a ride?" Sam McCalahan bounded out of the cab and whisked her inside before she could reply.

"Where to?" He relieved her of her dripping umbrella and shook it over the matted floor.

"I can't take you out of your way," Helga protested.

"We'll have to see about that." Sam wrinkled his brow.

"The Mayflower." Helga felt like gulping for air.

"You're in luck." Sam leaned forward and whispered something to the driver, then he leaned back in the seat and stared straight ahead.

Helga glanced at his stony profile. He seemed deep in thought, impenetrable and far beyond her. She had been foolish to think he had been phoning. She had been deceiving herself, playing some childish game of not answering the phone in order to keep some small hope alive. She wasn't used to living and that was the truth.

She averted her eyes from his broad shoulders and felt the dull sickening ache of disappointment as the cab inched through the traffic.

After a moment she gathered her reserves and turned to him with a smile that was at once genuine and poignant. "This is nice of you. Thank you."

"I couldn't very well leave you dripping there on the corner of Fifteenth Street." His manner was friendly but detached.

"Oh, yes, you could have," Helga responded wryly and noted

a glint of humor in his hazel eyes before he turned away to reach for something in his briefcase.

"I have a business meeting." He waved a few papers by way of explanation.

"Oh, yes!" Helga said quickly. "By all means. Study them . . . whatever. I need time to recover myself."

He gave her a quizzical look then directed his attention to the papers.

The worst was over, she told herself. She had seen him and there was no longer any reason to dread the encounter. Then why couldn't she shake the terrible sadness?

The business breakfast with Mr. Coley and Mr. Lamreci went well enough, especially considering that Sam McCalahan and three distinguished men she recognized as senators were seated within earshot. By the time Helga sank into her office chair she was drained. It had been like doing business under a microscope; she had never felt so acutely self-conscious in her life. Still, Mr. Coley and Mr. Lamreci both expressed encouragement after listening to her summarize the new line of attack. Mr. Lamreci, who was more than a trifle hard of hearing, complimented her in a voice that she was certain reached the adjacent table.

But why did she care? Why did it matter what he thought of the way she conducted her business? Good heavens, he'd imposed himself in the one area of her life in which she had felt absolute confidence.

At about three in the afternoon Tate Brown burst into her office unannounced. "Helga, you've got to get right on over to the Hill and sit in on an impromptu meeting at Senator Wiley's office."

Helga looked up from her desk with a cool expression. Perhaps he hadn't meant to issue a command, but that was certainly the way it had come across. "Isn't Kenyon here?"

"Didn't he tell you? He flew home for the weekend." Tate turned to rush out of the room.

"Why?" Helga's question stopped him.

"Why what?" He grimaced then pasted a quick smile on his face.

"Why am I going over to the Hill now?" Even Kenyon, who was not always known for his tact and consideration, did not issue ultimatums.

"Just to cover the meeting." Tate could not hide his impatience. "I'm not sure if they're going to touch on the transportation issue, but it's likely. I just got wind of it, Helga. Don't be difficult."

Helga looked at him evenly and stifled a biting retort. How dare he accuse her of being difficult? She had only asked. And what right did he have to give her orders? She still didn't know what his function was. He acted as if he were suddenly in charge here. And if he were why hadn't she been told.

"Fine." She gathered up the papers on her desk and reached for her handbag.

"It may be a wild-goose chase." Tate moved hastily to help her on with her coat.

"Thank you." Helga started for the door without glancing at him. If he had only asked. If he had approached her as a colleague and said he thought such and such was going on at Senator Wiley's and maybe it would be a good idea to sit in. She felt suddenly protective of her domain, her office, her job as Washington liaison for the Northern Railway case. Tate Brown was too pushy. He had his fingers in too many pies; he was always looking off sideways as if something better might come along. She had felt that way even before he had dismissed her as a boring person.

The rain had finally let up and Helga flagged down a cab with no difficulty. As always she felt a rush of excitement as the massive baroque dome of the Capitol appeared in the distance. There was so much about Washington she liked. If only . . . if only she had not . . .

She glanced quickly at her watch to distract herself. The sun was beginning to break through the steely low clouds. It really was time to stop thinking about Sam McCalahan. She hated mopers and that was all she'd done for nearly two weeks.

She paid the cab driver and marched resolutely toward the Senate Office Building with a growing sense of determination. She had been indulging herself in all kinds of nonsense and from this moment on she was going to stop!

Chez Bosc was a tiny elegant French restaurant in Foggy Bottom, that now-famous area of Washington between Rock Creek Parkway and Arlington Memorial Bridge that includes Watergate.

"I'm so glad we're doing this!" Marilyn had insisted on splurging on an excellent bottle of red Bordeaux, a Chateau Beychevelle. She poured them each a glass and swirled the deep-red liquid thoughtfully.

Helga inhaled the deep musky bouquet. She had never heard of Chateau Beychevelle before, but even without tasting the wine she knew she would never forget it. She had not stayed at Senator Wiley's office long. Tate Brown had been wrong. There was nothing at all relevant to the case going on there, so she had taken her own advice and indulged in some positive activity by going home early and soaking in a scalding tub doused with pine-scent gel. She smiled now and her clear complexion glowed from the leisurely hour in the tub. Her blond hair was swept back behind her ears and fastened with two narrow tortoiseshell barrettes.

"I'm glad too." Helga raised her glass and the two women clinked in a toast. She was wearing a pale icy-blue mohair sweater that was an almost perfect match to her blue eyes. Her long legs were encased in a pair of black satin pants and her shoes were a favorite pair of flat black balletlike slippers.

"Michel!" Marilyn signaled the maître d', who appeared promptly with a slight bow and a friendly grin. Marilyn was clearly a favorite at Chez Bosc. The chef had even emerged in his white uniform to pay his respects and congratulate Marilyn on her own culinary success.

"Michel, *ma cher,* Helga must taste the pâté maison. Now I know we've ordered already but just a sliver?"

Helga sipped her wine thoughtfully as Marilyn made several other last-minute requests in their dinner order. The decor at Chez Bosc was exquisite and perfectly suited to her temperament. The thick luxurious pale gray rug seemed to absorb every sound and the white upholstered easy chairs that surrounded the dining tables were so comfortable she could imagine sitting there for hours. Which, according to Marilyn, was precisely what people did when they came to Chez Bosc. Here dining was treated as an event, an occasion that stretched on for hours. And Helga, as her eyes moved around the room taking in the slender flickering white candles, the crystal vases with their sparse pale pink oriental floral arrangements, was satisfied that there was no better place to spend an entire evening. It was restful and refined, just as Marilyn had said it was.

"I hope you're hungry!" Marilyn giggled irrepressibly. "I'm around food all day. Wouldn't you think I'd want to do something else during my time off?"

"There is no one who loves food more than you do." Helga smiled. "I marvel that you don't weigh a ton."

Marilyn made a face. "Let's not talk about weight."

"But you're not fat!" Helga protested.

"Let's talk about your job," Marilyn insisted. "Actually I have lost a pound or two since the business took off. Now, what's new . . . or what's what for that matter. I don't know what you're doing except battling unions."

"I'm not battling unions," Helga corrected her with a smile. "That's the way people who want to divide the ranks describe the case. That's why so many of our public transportation systems are in trouble. We, that is, Matthews, Matthews, and Stubbs, are representing the railroad. That's true. But we're not representing them against the unions. We're trying to put together an entire package which the government will support . . . a package that will keep the railroad alive. Do you realize how many railroads have collapsed in the past twenty years? This country was built on railroads. When John and I were first married we took a train to Los Angeles. That train no longer exists. And it's not just passenger trains, though I believe with all my heart that we need to revive that aspect of the railroads too. But even the freights are endangered."

"You're really involved in this." Marilyn smiled. "I'm so glad. You really care."

"I think a viable, modernized railroad system could help turn this country around," Helga stated firmly.

"You should see the trains in France!" Marilyn pounced on the subject with her usual gusto. "You and I should go to France. Next summer! Okay! Maybe, if we're brave, we'll take the kids for part of the time. Promise?"

"You haven't changed at all." Helga laughed. "How can I promise a thing like that?"

"You don't have to mean it." Marilyn laughed as she took a sip of wine. "You have to mean it now, of course. That's how things get done . . . in my life anyway. You promise something and with all your heart you mean it. But you never know. And obviously you promise things that are . . . way-out sometimes."

"You've always been way-out," Helga said admiringly. "And I've always been way-in. Whatever the opposite of trendy is, that's me."

"You're beyond trends," Marilyn observed. "You're the sort of person who starts trends. You just don't know it. Just look at you in that fuzzy blue sweater and black satin pants and flat shoes. You look like the cover of *Vogue*. No, you look better than the cover of *Vogue* because you didn't plan it. You just did it because you wanted to."

Marilyn paused a moment, considering. "Listen, Helga, if you're so involved in this case . . . do you ever think of going to law school anymore. Why work for somebody else?"

Helga shrugged. "I love my job. Usually. Today I had a bad moment with someone but that's rare. And I love the firm, I love where their allegiances lie. Willard Matthews was like a father to me when John died."

"He just knew a good thing when he saw it." Marilyn narrowed her eyes pointedly. "You've always thought he did you a favor by offering you a job. You practically graduated Phi Beta Kappa for heaven's sake! You would have if . . ."

". . . if John hadn't died. You can say it." Helga gave her a reassuring smile.

"The thing is"—Marilyn poured them each another glass of wine—"I think you should be a lawyer. You yourself. Now, don't make a face like that. Helga, look at Lauren and me. We started Food Fancy on a shoestring and look where we are now. Bloomingdale's wants us to do a boutique! We can't keep up with all of the business we have."

"That's wonderful," Helga said, "but I don't get the connection. I love working for the firm. I can't imagine anything I'd like more."

"It's just that two years ago we didn't think we could do it. Lauren's older than we are. She'd never made a success at anything, including two marriages. The business has changed her life and given her confidence to reach out for what she wants." Marilyn giggled softly. "She's just decided by the way that she wants a particular man. You've heard of Big Sam?"

Helga raised her eyes with a coolness that amazed even her. "I . . . I think so."

"Well, Lauren, who is wonderful . . . You're going to love her, but she's usually quite cynical about men. Anyhow, she's gone around the proverbial bend for the Texan."

Helga placed one smooth hand gracefully on the white tablecloth, regarded it pensively a moment, then looked back at Marilyn. "I wish her luck."

Marilyn chuckled. "She'll need it. I've only met the man once but I wouldn't want to tangle with him. I prefer the more docile

78

variety . . . like Neal, bless him! I keep telling Lauren she's falling into the same trap again. She always gravitates toward handsome men with an eye for the ladies."

Helga gave Marilyn an enigmatic little smile. "And the Texan has a reputation for being a ladies' man . . . is that it?"

"You asked the right person!" Marilyn, ever the clarion for a juicy tidbit of gossip, leaned across the table with a conspirator's gleam in her dark eyes. "The man has galloped through the cream of Washington's crop. Neal and I used to try and guess who would be next. For a while it seemed like his picture was on the society page every single day . . . with a different woman."

"It must have been exhausting for him," Helga observed dryly.

"Apparently," said Marilyn, "he's one of these high-energy types who can live on a few hours' sleep. There are people like that, you know. People so potent and well-oiled that they just never seem to run down."

"Or driven," Helga offered smoothly.

"Not *just* driven," Marilyn objected. "It's probably in the metabolism, but I've met people, healthy, nonneurotic people, who simply live life at an accelerated speed . . . on a continual high peak. Well, I'd imagine it would take that kind of energy to be president of the United States, which is really what they're grooming the Texan for."

President of the United States? How remote and unreal it sounded especially in relation to someone she actually knew. Helga Tarr was not one to revere or idolize public figures. Being reticent by nature, she was just as likely to withdraw from a conversation with the senator's chauffeur as with the senator himself. Still, the idea of Sam McCalahan as an actual contender for the presidency of the United States gave her a vague, unsettled feeling that she did not fully understand. She thought of him as he had greeted her in the cab that morning, friendly and congenial as ever but very intent on utilizing every second of time to prepare for his meeting. During the ride his concentration had been entirely focused on the papers he had taken out of his briefcase. She had assumed his withdrawn behavior had something to do with her, that he was politely but firmly letting her know that while he would not let her suffer in the rain, there was nothing more to his gesture. But perhaps he had simply had something else to do, something that nothing or no one could intrude upon.

"There's no question the man has enormous political potential," Marilyn went on as the waiter brought an assortment of puff pastry hors d'oeuvres. "And, according to Lauren, he's even got integrity, which is rare. He's not just another pretty face. But you never know. At the moment he's a local item—something for the political sharks in town to sink their teeth into to test his durability."

"And how does Lauren feel about . . . politics?" Helga tasted one of the delectable morsels despite the growing feeling that everything that was being said, everything that was happening around her was unreal.

"I think she's a match for McCalahan." Marilyn munched blissfully. "She's very ambitious herself, and very game. Actually Lauren would be a perfect first lady as far as I'm concerned. Only thing is . . . two divorces? The men who write the rules frown on that, unless they can hush it up, which is the way most things are handled."

Helga devoured two morsels in rapid succession, and when Marilyn poured the remainder of the wine in her glass and suggested ordering another bottle Helga did not object. Earlier that day she had promised herself she'd shake off her boring old mopey depression and she was more determined than ever to do exactly that.

The wine helped enormously and so did the gratin aux fruits de mer, which was the first course, followed by a crisp and quite incredible roast duck with peaches. By the time Helga had finished the tender watercress and endive salad that Marilyn had requested be served at the conclusion of the meal, their earlier conversation seemed as distant and irrelevant as one of the suspense novels she had taken to reading before bedtime.

"I needed this!" She reached for her wineglass, enjoying the sense of well-being that flowed through her body.

"I don't want you to leave," Marilyn said, and Helga smiled and wondered if her own face was as flushed and her own eyes as glazed with inebriated contentment.

"You never wait to cross a bridge," Helga began, then giggled softly as she tried to correct herself. "You *always* cross a bridge before you come to it. Anyway you'll be sick of me in another month."

"I doubt it," Marilyn mused. "Betsy adores you."

"And I love her." Helga smiled fondly, thinking of the little girl. "It's nice liking your friend's children. It doesn't always happen that way."

"Amen!" Marilyn breathed. "You should get married and have one . . ."

"You are so full of advice." Helga blushed. "First I'm to be a lawyer, then I'm supposed to have a baby."

"I like to see all of my friends happy and taken care of," Marilyn announced cheerfully. "I am shameless in my ability to make a pest of myself with advice."

"Well, I honestly wouldn't mind," Helga confessed. She drew her lips together for a moment as she considered telling Marilyn about what had happened between her and Sam. But that would mean putting Marilyn in an awkward position with Lauren, or so she told herself.

"Do we dare have a cognac?" Marilyn asked with mock trepidation.

"We didn't have dessert," Helga replied sagely. "It seems we might indulge a bit more."

By the time they finished the cognac they were both quite tipsy.

"I think!" Marilyn assumed a declamatory style. "I think! I think, I know, I foresee that you are going to fall madly in love."

"Marilyn"—Helga kicked her gently under the table—"you're soused."

"I mean it," Marilyn said. "I told you I'm convinced that people who've had a deep love, a good marriage the first time around are destined, yes destined . . . to find a second love. Even if the second love is different."

Helga sighed and a faraway look came into her eyes as she thought of Sam. Nobody could have been more different from John than the Texan. John had been small, slight, tweedy, and intellectual. He had an endearing sense of humor that reduced people to gasps of laughter, but only if they were quick to catch the subtle innuendos that he delivered in a soft, understated tone of voice.

Under the influence of the wine John and Sam seemed to inhabit the same space, the same time. In Helga's imagination she saw them both very clearly, without sentimentality, without even a suggestion of guilt that she was comparing the two. There was no need, no reason to compare them. They would have liked each other, she was sure of it. As loud and boisterous as the Texan could be, he was not a self-absorbed man. He was attuned to what was going on around him, to birds hopping on the ground, to the voices of men that did not shake the rafters as his did. He would have heard John Tarr's gentle quips and he would have laughed.

Perhaps she had made a mistake in lashing out at him so sarcastically. It had all happened so fast, but perhaps she could rectify the situation. She had never in her life pursued a man. But then she had never in her life shared two bottles of wine and a cognac over dinner!

"I love getting tipsy with my women friends," Marilyn confessed. "It always makes me feel chic and very with-it."

A low purr of agreement escaped from Helga's softly parted lips. "How long have Sam and Lauren been seeing each other?"

"A few months." Marilyn was suddenly alert. "Why don't I arrange a small dinner party, something very casual for the coming week? You can meet Lauren and the fabled Texan. I'm willing to bet you'll find him a bit too loud and overpowering."

"Well," Helga mused languidly, "that should be interesting." She had probably consumed too much liquor, but it didn't seem to matter. It had been a long time since she had felt so expansive, so receptive to whatever life might offer. Possibilities, suddenly her world was full of them.

"But I take it . . . there's nothing exclusive between Lauren and . . ." Helga waved her hand limply as if his name had escaped her.

"Heavens no!" Marilyn confirmed.

Helga settled back into her chair with a contented smile and allowed her mind to drift in a future of whimsical romantic possibilities while Marilyn, who insisted this evening was to be her treat, took care of the bill. She was thankful Sam's relationship with Lauren was in the preliminary stages. She would never have been able to proceed without ascertaining that.

The word *proceed* brought her up short. There was nothing romantic about the word proceed, and that was precisely what she would have to do if she was serious, if she was not just off in some intoxicated fantasy. She was going to have to *proceed* . . . make a phone call, write a letter. If she was ever going to get his attention again, she was going to have to take matters into her own hands. She was going to have to proceed!

She was so lost in her own thoughts that she did not feel Marilyn's foot nudging her beneath the table or hear the deep, mellow laughter coming from the bar. Six distinguished men, all in evening clothes, had entered in the spirit of vociferous male camaraderie to share a nightcap after an earlier function. Sam McCalahan was among them.

Helga frowned slightly; she knew herself well enough, even under the haze of liquor, to know that proceeding would be no easy matter. She had never in her life phoned a man, and while she believed, ideologically, in a woman's *unalienable* right to proceed, she could not imagine phoning Sam McCalahan. And yet she was going to. She had made up her mind, was, this very minute, making herself a promise that tomorrow morning, cold sober, she would fish out the little card he had handed her that first day by the river . . . and *proceed.*

"Helga Tarr, this is Sam McCalahan." Finally Marilyn's voice penetrated her intoxicated concentration, and she looked up just as the Texan, dressed in black tie and tuxedo, slid into the chair next to her.

"Hello." She did not have time to mask her feelings. When she clasped his outstretched hand the ripple of pleasure that flowed into her was mirrored in her eyes.

"You two ladies having a nice night out on the town?" Sam gave Helga's hand a warm squeeze before he released it.

"Yes!" Marilyn looked from Sam to Helga with a shocked expression. The electric glances that shot between Helga and the Texan had not escaped her for a moment.

"You know Tate Brown." Sam motioned for Tate to join them.

"How are you, Marilyn." Tate hopped off the bar stool and extended his hand first to Helga, then to Marilyn.

"I've been meaning to call and compliment you on that carrot cake with sour-cream icing." Tate smiled as he declined Sam's offer to join the women. "Lauren sent me over a huge slab and I must say, she refused to take any credit whatsoever. Said it was one hundred percent your creation."

"Well, well . . ." Marilyn, who was never speechless, was still recovering from the impact of witnessing such torrid currents passing between Helga and Sam. "That's Lauren for you . . ."

"Wonderful woman!" Tate nodded. "Sorry about the wild-goose chase today, Helga."

"That's all right," Helga replied quickly. Beneath the table Sam's trouser leg brushed against her black satin pants and she felt him shift farther away. Too quickly, she thought, as if the proximity was having the same stupefying effect on him. She glanced at him briefly and her heart accelerated madly. He hadn't changed! He hadn't changed at all. He was staring at her with the same warmth, the same appreciation he had lavished on her by the river.

She was only peripherally aware of the conversation that was taking place between Tate and Marilyn, and though she did not look back at him, she was sure that Sam was having the same difficulty concentrating. The back of her neck began to perspire and the palms of her hands as she pressed them together were like ice. The wild sensations that assaulted her body were strangely sweet, for even as she felt herself throbbing with hot impatience, she knew for certain now what she had sensed from the beginning. There was something rare between them, something that, though it might be frightening in its intensity, could not be denied. They would be lovers. There was no question.

CHAPTER FIVE

Helga sat in the backseat of Sam's littered blue Oldsmobile and tried to concentrate on Marilyn's bubbling nonstop conversation. Poor Marilyn was totally flabbergasted by what was going on. She drew in a deep breath and sank back amongst the leaflets and tennis balls.

Sam had insisted on seeing them home. Helga smiled softly as she stared at the back of his sandy head. He hadn't fooled anyone with his suddenly traditional insistence that the two ladies needed to be escorted to their door. He hadn't fooled Marilyn and he certainly hadn't fooled her. And *she* probably hadn't fooled anyone by hopping into the backseat of the car.

Marilyn twisted around in the front seat and gave Helga a quizzical look, but Helga only shrugged and shook her head. What could she say? Marilyn rolled her eyes in Sam's direction before turning back around in the seat.

As they approached the Sell residence, Helga felt a fluttering of nerves in the pit of her stomach. What now, what now? She felt as if she were on the edge of a high diving board, blindfolded. Would he invite himself into Marilyn's? Would the three of them sit around talking all night?

But Sam seemed to know exactly what he had in mind. No, it would not do to drop the two women at the curb. He parked the car and kept up a steady charming banter of conversation as he walked them to the front door.

"This is very nice of you." Marilyn's tone was genuine if still bewildered. She glanced quickly at Helga, then back at Sam. "Helga lives around there . . . through that little gate. I'm fine now but—"

"I'll make sure no frogs hop out to scare her." Sam grinned as Marilyn went inside the house.

Helga's heart seemed to have stopped as they stood for a moment. The two gaslights that flickered on either side of the front door cast mysterious shadows along the porch.

"Timeless," Sam said watching the flickering lights.

"Yes," Helga agreed softly.

"Your friend is very sensitive." Sam placed his hand gently under her elbow and began guiding her along the width of the porch.

"You mean because she knew you wanted to see me to my door?" Helga smiled. "I'm not sure that either of us, you or me, that is, was very subtle."

Sam stepped in front of her and placed his hands on her shoulders. "You seem so different than when I saw you this morning."

"I could say the same about you." Helga's pulse raced as she looked into his face.

"Why?" he peered at her closely, absorbed in the moment, just as he had been totally absorbed in his papers that morning.

Helga felt galvanized by his gaze. "I was convinced that you had written me off."

Sam looked at her for another long moment. "How could I do that?"

"Maybe we should go on to my room." Helga pulled away from him and led the way down the porch steps and into the backyard garden. The night was crisp, almost cold, and the moon, which earlier had been a fat orange harvest moon, had turned milky pale.

Helga opened the door to the stone cottage, flicked on the floor lamp next to the couch, and stood aside for him to enter.

"I wouldn't have written you off." His expression was serious as he stepped inside.

"Really?" Helga stared at him and her question hung in the air between them.

"I tried to phone you." A shiver ran down her spine and she stopped herself from asking when, what time? Was it possible that she was so attuned to him that she had known when he was phoning?

She moved away from him suddenly and shrugged off her coat. She did not believe in mystical synchroneity, she did not want to believe in it.

She turned back to him. Dressed in the formal tuxedo with his bow tie primly at his neck, he was the very picture of a presidential hopeful, elegant, dignified . . . yes, even heroic. She wouldn't have thought he would feel comfortable in such formal attire, yet he wore the clothes, the way she was beginning to see he did everything, with complete abandon and ease. Each time she saw him she thought she had seen another part of the kind of man he was—a casual, boyish man by the river waiting for a bird, a rather boisterous handshaking man moving through the crowd at the Phillips Gallery. And now this man, intense, compelling, and even more handsome than she remembered.

"I had to go back to Texas on business." He sat down on the sofa but his eyes never left her face. "You really didn't think I wouldn't phone?"

Helga felt suddenly nervous. His propensity for candor was unlike anything she had ever known. He had from the start put all of his cards on the table where she was concerned, and yet it was almost more than she could accept from a man of his stature.

"I thought you would." She forced herself to rise to his example. "But then when I didn't speak to you I was convinced you thought my behavior at the Phillips was . . . silly. I don't know, that I was . . . too old-fashioned."

"No." He shook his head agreeably and waited for her to

continue. She had the sense that she might say anything to him, anything at all, and he would accept her.

"I'm an impatient man," he said when she did not continue, "but I'm also a man who likes to get what he wants. I want you. However long that takes is how long I wait."

He folded his hands on his lap and looked at her with a mysterious half smile that made her breathless.

"I thought you would call." Helga moved slowly over to the couch and sat down at the opposite end, kicking off her shoes and tucking her feet under her as she faced him. "I was so sure that you would that sometimes I didn't answer the phone."

He was momentarily startled by her confession, but then he smiled and nodded as if he liked that added twist of complexity. "I had the feeling you were in that position. That's why I never called you at the office. Did that detail never arouse your curiosity?"

He eyed her narrowly and she laughed. "Of course it did. I said, how badly can he want to talk to me if he doesn't call me at work?"

"You wanted to make things hard for me." He looked at her a moment then leaned over and began untying his shoes.

Helga studied his broad shoulders as he hunched over his shiny black shoes. The black jacket strained over his broad shoulders as he eased his feet out of their confinement and wriggled his toes.

"New shoes?" Helga experienced an unexpected palpitation at the sight of his large black stockinged feet.

"Man, do they ever hurt . . ." Sam continued unabashedly massaging his toes. "All evening I've been wanting to do this!"

Helga stared at his huge hands as they manipulated and rubbed his aching toes. It was an ordinary enough act, yet it triggered in her a desire so fierce that she averted her eyes in embarrassment. Despite his comical moans of relief she could do nothing to quell the persistent fluttering. She was suddenly aware of the sensual texture of her black satin slacks and she shifted her legs out from under her to dispel the giddiness that swept over her at the rich sound of his voice.

She hugged her arms in front of her fuzzy blue sweater in a gesture entirely foreign to her. The fire in her breasts did not subside, and when he sat back up against the couch and their eyes met, she felt she was bursting with desire for him. She thought vaguely of all the things Marilyn had unwittingly revealed about him . . . of the many women who passed through his life, of Lauren, of his political future. None of those things seemed real.

What was real was the man. And the myriad feelings he aroused in her—those were real too.

"Mind if I light the fire?" Sam was the one finally to break the spell and to tear his eyes away from hers.

"I haven't tried it." Helga glanced at the brick fireplace that was already set with kindling and paper.

She watched him crouch on his haunches as he struck a match against the bricks and ignited the paper. Once again the massive power of his broad shoulders set off a series of tugging spasms and she sprang to her feet, stretching her arms above her head in a futile effort to gain control over her senses. She stood behind him and a bit off to the right. The glow from the fire cast a faint pink shadow across her face as the flames licked and curled around the twigs.

"It wasn't that I was playing hard to get." She spoke the words instinctively, without thinking.

"I know." Sam fell to a sitting position and with his back still to her sat cross-legged in front of the fire.

"I mean it wasn't premeditated." She stared down at the top of his head. "I wanted to hear from you and didn't want to. It was easier, in a way, to believe you'd written me off."

"You didn't seem like the sort of woman to read Helen Gurley Brown's advice on how to snare a man." He chuckled softly as if the idea amused him greatly.

Helga smiled and sank down onto the floor next to him. The

heady euphoria she had experienced at Chez Bosc had all but vanished, and in its place there was a new, more provocative intoxication. It amazed her that after consuming so much wine she could feel such extraordinary clarity. But then she had made a decision, a decision to *proceed,* to take matters into her own hands. That he had appeared so unexpectedly just after she had arrived at that momentous decision made everything that much easier.

"I spend a lot of time considering what people's motives might be," he remarked as he casually removed his tuxedo jacket and tossed it onto the couch. "The whole political game is a question of second-guessing, of out anticipating the other side. If you're going to be effective in the legislature you have to have your antenna out and be able to put yourself in the other guy's shoes."

"And you put yourself in my shoes?" Helga watched the shadows flickering across his strong, handsome face.

"I offended you at the Phillips Gallery. I came on too strong, got carried away. You had every right to call me on it"—he turned to her with a grin—"which you did, and roundly, I might add. For a delicate-looking creature you have a tongue which would rival, both in speed and acridity, those of some of our most wily congresspeople."

"May I consider myself complimented?" Helga stifled a smile.

"You may consider yourself . . . complimented may be too generous a word . . . You may consider yourself pigeonholed!" Sam gave a robust laugh as he fumbled to loosen his tie.

"I don't usually insult people." Helga watched in amusement as he struggled with the tie. "I'm rather known for being un-ruffled."

"And I ruffled you? Am *I* complimented?" Sam gave a hard jerk and tore the tie off. He stared at it a moment, waded it into a ball, and tossed it into the fire.

"Why did you do that?" Helga turned to him with an astonished smile.

He gave her a coy look, lifted both of her hands up to his lips, and kissed them each lightly. "To surprise you. To see your eyes light up, catch you off guard and shatter that cloak of mysterious, unruffled calm you wear so with such panache. I always like to catch my opponents off guard."

"Am I an opponent?" Helga asked weakly as he moved his mouth over her knuckles.

"We'll have to see about that, won't we?" Sam leaned forward and kissed her tenderly on the lips, then pulled away.

She closed her eyes briefly. The sensation of his full, dry lips pressing chastely against hers unleashed a torrent of scalding waves. She had stopped herself from responding, but she could not stop the breathlessness, the almost painful yearning to feel all of his solid manly form pressing into her. She was beset by images that drove her to a higher pitch of desire—images of herself as a totally abandoned woman, a woman who would strip off her icy-blue sweater and toss it into the raging fire, just as he had done with his tie. She imagined the look on his face, the mixture of shock and raw lust. She thought of his eyes devouring the splendor of her ample breasts and felt the agonizing suspense of his large hand hovering over her prickling flesh.

Her pulse accelerated wildly as images of their naked bodies entwined and undulating with uninhibited passion flashed in on her. She drew in a deep breath. She was not that sort of woman, and however much she wished it she could not overcome a lifetime of control and propriety. She stared at the flames and listened to the crackle of the fire. Despite the serenity of her expression each flicker, each sound was fuel to her fantasies. She saw her pale, slender body moving in front of the flames in a slow, hypnotic dance. To dance naked before him? She blinked her eyes hard. She had never in her life entertained such lustful thoughts.

"What are you thinking?" His husky voice interrupted the voluptuous images.

Her heart raced at his intrusion. She shook her head and continued staring into the fire. She had made the mistake at the

Phillips Gallery of sending out signals that, in the end, she had been unwilling . . . or unable to act upon. Tonight, in deference to her, his kiss had been restrained, not out of lack of passion but because, as he had said, he was waiting. She craved the sensation of his hands on her breasts, wanted that slow, stroking tongue tasting her flesh, but this time there would be no stopping. She frowned, struggling with convention, with details that had nothing whatsoever to do with who she was and who he was. What it came down to was she had not known him long enough. She knew it was absurd, but she could not shake some far-off insistent voice that kept reminding her that this was only the fourth time they had seen each other.

"I was thinking . . ." Her voice trailed off. "I was thinking . . ."

He reached for her hand and gave it an urgent squeeze.

"Thinking," she continued after a moment, "that it's late and you should leave, but I don't want you to. I was thinking so many things."

He pulled her close and cradled her against his chest so that they were both facing the fire.

"Maybe you do too much thinking. I know that must sound like a trite male approach to seduction, but I think it has particular significance for you. All you cerebral types are alike."

There was a soft, humorous note in his voice. Helga studied one small, narrow flame as it shimmered into several orange points then widened into a single bluish triangle. It felt good to lean against him, to feel the steady, even throbbing of his heart.

"But there's no rush," he murmured against her hair, then sweeping the strand aside he kissed her ear gently. "We could have dinner tomorrow night." His hand moved slowly down her arm, grazing the side of her gently rounded breast ever so slightly.

Tomorrow night seemed like an eternity. Helga shifted in his arms, burying her face into him, still staring at the dancing flames.

She had known only one man in her life. She took Sam's hand in hers and studied it intently, again struck by the sensitivity of his long fingers, the smoothness of his palm, and the light sprinkling of sandy hairs on top. She had thought of his hands many times during the past two weeks. It was hard to imagine those same hands holding the reins on a bucking bronco or lassoing a steer. She raised his hand to her lips and tested the wiry hairs with softly parted lips. She felt him draw in a sharp breath, and that sound sent her beyond the point of no return. His reaction banished all of her fears.

With a certainty she had experienced only once before as a girl she turned against him and rose to her knees. Her eyes were as alive as the flames that leaped behind her. He sensed the change in her immediately and tensed in anticipation.

Helga quivered as Sam's mouth sought hers. There had been no mistaking her signals. She steadied herself on her knees as his mouth opened on hers, hot and damp, as forceful and dynamic now as she remembered. His tongue moved furiously in long, rapid strokes that seemed to dive down into her core to inflame her there. They were both on their knees, their bodies seared together as if by some pull beyond their control.

Helga moaned her acquiescence and swirled her tongue around his, enticing him, matching his rhythm, which grew more frenzied and powerful with each thrust. With her arms flung around his neck she felt herself suspended, lost in all of the wonders of his huge, muscular body. His breath tasted faintly of fine cognac. Or perhaps it was her own breath intermingling with his. It was difficult to tell. It was enough to drink in all of the dizzying sensations, to feel the sharpness of his teeth, to run her hand over his cheek, which was coarse and pleasingly abrasive for want of a shave after a long day.

Helga moved her hands around his face, relishing every detail, memorizing with her fingers the heavy bones above his brows, the high cheekbones and the sharp, straight nose. As his mouth moved hungrily on hers, she felt herself bursting inside. She was boiling, rising ever higher and higher, on the point of overflowing.

When his hands moved adroitly down the front of her sweater to cup her breasts, she could only sway into him, accommodating his searching fingers. Her head fell to one side and she began to pant softly, rhythmically as he skillfully slipped both hands beneath her sweater. The sensation of his hands on her bare flesh brought a moan of gratitude to her lips, and when she felt his nimble fingers inching around her back to unfasten her bra, she was on the point of crying out.

"You are so beautiful." He gazed at her for a moment as his hands stroked her silky back. Then he deftly unfastened her bra and in one fluid movement his hands were pressed against her breasts, testing their softness with a delicate finesse that took her breath away.

She raised her arms above her head, and as if in a dream she felt him strip off the blue sweater and toss it on the couch next to his jacket. She could not believe what was happening, could not believe that the woman she had been all of her life was sitting half naked in front of a roaring fire offering her breasts without the least twinge of modesty.

Sam stared at her smooth ivory torso. He caught her eye for a moment and her fever soared higher. The heat from the fire warmed her back, and as he buried his head in her breasts, she closed her eyes to savor all of the luscious sensations. His mouth found one nipple and deliberately he placed his tongue on the hard center tip and made light flicking strokes. He swept the other hand along the length of her torso, stopping to test her delicate rib frame, memorizing the silky smoothness of her body as she had done moments before with his face.

She shuddered as his mouth slid along her breasts, which were now damp and warm. His tongue swirled and sucked, propelling her into a world of erotic splendors so intense and varied that she could not begin to imagine what might lie ahead. Each artful foray drove her into a new realm. He showered her neck with light kisses and found her mouth again. This time his kiss was deep and provocatively thoughtful, as if he were dipping into her very soul.

His expression when he looked at her was quizzical.

"It's all right." She lowered her eyes in answer to his unspoken question. "I want you to stay with me. I want . . ." She could hardly speak for wanting him. "I want us to make love."

Sam caressed her cheek tenderly as he unbuttoned his shirt, and she was aware of many things as she watched him strip naked before her. She was aware of the crisp November night outside the door to the cottage, of the crystal stars, the bursts of orange marigolds still blooming, the occasional hissing of the fire, the heavy woody aroma, and the shadows that had deepened, plunging the room into near darkness as the fire burned more slowly.

The contrast of her pale breasts and torso against the black satin pants was intensely erotic, and it seemed to Sam McCalahan that nothing so strange and sweet as this had happened to him in his entire life. The unexpected blond creature who continued to stare up at him so boldly had astonished him from the first moment he had laid eyes on her, but this turn of events had taken him completely by surprise. He had imagined a cup of tea, talk, and plans for another evening . . . he hoped soon. With a woman as obviously intelligent and controlled as Helga Tarr he had envisioned weeks, perhaps months even of courtship. Yes, he had even thought of the word courtship in reference to her. And now this. It was baffling, like something from a dream.

Helga smiled languidly, taking in the magnificence of his manly form. Her face was flushed from the heat and strands of damp blond hair clung to her neck. Because he wore his clothes with such style and verve she had not anticipated such an athletic body. The muscles in his upper back were thick and well-defined, almost as if he had spent time in body building, an idea that caused her to give a low throaty laugh. She could not for an instant imagine him jerking barbells up and down.

"What is it?" He had turned his back to remove his trousers and now he glanced at her over his shoulder.

Helga reached for the plaid blanket that was draped over the sofa and spread it in front of the fire.

"What's so funny?" Wearing only his blue boxer shorts, Sam leaned back down to kiss her forehead.

"You." Helga ran her hands over his broad chest, which was sprinkled with tightly curled sandy hair.

"I'm funny, am I?" He gave a low laugh and nuzzled her neck playfully. "A man undresses and gets a laugh?"

"Yes." Helga wiggled away from him and stared again at his broad, magnificent chest. His legs, too, were the legs of an athlete, with thick, sinewy thigh muscles and hard, bulging calves.

"Wait till you hear me laugh at you," Sam told her with a long, sexy look. "You don't know what laughter is until you've heard me laugh!"

Helga's breath quickened at his suggestive promise. The playful teasing made her giddy with desire, with an abandon she could scarcely believe. There was such ease, such a naturalness to his movements as he stalked over to the sofa and laid his trousers out flat. He was at home. Yes, he seemed as comfortable here in his role of ardent lover as he had been on the banks of the Potomac, or shaking hands with his colleagues, or submerged in his work in the cab. He was a man at home in the world, a man who seemed to know who he was and was at peace with that knowledge. His was no rushed, fumbling attack, but a long, extended erotic moment . . . something to be savored and prolonged. Helga ran her hands down the sides of her black satin pants. There was a sanctity to the silence, to the flickering shadows. When he sat down beside her, stroking her breasts lightly as he gazed at her, she knew that he felt it too.

They stared at each other as if they were listening or as if they were *hearing* something exquisitely rare, something that only they could hear. It was their world at that moment.

Helga lay back on the plaid blanket and closed her eyes, her breathing more measured now, as if she had primed herself to contain the high pitch of passion. She felt his hands at her waist, felt him release the small hook and heard the soft sound of the zipper. She lifted her hips up slightly as he skimmed off the slacks and sucked in her taut stomach when his hand caressed her bare skin just above her scant black bikini panties.

Behind closed eyes she had the sense of herself spinning wildly far far out into the galaxy amidst stars and moons all traveling, like herself, at breathtaking velocity. His hand caressed the sensitive inner line of her thigh then slid around beneath her buttocks to explore each curve and crevice. She soared, spinning and whirling and offering herself to the pure sensuality of his inquiring fingers as he stripped away the final barrier. She heard a low moan, like distant thunder, and she opened herself willingly as he stroked her.

His touch was tender. She had known it would be and she swiveled her hips in answer to the titillation as his fingers sought that fine, hard point of pleasure.

"Sam!" She called to him and reached out to draw him down on top of her. She had gone beyond the whirling darkness into white heat. Her hand grasped him and he shuddered as she guided him closer and closer. They were both delirious with anticipation but still the moment was prolonged. His weight fell full upon her and they both gasped in recognition before they began to undulate and tremble, each giving total access to the other, their mouths moving feverishly, their legs and arms entwined.

"Helga . . ." He breathed her name as if it were a prayer. "I've thought of you . . ." He broke off and his hands clutched her almost frantically, and she knew she was seeing yet another side of him. He murmured her name again and again as he took full possession of the remaining darkness, filling her with throbbing fire and moving against her with a fury that stirred her soul.

When they finally lay drenched and trembling in each other's arms, the fire was a mere glow of red embers. Sam wrapped the blanket around them and they snuggled against each other still lost in an erotic haze. They lay that way until the fire was ash, until they were clinging to each other to stave off the chill of the autumn night. Reluctant to move they nestled closer.

"We're both going to catch pneumonia," Sam whispered but made no move to get up.

"Hansel and Gretel," Helga said groggily. "There's a bed up there." She started to gesture upstairs to the loft but thought better of disturbing the warmth of their cocoon.

"I should go." Sam's breath was warm in her ear and she shivered. "I don't want to."

"Mmmm." Helga snuggled against him, wanting to shut out the world, wanting not to think of anything that existed outside of their world.

"We'll have dinner tomorrow night," he whispered. "I should say . . . tonight. It's nearly two."

"How do you know?" Helga opened her eyes and gazed at him.

"Inner clock," he told her. "I always know what time it is."

"That's why you were late the day we first met," Helga observed mischievously.

"You got me off my track." He kissed her lightly on the mouth. "You're a surprising woman."

Helga nodded. "You didn't expect this . . . to happen tonight."

Sam smiled. "I sure as hell didn't!"

Helga laughed softly. "Me neither."

Sam regarded her for a moment. "I didn't figure you for the impulsive type."

"I'm not." Helga nestled more deeply against him. "I've been thinking about you for two weeks. Tonight, before you showed up at Chez Bosc, I'd made up my mind . . . I was going to call you tomorrow . . . or rather today."

"I'm not home." Sam hugged her close.

"It's too cold for you to leave." Helga wrapped her arms around him more tightly and his flesh warmed her.

99

"I thought you might be sensitive about . . . Marilyn," he said after a moment.

Helga felt a faint flutter of anxiety intrude upon their world. "You're sure that's the reason?" Lauren. Lauren was the reason.

Sam felt her tense and looked closely at her. "There's no other reason," he said sincerely.

"It's too . . . too bizarre for you to leave!" Helga told him evenly. "Unless the press is lined up outside my door."

"I don't want to . . ."

"Then don't!" Helga turned into him and pressed her lips against his until she felt a thrill of pleasure ripple through his body.

Helga awoke the next morning with the same rapturous smile on her face. Sam, his feet hanging off the bottom of the bed, was sleeping soundly with his head practically buried underneath the pillow. She had no recollection of how they had climbed the ladder to the loft, though she must have climbed up herself since there was no way he would have been able to carry her. She remembered a lot of giggling and pinching, and several bad jokes about Hansel and Gretel and breadcrumbs. And it seemed as if the sun had been coming up but she couldn't be sure of that either.

But she was sure of one thing. She was absolutely one hundred percent in love with Sam McCalahan. She felt a wild, unfettered excitement as she bounded out of bed and scurried down the ladder into the main room to put on some water for tea. This was a man worth waiting for. She ran back over to the ladder and scrambled up to have another look at the huge lump in her bed.

She put on the tea kettle and went into the bathroom to brush her teeth. She was tousled and flushed, and though she had had less than five hours of sleep, she looked radiant. Most incredibly, she could not stop smiling. Even with the toothpaste dribbling out of her mouth she looked smug and satisfied. She doused her face with cold water and watched the rivulets run down her face.

She had never laughed so much in her life and the laughter had been like some erotic nectar. Even thinking of him made her feel the swell of laughter welling up. And right alongside the laughter . . .

She shook her head at her disheveled image. All she wanted to do was pounce right back in bed with him . . . and talk, and laugh . . . and make love.

Just as she was about to step into the shower, the phone rang, and she dashed into the living room to answer it. Probably it was Marilyn . . . inquiring.

But it wasn't Marilyn. It was Tate Brown and Helga stiffened when he asked to speak to Sam.

"Why would he be here?" She despised lying, especially under such circumstances as these.

"It's important, Helga." Tate skipped the preliminaries.

Helga's face was expressionless. "I'm sure it is, Tate. Otherwise you wouldn't have called. But he's not here."

Tate paused and she could practically feel his suspicion in the empty air. "If you talk to him tell him I need to see him. Before noon. It's urgent."

Helga resisted the urge to make some cynical retort, but she needn't have bothered because after a brief pause the line went dead.

Her face was livid when she replaced the receiver. How dare he call at ten in the morning. How dare he not even bother to disguise his innuendo? He had been blunt and rude and given her no choice but to lie.

"Who was that?" Sam peered sleepily over the edge of the loft.

"Someone I detest," Helga said coolly.

"Oh." Sam ducked his head as if he'd been shot. "I'm going back to sleep. Let me know when the coast is clear."

After a moment he appeared again wrapped in a blanket. "Helga? I'm not really going back to sleep. Don't you want to tell me? You don't seem like the sort of person who could despise anyone."

101

Helga's face was set as she went over to remove the whistling tea kettle from the stove. "It's not your fault." She looked up as he joined her next to the stove. "It was for you. Tate Brown."

"How the hell'd he know where I was?" Sam scratched his head, still looking dazed and sleepy.

Helga censored a bitter reply as she plunked two tea bags in two cups. Maybe it was to be expected that any woman Sam McCalahan left with he slept with. No, she refused either to believe that, or even if was true, to believe that Sam's past had anything to do with her. She knew that what had happened between them was as rare for him as it was for her. It was important to keep the lines of demarcation clear here. It wasn't Sam's fault that Tate Brown's diplomacy left a lot to be desired.

"I love you." Sam looked up from blowing on his hot tea with a boyish grin.

"I love you," Helga said softly and lowered her eyes.

"Well!" Sam slapped his bare knee where the blanket had fallen away. "One hellofa night. I'd say we had one hellofa night!"

But she could not shake Tate Brown's presumptuous interruption. It wasn't even that she cared if people knew about her feelings for Sam. Of course she wanted privacy, and maybe it bothered her that Washington was a town that thrived on gossip, but it had never occured to her to indulge in secrecy. Obviously it hadn't occured to Sam either. No, what concerned her was Tate's belittling tone. He had to have known she would deny it. Therefore, she reasoned, he had intentionally put her on the defensive. He might just have easily said, *if* you see Sam before noon, would you please ask him to call me. That would have left her options open. She would have said, sure, and Sam would have called back leaving his precise whereabouts out of it. Only an idiot would not see the difference and Tate Brown was no idiot.

"I should go to my office for a couple of hours this afternoon." Sam gave her an apologetic look.

"Of course," Helga crossed her legs as she sat at the round oak table sipping her tea. Her blue robe parted as she swung one leg slowly back and forth. Sam's eyes were drawn irresistibly to her long shapely leg and she smiled softly, experiencing a rush of desire. Sam caught her eye and gave an acknowledging smile.

"You got a swimsuit around here you can model for me?" He gave her a lecherous smirk and she tossed her napkin at him.

"People from Minnesota don't swim. We ski."

"What a shame." He pretended to pout. "You'd look great in a swimsuit. But I'll settle for what I can get."

He reached across the table for her hand. "But we will have dinner tonight."

Helga nodded. "Don't worry about working. I understand. I've got some work to do myself and I told Marilyn I'd stop by Food Fancy this afternoon."

She paused a moment to see how that piece of news had affected him, but he gave no sign that anything or anyone connected with Food Fancy was any concern of his. With her flare for exaggeration Marilyn had probably blown the whole Lauren-Sam thing out of proportion.

"We have the rest of the morning." Sam pulled her to her feet and pressed her against his body until she was keenly aware of his intention.

She felt her body begin to melt into him, felt her soft, supple curves grow pliant against his hard, powerful form. How easy it was to surrender to him. And yet it was not surrender really, for in the end she was left feeling more powerful. She slipped her hand beneath the blanket that he wore like a cloak and massaged his bare back. They had said they loved each other as simply and casually as if they said it every day. There had been no false start, no hesitations, no draining complexity. It was like a miracle. There was no other word for it.

As they started slowly for the loft bed, Sam leaned down and kissed her on the side of the neck. "I should probably make one phone call."

"Fine." Helga smiled. She knew who he'd call and that, she told herself, was fine too. Better for Sam to phone Tate than to have Tate call again. She went into the bathroom to give him privacy, and also because her disdain for Tate Brown precluded even being in the same room with someone who was speaking to him on the telephone. Why was she reacting so violently to him? She closed the bathroom door and sat on the edge of the tub, pondering the question. It wasn't like her to have problems with people. She was always capable of figuring out a way to deal with difficult people. Well, perhaps she just hadn't figured out a way to deal with Tate Brown yet.

She busied herself brushing her hair and smoothing moisturizer on her face. She could hear Sam shouting about something in the other room, but she made it a point not to listen. After a long silence she decided the phone conversation had ended and came out.

"Twenty-five percent is just too much." Sam was still on the phone, only now he was speaking in a low, tense voice. "No, I don't care what the senator says, I won't go for twenty-five percent. I will not back any legislation that smacks of that kind of nepotism and I'll be glad to tell him to his face that it's a fraud."

Sam frowned and pulled the blanket around his hefty body as he sat hunched forward in a wood chair that was too small for him. "Damn it Tate, I know what you're saying and you're right but I don't care. It doesn't change my mind. Now just set up some brunch thing and I'll be over there as fast as I can. I don't care what you tell them to get them there. Just get them there! And phone . . . I don't know, some hotel in New York, I don't care which, and book me a room. Damn right I want to be in New York for the fireworks. See you in half an hour!"

Sam slammed down the receiver and sat scowling. His large bare feet were planted firmly on the rug in a widespread position and the blanket had slipped unnoticed off one shoulder. The thought that he looked like an omnipotent Roman emperor whose toga was slightly askew did not amuse her. She stared at him a moment, but he was too absorbed to notice. When she wandered back into the kitchen area, he did not look up.

As she stood at the kitchen sink she heard him dial another number.

"Hey, Bob . . . Sam here." Helga wheeled around and gaped as he embarked on a jovial, enthusiastic conversation that bore no relationship whatsoever to the irritated scowl on his face.

"Looks like I'll need a few more days before our meeting. Something's come up back home in Texas. I'm at the airport now. Rotten luck too 'cause I just managed to get back."

Helga caught her breath and turned back to the sink. Politics. The shifting around of facts to suit the circumstances . . . she had known all along that was the way things were done. But somehow hearing how quickly and easily he could lie made her suspect. She shook her head, trying to dispel the fear that was inching in on her. In the background Sam continued some inane conversation about the Dallas Cowboys, covering his tracks by captivating whoever Bob was with his enthusiasm over tomorrow's game. Bob thought Sam was at the airport, when in fact she had heard him tell Tate he would meet him in a half hour and was going to fly to New York later in the afternoon. The logistics made her dizzy.

"I'll just be a minute," he called to her as he replaced the receiver and began dialing another number.

Helga moved serenely to the round oak table and sat with her hands folded in her lap. That he was probably involved in something important, that the shifting of facts was in all likelihood a political strategy that would in the end precipitate something beneficial did not matter. She did not question his integrity . . . not even when his business involved Tate Brown. Her questions went even deeper than what side of the political fence he might be on.

She listened with a detached look as he discussed lobbying tactics with another congressman from Texas. His gregarious good nature was such an integral part of his character that until now she had never been fully convinced that he was truly ambitious. In that regard she had discounted Marilyn's description of him. Ambition of the sort that makes presidents was something she never would have attributed to a man who would sit by the river and wait for a bird. Only now she saw it. Now she saw the full magnitude of the political animal at work. And the ambition of the burly man cloaked almost comically in a red plaid blanket was formidable.

Although she did not know the precise nature of the problem Tate had phoned about—something to do with oil quotas in Sam's congressional district—she had witnessed how instantaneously and efficiently he had focused on the issue. There had been no ambivalence. He had proceeded methodically with a fierce, almost deadly intensity. As she sat half listening to the phone conversation that was still in progress, she tried to reconcile this dynamic figure with that of the man she had cradled in her arms. This was a man hell-bent on success, a man whose priorities would always . . . always be public.

How ironic that she, a person who valued privacy and solitude above all else, had been drawn to a man destined—yes, she saw that now—destined to be a public figure. She could no more imagine herself on the campaign trail than she could see herself joining the circus as a clown. The idea of being in the limelight was not only foreign to her nature, it was frightening.

For an instant she struggled with her growing conviction. Wasn't she jumping ahead of herself? They were still in the beginning stages here. Wasn't she being just a bit premature to entertain thoughts of herself as his wife?

No. She had many flaws in her character but ambivalence was not one of them. Like Sam, she, too, had a talent for evaluating situations . . . even when they concerned her. She would not deceive herself into thinking that what had happened between them was casual. She was not a casual person. And Sam? Well, whatever he was or had been with other women, with her he was anything but casual.

No, she would fall into an even greater trap if she did not look the situation full in the eye and perceive reality for what it was. The painful truth was that she would never choose to become seriously involved with a man like Sam McCalahan. How fortunate, she told herself, that she had made the discovery now, before it was too late.

CHAPTER SIX

"You'll have to forgive me this time." Sam grabbed her around the waist and planted a quick kiss on her cheek as he rushed over to the couch and picked up his tuxedo jacket. He slipped it on with an impish grin and looked none the worse for having whirled like a cyclone getting dressed.

Helga gave him a cool smile. "There's nothing to forgive."

"I'll phone you from New York tonight . . . unless you'd like to come along." Sam began pawing through the cushions on the couch.

"You threw it in the fire last night." Helga felt a twinge of sadness as she reminded him about his necktie.

"Right!" He slipped his arm around her waist as he started for the door. "How about it? You could take a later flight this afternoon."

"I'd better not." Helga felt herself stiffen defensively at his touch.

"You're angry?" Sam pulled her close.

"I'm not." Helga replied succinctly. "You're late."

"You're upset." Sam stood with his hand on the doorknob. "This is important, you know. I wouldn't just fly off if wasn't important. Fact is . . . I'd like to tell you about it sometime. I think you'd be interested."

"I'm sure it's important." Helga tightened the sash on her robe. Something inside had gone all cold but that was good. It made things easier.

"You really must go." She patted his arm in what she hoped was a friendly gesture.

"Well, damn it . . . you're like somebody else! What the hell is going on here?" Sam roared.

"I swear to you," Helga said in a low, controlled voice, "I am not angry at you for fullfilling your duties as a congressman. I know how seriously you take your responsibilities. I don't question that."

She smiled tightly as if that would make things easier. "I wish more people in public office were like you—" She broke off aware that she sounded stilted and formal, as if she were addressing him from across her desk.

"I guess you mean that as a compliment, Helga . . . but it scares me."

"It's just that it's impossib—"

"What the hell do you mean impossible?" Sam exploded.

"Stop yelling." Helga looked at him with a placidity that made him flush with anger.

"I can stop yelling anytime I want," he told her in a voice that was no more than a whisper. "I can control my emotions if that's what you want. You seem to prize that so highly. Now look, I've got about four minutes . . . I know that sounds brash but—"

"You have to be someplace." Helga finished his sentence. "I honestly didn't mean to upset you before—"

"Why wouldn't I be upset?" He grabbed her impulsively.

"We're opposites," Helga began.

"Damn it! Of course we are. So what?" Sam glared at her.

"I didn't want to get into this . . ."

"Of course you didn't," Sam fired. "You don't like to get into anything. You don't like confrontations."

"There's no need for a confrontation." Helga felt her patience about to snap. She wasn't angry! How could she be angry at him for being who he was? She admired him, respected him . . . she just couldn't be a part of his life.

109

"Come to New York with me?" he placed his hand lightly on her shoulder.

She shook her head and lowered her eyes.

"All right damn it! Then don't!" He threw the door open, gave her one final glare, and with a bitter smile made a show of closing the door slowly, with infinite care, so that it latched shut with scarcely a sound.

The following week was a busy one. With both Willard and Kenyon in the office Helga worked late every night typing depositions. By her own choice she spent long hours at the library in search of obscure legal data that might advance the case. Since Tate Brown's open act of hostility toward her, he had ceased to be a problem. Whereas before she had been confounded by her inability to deal with him, now she simply ignored him except for polite greetings. She saw this new strategy not as a defeat, but as a step in the right direction. She was learning to play her own tactical game and there was some satisfaction in that. She had never wielded her aloofness with such a sense of abandon.

Apparently Tate had not even phoned Marilyn before calling to find out if Sam was with her, and ironically Marilyn, usually one to sniff out the most subtle indiscretions, suspected nothing. Secure in her image of Helga as a prudent, unimpulsive, rational woman, she assumed that Sam McCalahan had come in for a cup of tea and left with, at the most, a fiery good-night kiss. She had naturally been curious about when Helga was going to see the Texan again, but had evidenced no surprise at all when Helga said that while she had found Sam amusing, she was simply not interested in seeing him again. As if to emphasize her decision, Helga accepted a date with Marilyn's candidate, the French attaché, and with a lawyer whose acquaintance she had made on her own while working on the case. She was more determined than ever not to slip into Nordic lethargy. She was relieved that Sam hadn't called but not surprised. It was unfortunate that their brief affair had ended on such a sour note, but, she repeat-

110

edly told herself, even that was for the best. It had facilitated the emotional break. She knew, unquestionably, that she had made the right decision. This time she did not even have to rely on her supply of gory thrillers to fall asleep at night.

"You're losing weight." Marilyn looked up from her autumnal gardening as Helga came out of the stone cottage bundled up in a navy blue jogging outfit with a plaid scarf around her neck. It was a Sunday morning, exactly eight days since she had last seen Sam McCalahan, and for the first time she was aware that winter was here.

"I don't think so." Helga hopped up and down, readying her body for the five-mile jog she had set for herself.

"Have dinner with us this evening? Family style with lots of turmoil and all the McDonald's you can eat."

"You're not going to McDonald's?" Helga bent down next to Marilyn and pulled up one of the marigold plants, which was limp and faded from the frost.

"If you have kids . . . you *must* occasionally go to McDonald's no matter how you feel about it. My kids hate the way I cook . . . well, not hate. But what do they want to know from pâté en croute and salmon mousse?" Marilyn grimaced. "Maybe I should take up jogging."

"When would you have time?" Helga tugged at clump of dead flowers.

"I guess." Marilyn was not her usual exuberant self.

"Something wrong?" Helga asked.

"Oh, I don't want to bore you with my domestic trivia."

"I don't think you'd bore me," Helga urged.

"I wish I was self-sufficient like you." Marilyn chewed the inside of her lip thoughtfully.

"I'm not really," Helga said.

"Yes, you are," Marilyn insisted.

"The last time we talked you said you thought I should be a lawyer and have a baby . . ."

"But *you* could do that." Marilyn jerked a plant out by the

111

roots and tossed it in the heap. "You could do anything because you would always be your own person and you would keep your autonomy and never get confused. You know what you want, you know what's good for you. I mean, I even think I was wrong when I said you were hiding all those years after John died. I think you were doing what was best for you. Now you've changed . . . you're dating. You waited for the right time, until it was right for you. You didn't let convention dictate to you. You just seem to know what you should do and you do it."

Helga stared up at the steely-gray November sky and a strange melancholy feeling swept over her. "What's the matter, Marilyn?"

"Neal and I . . ." Marilyn swallowed hard and shook her head.

Helga felt as if a cold hand had closed around her heart. Marilyn and Neal were the perfect couple—they were friends, they laughed together, shared . . .

"We've been married twelve years," Marilyn said. "Maybe that's too long."

"But you two always seem so happy."

"There's no spark." Marilyn looked ashamed for saying so.

"You never see each other," Helga said. "Marilyn, you're both always on the run."

"You think I should give up the business, don't you?" Marilyn frowned as if she'd heard that argument before.

"No, I don't . . . but maybe you two need time together. I could stay with the children. I mean you have Libbie, of course, but I could be the . . . official figure in your absence. You know I'd be glad to."

"Lauren would kill me if I took time off now. Before Christmas? No way."

"So take off *one* night. Fly to New York and promise each other you'll take more time in the spring. Take your own advice. You told me it was important to make promises even if you didn't know for sure you could keep them." There was an urgency in Helga's voice; an unexpected tide of emotion swept over her and she felt herself close to tears.

"Thanks." Marilyn stood up and brushed the dirt off her jeans. "It's worth a try."

If you love someone anything is worth a try. The thought spun round and round in Helga's mind as she jogged along the Mall. In the distance the Washington Monument, that simple yet eloquent obelisk, was outlined against the gray sky. The sun was trying to break through. One minute a shaft of light would slice through the heavy layer of clouds and the next it would disappear, as if the elements were at war with one another.

Helga accelerated her gait, tucking her chin down against the plaid scarf. She had planned on flying home to Minnesota for Thanksgiving. Kenyon had assured her that everything would come to a grinding halt during the week preceding the holiday. There was no reason for her to stay behind.

She was ambivalent, something she never was, about going home. But it had seemed like the right thing to do—a gesture to her parents, a way perhaps of collecting her thoughts in the solitude of the snowy woods. Oddly, she was afraid she would begin thinking of Sam up there. Here there were distractions and a life that was, she realized, becoming more and more important to her. Marilyn wanted her to have Thanksgiving dinner with the family. She had suggested that if Neal agreed she would take advantage of Helga's offer to oversee the children. They could leave the day after Thanksgiving and have the whole weekend alone together. So it was settled, just like that she was staying in Washington over the long holiday weekend.

Helga was gasping hard as she approached the stark monument. Marilyn had not mentioned Sam. But there was no reason why she should have. It was as if that magical night in front of the fire had never happened. She had been so successful at cooling her emotions that until an hour ago in the garden she had believed herself to be free of him.

113

She slowed her pace and walked along huffing, oblivious to the admiring glances of strangers as they took in her rosy cheeks, the beguiling intensity of her expression, and her pale blond hair, which the wind whipped straight back from her face.

As long as she was staying in Washington, she might as well even agree to go to New York with Marilyn and Lauren on the Tuesday before. Maybe meeting Lauren would settle something. Maybe knowing that Sam was involved with another woman would make things easier. If he were off limits . . . Yes, she would be able to handle that. She had the discipline for that sort of thing. She could deal with concrete facts; it was the ambiguities, the loose ends that were making her . . . well, not quite miserable.

"I can't believe you've never been to New York." Lauren Richards was as vivacious and beautiful as Marilyn had described her. Dressed in a voluminous black cape that billowed as the three women walked down Fifth Avenue, Lauren let out squeals of approval or groans of aghast horror at the variety of fashions displayed in store windows. The avenue was jammed with acquisitive holiday shoppers, and it seemed to Helga that everyone was smiling in amusement at Lauren's running commentary.

Lauren made no bones about her age. At forty-one her dark hair was liberally streaked with silver, her face delicately etched with laugh lines. There was a boldness about her that might have put Helga off had it not been so irresistibly tempered by an irrepressible sense of humor. Lauren's laughter welled up at the most unexpected moments, enticing everyone around to, at the very least, smile.

"I told you you'd love her." Marilyn nudged Helga as they stood on a corner outside of St. Patrick's Cathedral and waited while Lauren darted into a phone booth to verify the time of the meeting with their colleague at Bloomingdale's.

"I do like her." Helga looked around at the bustling crowd.

"I always thought you were the most talkative person I'd ever met . . . I see I was wrong."

Marilyn grinned. "The first time Lauren and I met our mutual friends were taking bets on how much we'd hate each other. Two yappy, aggressive broads in the same room, vying for power? Nobody could believe it when we hit it off and decided to go into business together."

Lauren was gesturing wildly from inside the phone booth and Marilyn ran over and squeezed in next to her. It was a glorious day for an outing, quite cold but with a warm, brilliant sun overhead. Helga climbed the steps that led up to the cathedral. Later in the afternoon while Marilyn and Lauren were at their meeting she would return. Actually, she had a long list of sights she wanted to see and was still wondering if she shouldn't let the other two women return to Washington and spend the night in New York. But Marilyn was lobbying strongly for her return to Washington where the Danish Ballet was giving a special gala benefit concert at Kennedy Center. Helga was acutely aware that her reasons for not wanting to attend the concert had to do with Sam McCalahan. Under any other circumstances she would have loved nothing more than an evening at the ballet. However, Marilyn, in her innocence, kept arguing that *everyone* in Washington would be there. And everyone, though Helga was loath to admit it, meant the Texan.

"All set!" Lauren took the steps to St. Patrick's two at a time and slipped her arm through Helga's. "Do you want to eat first or snoop around that boutique on Madison Avenue I told you about?"

"Snoop first, eat later?" Helga ran down the steps with Lauren, and Marilyn linked her arm through Helga's other arm en route to a boutique that Lauren had promised would be perfect for Helga.

An hour and a half and a full week's salary later Helga was finishing the last of the most delicious omelet she had ever tasted while Marilyn and Lauren ran down some of the last-minute details prior to their business meeting.

"You're sure you don't want a glass of wine?" Lauren asked the question for the third time.

"Positive." Helga smiled. "I have a million things to do while you two are busy."

"She has over forty nieces and nephews." Marilyn laughed.

"She's not exaggerating by much," Helga told Lauren.

"I'm nervous." Lauren twisted in her chair and signaled the maître d' for the check. "I don't want any problems with this meeting. I want Bloomies to swallow the whole proposal."

Helga took a sip of coffee. She would be willing to bet that Bloomingdale's would do just what Lauren wanted them to do. It seemed impossible that anyone would turn her down. And of course the main "anyone" who came to mind was Sam McCalahan whose name, so far, had not been mentioned.

Helga shifted in her seat feeling a trifle uneasy about what her real motives were in flying to New York with Marilyn and Lauren. The thing was, having met Lauren, she was convinced that the older woman was a perfect match for the Texan. Lauren was everything she wasn't. Like Sam, Lauren's gregariousness stemmed from a genuine interest in other people, and also, like Sam, she seemed to take delight in being in the spotlight. Helga could imagine Lauren on the campaign trail, captivating the dubious, paving the way with her bright, decisive charm. It was not in the least difficult to see why Sam had been drawn to her.

"So . . ." Lauren fastened her sparkling brown eyes on Helga. "I hear Sam McCalahan gave you a taste of the Texas rush?"

"I guess you could say so." Helga's heart did a quick flip.

"He's really something, isn't he?" Lauren shook her head with an awed expression.

Helga nodded hesitantly. "Yes . . . yes, he is." She glanced quickly at Marilyn but her friend was oblivious to any innuendos. Helga felt the muscles in her neck loosen. There was nothing

116

really at stake here or Marilyn would be sending her warning looks like mad.

Lauren turned to Marilyn with a suggestion for the meeting, and it seemed as if the subject was closed. Helga picked up the glass coffeepot and poured herself another cup. Her heart was racing. Despite Lauren's casual tone, she felt like a two-bit Mata Hari. Here Lauren was being open and generous, while all the time she had been waiting like a thief by the side of the road, hidden in bushes ready to leap on the subject of Sam McCalahan. How disgusting!

"You're still seeing him?" Helga inquired in a low, unruffled voice.

"Sam?" Lauren turned back with a surprised smile. "You've heard of a hot potato?"

Helga stared blankly at her.

"I"—Lauren thrust her thumbs beneath a pair of imaginary suspenders—"am the hot potato."

"I'm sorry . . ." Helga felt a flutter of excitement in the pit of her stomach. At the same time she was truly sorry for the other woman. It was confusing.

"Oh, don't be sorry!" Lauren patted Helga's hand fondly. "I had my eye on him, of course, but I was a fool to think it would work out . . . in the long run, that is. Guys like Sam McCalahan have to be careful. I mean, if he'd married before he hit the big time in Washington he could have done what he wanted. But believe me when Big Sam bites the marital dust it will be with the approval, whether he knows it or not, of the men behind the scenes.

"I have a habit of deluding myself." Lauren reached in her handbag and pulled out a pack of cigarettes. "Do you mind if I smoke?"

Helga shook her head and took another sip of coffee. She hoped that Lauren didn't notice that she was a bit too fascinated by the story.

117

Lauren took a deep drag off the cigarette and exhaled thoughtfully. "Nobody is going to allow a presidential possibility to get too involved with a childless woman with two divorces. You know, after Sam dropped me like . . . a hot potato, I started feeling how lucky I was. I could have been bumped off, huh? If things looked too serious."

"You're joking . . . ?" Helga's mouth flew open.

"Yes!" Lauren roared with laughter. "I'm joking, of course. These are not medieval times, after all. We are modern women with rights. We cannot be executed because we do not bear male children. We cannot be murdered on a whim."

And that was the extent of the unsettling conversation about Sam McCalahan. Life, thought Helga several hours later as she meandered aimlessly around the perimeter of Central Park, was amazingly unpredictable and bizarre. Certainly it was more unpredictable here than it had been back in Minnesota. She realized with a jolt that for the first time she had not added the word "home" to the phrase back in Minnesota. In little more than one month she had already begun to break away. It was as if the woman she was now was only partly the Helga Tarr of the past ten years. Sometimes she had the distinct impression that there was a new person inside of her. Only maybe the person wasn't new because in a sense she seemed familiar.

Helga sank down on a park bench and watched the squirrels scurrying around. They were so tame, so expectant sitting there on their little haunches. After a moment she got up and bought a bag of peanuts from one of the street vendors. In an instant she was besieged with pigeons waddling aggressively at her feet. She did not want to think of Sam McCalahan, but the little animals brought him to mind, and suddenly she felt a deep physical yearning to feel his bulky body next to her on the bench.

She tossed the peanuts behind the bench onto the grass, gathered up her packages, and headed for the Plaza Hotel, where she was to meet Marilyn and Lauren to catch a cab to the airport.

Lauren's exaggerated account of how the political bigwigs could manipulate peoples' lives should have added fuel to her decision never to see Sam McCalahan again. But somehow it had the reverse effect. All the while she had been sorting through fuzzy stuffed animals and video games to be mailed off to her nieces and nephews for Christmas, Sam McCalahan had been uppermost in her thoughts.

Back in the stone cottage in Washington Helga ran a comb through her smooth blond hair and stood back from the mirror to gaze at her reflection. The red evening gown clung seductively to her strong, lean body, and its single wide strap accentuated the graceful lines of her pale shoulders. She never wore red, yet in the presence of Marilyn and Lauren she had allowed herself to be convinced. She turned to her profile and studied the result. She had wanted to buy the dress in black, "To go with the rest of her black dresses," Marilyn had pointed out with a laugh. How many basic black dresses could a woman have? And navy! Helga had responded by poking fun at herself, but now looking at herself draped in slinky red, she was on the verge of being embarrassed. Was she really going to go to Kennedy Center looking like a siren?

She turned away, annoyed with herself for being so safe and provincial. Her eyes told her the dress looked good on her. She was no fool about aesthetics. The only thing was that people would notice her, people would stare. She was convinced that in black no one gave her a second thought. Marilyn had laughed at that too.

She fastened a delicate gold chain around her neck and then took it off. The red brought out the natural rosy color in her cheeks. She had to admit she did not look quite so pale in red as she did in black. Marilyn was wrong—she did have a few other hues in her wardrobe: greens, navies, browns, subdued, safe colors.

119

She switched on the radio to her favorite jazz station and toyed with the idea of backing out of the whole evening. She could save the dress and wear it to somebody's Christmas party.

She could dye her hair green, she thought ironically, and go as a wreath. She was too much on edge. She walked back over to the mirror to assure herself that her nervousness did not show, but the image of the tall, stately blonde with the steady, slight smile did not significantly alter her rattled condition.

She sat back down on the sofa and stared at the empty fireplace. She had cleaned the ashes out. It was bare now. She hadn't even bothered to lay another fire.

When the phone rang she reached over tentatively to answer it. "Meet you out front at the car," Marilyn chirped.

"Marilyn . . ."

"No!" Marilyn jumped in at the reluctant sound in Helga's voice. "You said you'd go!"

"Why is it so important? You can hardly accuse me of being a hermit lately? I've practically been a social butterfly."

"Your idea of a social butterfly, not mine," Marilyn said.

"I'm having second thoughts about the dress." Helga twisted the telephone cord in one hand and glanced down at the watch she was not wearing.

"Of course you are. You're just not used to it. We didn't exactly twist your arm, Helga. You know you look fabulous in it."

Helga laughed. "Okay. But just the ballet. I don't think I'll have the energy to go to Senator Wiley's afterward."

"Helga, you talk like you're ninety going on two hundred. This is a party . . . not work. It's the beginning of the holiday season with good cheer flowing from every heart. Hurry or we'll be late." Marilyn hung up before Helga could dredge up any further objections.

Kennedy Center, which up until now Helga had only seen

from a distance in her biweekly jogs around town, was not far from the Sells' Georgetown residence. Wisely, Neal suggested they walk to avoid the crunch of traffic. He would return home after the ballet, pick up the car, and drive them to the party that Helga continued to insist she would not be attending.

As they walked toward the gleaming white building, Helga was aware for the first time of the colossal, heroic quality of the structure. There was a spiritual solidity to the building, and tonight, bathed in moonlight, it gave the impression of some oversized ancient Greek temple. She hung back a bit to admire its proportions. A warm feeling flooded over her as she saw Neal slip his hand in Marilyn's. Apparently their decision to fly to Bermuda after Thanksgiving had already eased some of the tension between them.

Helga drew in a deep breath and told herself not to be nervous. But she was nervous and the line of official black limousines creeping up the short rise to drop people off at the bronze and marble portico that wrapped around the monolithic structure only added to her conviction that Sam McCalahan was certain to be here.

And what would he say? What would she say?

Marilyn and Neal waited for her at the door and together they entered the Center's foyer, which was already teaming with men in formal attire and women in evening gowns.

"See," Marilyn whispered. "I told you the red dress was perfect. Now if I can get you take that black coat off . . ."

Helga cast her friend a wry look, shrugged off her coat, and handed it to Neal, who went off to check it.

A colossal bronze head of the late John F. Kennedy dominated the long, narrow foyer. An eerie feeling swept over Helga as she studied it. No, she did not want to think those thoughts. They had nothing to do with her, nothing at all.

But the analogy between Sam McCalahan and the late president was too obvious. It had been made many times by

121

people less emotionally involved and more politically astute than she.

As they wound their way through the lobby they were intercepted by various acquaintances of the Sells'. It wasn't until Helga was seated between Marilyn and Neal that she realized she had managed to forget her self-consciousness about the red dress. Well, perhaps there was hope for her yet, she thought wryly as the lights dimmed and a hush fell over the audience in the Opera House.

But she was all raw nerves and tension by the time intermission arrived. In the lobby she found herself standing in the center of a group of Marilyn's and Neal's friends. Most of them were young married types except for a dignified man in his late forties who introduced himself as Julio Martin and insisted on bringing Helga a glass of champagne. When someone called her name and she turned to see Willard Matthews, the sight of the familiar fatherly face brought a blush of gratification to her face.

"Willard . . . what are you doing here?" With a polite nod at Julio Martin Helga turned away from the little group.

Willard shook his head incredulously. "I didn't recognize you. I said to Mimi that girl looks like our Helga." Willard nodded his approval.

"The new me." Helga raised one slender eyebrow. "I didn't know Mimi was in town."

"For Thanksgiving," Willard explained. "Say, why don't you join us. I should have thought of it sooner but . . . well, I wasn't sure Mimi would agree to fly out."

"I have plans." Helga smiled. "You've met the Sells? Marilyn and Neal."

A gong went off signifying the end of intermission. As Helga turned to return to her seat, Willard Matthews caught her by the elbow.

"Helga, won't you join Mimi and me at Senator Wiley's?"

"I hadn't planned . . ." Helga caught Marilyn's disapproving eye and laughed. "I'll join you. I want to see Mimi. Shall I meet you outside?"

"Next to the box office." Willard backed off, gesturing toward one of the windows at the far end of the lobby.

And so it was settled. She was going to Senator Wiley's after all, and as Marilyn had said when referring to the red dress, no one had twisted her arm.

CHAPTER SEVEN

Just as Helga had anticipated, the party at Senator Wiley's was exactly the sort of overcrowded, sumptuous affair she usually avoided. It was true that the senator's rambling Victorian mansion, which was not far from the Japanese embassy on Massachusetts Avenue, was one of the most elegant in town, and it was also true that the senator and his wife were known to be among the most congenial hosts in Washington. Even so, thought Helga, as she found herself wedged against the back of a strange man while Willard Matthews twisted his way toward her with a glass of wine, it was not her idea of fun.

Willard handed her the glass and signaled for her to follow him to the wing chair where he had left his wife. When they reached the chair it was empty and he turned to Helga with a shrug.

"That's Mimi for you. Never wants to go till she gets there, then she gets swallowed up by the crowd and it's all I can do to get her home. Good Lord, I can't get over the change in you." Willard set aside all pretense and stared at Helga.

"It's a new dress." Helga smiled at the white-haired gentleman, wishing he hadn't reminded her.

"No, no," Willard protested. "It's more than that. You've blossomed."

"Hardly." Helga denied it with a slow, contained smile.

"'Bout every fella I see here has his eyes on you." Willard's

124

eyes twinkled. "Who was that Julio fella at the ballet? Somebody I should know about?"

Helga laughed. "No. And not somebody I should know about either. I just met him."

"Ah . . ." Willard waved. "There's Mimi with a plate of something. Now you let me know when you want to leave, and I'll have my driver take you."

Before she could protest Bob Helman, one of the presidential aides who had made himself particularly helpful over the past few weeks, claimed her attention and whisked her off to meet his wife and several friends, one of whom just happened to be another eligible man. Well, it was certainly true that Washington was a city that rolled out the red carpet for a single woman. So far this evening she had been introduced to seven available men and the evening was still young.

"Aren't you glad you came?" Marilyn and Neal brushed by her on their way to another room where someone was playing a mellow jazz piano and a few couples were dancing.

Before Helga could reply they were swept along in the tide of moving bodies. Everyone, thought Helga, seemed to be moving, as if the floors were a mechanical turntable. After several thwarted attempts to locate the dining room, she finally found herself at the head of the long line that was filing by a gleaming mahogany table loaded with bowls of fresh shrimp, honey-baked ham, several varieties of quiche, salads, and a turkey artistically constructed out of assorted raw vegetables. As she filled her plate, she found herself tensed and listening, as if she would be able to distinguish the low rumble of his voice above all the laughter and conversation going on around her. She was both dying to see his sandy head towering above the crowd and praying that she would be spared the sight of him.

"I'll never eat all this," she remarked to an elderly gentleman who was behind her in the line.

"Try the mustard sauce," he urged. "It's one of Maureen's favorite recipes.

125

Walking with her heavily laden plate in one hand and a glass of red wine in the other was another matter. She had never understood the knack of eating and talking at the same time, of balancing plate, glass, knife, fork, napkin. Sometimes the logistics were so formidable that she went home hungry after this sort of extravaganza, but tonight for some peculiar reason she was hungry, starved to be precise. She stood amidst the flowing crush of guests, trying to determine where she would most likely find a quiet corner. After a moment she began moving cautiously through the crowd until she passed a door that was slightly ajar. Backing up, she peered in and, finding it deserted, tapped the door open with her knee and went inside.

It was an inviting, warm room with high arched windows at one end, a mammoth old cherry desk angled in one corner, and several leather chairs centered around a low magazine-laden coffee table in front of a crackling fire. Since there was a small white-clothed table set with wine bottles and glasses, she did not feel that she was intruding. Even so, she thought as she sank into one of the cushiony leather chairs, she probably would have taken refuge here anyway. The walls were lined with books and before she attacked her plate she got up again to peruse the lower shelves. Finding a volume of legal cases that intrigued her, she slipped off her shoes and settled down to eat her supper in the company of a good book.

It *was* a good book, and one case in particular triggered an idea for a possible new approach in the Northern Railway case. She wondered if she would have the nerve to broach the subject with Willard Matthews, wondered if he would think she was overstepping her bounds. Well, she would do it anyway. The case was too important not to investigate every possibility.

Several people drifted in and out of the library, but apparently the lure of solitude did not appeal to too many of the Wileys' guests. She smiled to herself, thinking that it really was a wonderful party and she really was having an absolutely fantastic time. She felt nothing but warmth and gratitude toward the Wileys for having such an elegant yet cozy room in their home.

She looked up as a young couple entered holding hands. They looked embarrassed, and before she could assure them that they had not interrupted her, they ducked back out again. Perhaps people thought she belonged here, that this was her room and that she was a special friend of the Wileys'. She nodded her blond head slowly as if in answer to a question. It was the sort of room that suited her best, and if she were ever fortunate enough to have a home of her own, she would have just such an inviting library filled with crusty old volumes, heaped with magazines and sundry professional journals.

She sipped her wine thoughtfully, enjoying the pleasure of her own company after the long day in New York with Marilyn and Lauren. Maybe she did like big parties after all. There was something relaxing and convivial in being a part of a large celebrating crowd yet at the same time being removed. Yes, she liked the muted laughter, the occasional sound of a voice in the hallway. She liked the hum of activity and the knowledge that people were having a good time. But she liked it most when she was on the fringe. She smiled, thinking that one day she might hostess such a gathering as this and then retreat to her bedroom to enjoy the sound of talk and laughter as it floated up the stairs. Yes, it was simply that she had a different perspective. Her smile broadened. It was a good thing though that most people didn't feel as she did. If they did there would be nothing for her to enjoy!

She drained the last drop of red wine from her glass and was debating whether or not to have a refill. The day in New York should have exhausted her more than it had. Marilyn was right. She did tend to treat herself like a premature geriatric case. This was a party after all, and if it pleased her to enjoy the Wileys' hospitality sitting alone in the study sipping wine and reading a law book, then that was precisely what she should do.

Her hand was hovering next to a bottle of Beaujolais when, out of the corner of her eye, she saw Sam McCalahan step inside the study and shut the door. He was carrying a plate mounded high with food, and when he turned around to walk into the room his mouth flew open.

"Oh . . . sorry!" He may as well have cursed at the sight of her.

"It's all right." Helga's fingers clutched at the bottle of wine as if for support. She expected him to turn around and leave. Sam glanced at the table in front of the fire, taking in her plate, which was empty except for a crust of French bread. "Loud party." He stood just inside the closed door holding his plate.

"You should eat before it gets cold." Helga poured herself a glass of wine and moved to the center of the room where she stood with one arm draped over the back of a leather chair.

"I suppose I should." Sam looked at his heaping plate with a surprised expression as if he had forgotten it was there. She had never seen this indecision in him before.

"I see you took some of the mustard sauce." Helga felt as if her voice were an echo inside her head.

"Damn right!" Sam nodded at his plate. "I've had Maureen's mustard sauce before. You can eat it on anything and it improves the taste. Not that this needs improving. You can eat it on beef, chicken or just on a plain piece of toast. Once I ate some for breakfast . . ."

He paused, still staring at the glop of mustard sauce. His sandy hair was longer. She wondered if people hadn't been tousling it all night. More likely he had been among those dancing in the other room, because he had also loosened his tie and had the manner of someone who was exhausted after a long race. He wanted to leave the room. She knew he did, and she wished she could think of the right words, or at least of a few reasonable words, to detain him. She started to tell him for the second time that his food was getting cold. Beyond that obvious observation her mind was blank.

"I ate the mustard sauce by mistake." Without warning he

128

strode across the room and sat in one of the chairs that faced the fire. Taking her cue, Helga moved to sit facing him.

"You thought it was the jam," she offered with the hint of a smile.

"Damn right I did!" He jabbed his fork into a slice of ham, then just as he was about to put it into his mouth he looked at her and grinned.

"Haven't I seen you someplace before?" He slid the ham inside his mouth and chewed.

Helga held his glance. Her body was alive, registering none of the complex ambivalences that ran rampant in her mind. He had asked the question with his usual good-natured bravura but there was another color to it. He was caught, as she was. He wanted to test her. Perhaps he wanted to hurt her too, to make her pay. She didn't blame him. He certainly had his reasons. She ignored his rhetorical question and took a sip of wine.

"I see you're reading." He nodded at the book that was lying facedown next to her plate.

"The senator has a wonderful library. I couldn't help myself." Helga watched as he meticulously began to slice his ham into thin even pieces. He put a tiny dollop of mustard sauce on one piece, slipped it into his mouth, and chewed it thoughtfully as he stared into the fire.

"Never know how I can juggle my plate and my glass. Big eating parties like this put me on edge."

"Me too." Helga smiled, genuinely, for the first time since he had entered the room. "I wouldn't have thought it would have bothered you."

Sam savored another bite of ham before answering. "That's because you don't know me." He gave her a long, hard look.

She thought of the way he had closed the door that day . . . so gingerly, so controlled. He was acting out his anger for her benefit. Controlling the hostility, doling it out in a way that would be acceptable to her. Beneath his cautious behavior she sensed a seething, a confusion about what her motives had really been.

"I usually don't like large crowds." Helga skirted the confrontation.

"I would have thought as much." He munched away with a satisfied look that she found irresistible.

She wanted to be his friend. If all else failed . . . and she was still set on that score. But to lose this man entirely . . . to lose his friendship because she felt . . . What? Inadequate? No, she didn't exactly feel inadequate. She felt that whatever life he wanted, whatever life he was destined to have was something utterly foreign to her. She told herself that in time she would no longer be besieged by the throbbing, urgent physical sensations that swept over her in his presence. She would deal with that in time . . . if only they could be friends. That was important.

"I didn't call you." He didn't even look up when he made the statement.

Helga took a sip of wine. Odd how quickly she had grown accustomed to the blatant way he approached a subject. He was so unlike anyone she had ever known, so unlike her family, where everyone tiptoed around issues and never ever said what was on their mind.

"I know you didn't." Helga gave him a challenging look which he acknowledged.

"You didn't not answer your phone for . . . fear?" He was testing her again.

"I answered my phone every time," she told him.

"Have you ever thought of having a nice, easygoing affair with a man?"

This time his question shocked her. Her mouth flew open and he let out one of his huge guffaws. For an instant their eyes met and then, quite miraculously, they were both reduced to laughter.

"I really didn't follow you in here." Sam mopped up the rest of the mustard sauce with a piece of crusty French bread.

"I know you didn't." Helga experienced a twinge of regret, then she chided herself. After all she couldn't have it both ways. She had rejected him harshly, without any explanation, and he had taken her at her word. Wasn't that what she wanted?

"But I'm glad you came in," she said after a moment. "I'd like us to be friends."

"I understand." Sam took a long drink from a tall glass. "I really do understand." His face was friendly and relaxed when he looked at her.

It was not going to be easy to distance herself from him, to stay within her self-prescribed bounds of platonic friendship. She would not acknowledge the deep, primitive feelings he stirred in her, but what she could not deny was the almost irresistible urge she felt simply to reach out and touch his hand, to feel the warmth of his skin.

"I'd like it too." He stood up suddenly. "To be friends, that is."

She did not look up but she was aware, too aware of his long-limbed body and broad, magnificent shoulders. She was far, far too aware of how completely they had possessed one another. The skin on the back of her neck prickled as she recalled how audacious she had been with him. She had actually thrown herself at him.

He strode across the room and she heard the sound of water being poured into a glass. She was keenly aware of every move he made, and in the silence it seemed almost as if she could hear the cool, clear liquid as he took it into his mouth and swallowed. There was the sound of ice cubes clinking into a glass and again the sound of water being poured. When he returned he stood with his back to the fireplace sipping from the tall glass.

"Eight glasses a day." He toasted her with an almost shy smile.

"It really works." Helga slipped her feet back into her shoes. "If I feel a cold or something coming on and make it a point to drink my eight glasses I can actually nip it in the bud.

131

"It's one of those cures, one of those old adages that's so simple nobody really believes in it anymore." Sam eyed the glass a moment. In repose his face was drawn, and there was a weary sadness about him as he continued to stare at the glass. It occurred to her that he had been working too hard, that the problem that had interrupted them that Saturday morning was beginning to drain him. She resisted the impulse to ask him if that was the case. She did not particularly want to bring up anything relating to their one night together.

"Yes, yes." Sam turned the glass slowly in his hand with the same sad look on his face. "The simplicity of a certain time. I don't know. It's not that I think we should go back to the sort of life we had before the Industrial Revolution. Lord knows we can't go back in any case, but if we could only recapture that part of the past which has real value."

"Like the railroads." Helga shook her head.

"What a fight . . . what a battle." Sam nodded. "I talked to your boss, Willard Matthews, out there. Nice man . . . he and his wife, both nice people. It doesn't look too good for your case right now, I guess."

"Well"—Helga sat forward in the chair—"we have until the first of May. Nobody wants a strike. I've probably spent more time than either Willard or Kenyon talking to union reps. They don't want a strike."

Sam walked back to his chair and sat down. He spread his legs and leaned forward, clasping his hands together and moving them up and down in the space between his knees.

"The sad thing is," Helga went on, "in the end I think the employees will settle. Nobody wants a strike in this economic climate . . . nobody whose job is involved. Unfortunately nothing will be gained by settlement. The government, the unions . . . everybody will smile and pat each other on the back because a strike has been averted. But we'll still be left with a crumbling, deteriorating system and in the end both the government and the unions will have lost."

"You ever thought of being a politician?" Sam raised his eyes and looked at her.

"You know I haven't." Helga flushed and averted her eyes.

"You're very convincing." Sam sat back in his chair, and for a moment there was only the sound of the fire, a sound that sent a quivering sensation up through her stomach.

"The money has to come from somewhere." Helga forced her thoughts onto safe territory. "It would be wonderful if it could come from the private sector. But I don't hear any offers. And patchwork money won't mean a thing. The feds keep pointing to all the losses incurred by various railroads as if those losses were the final proof that the system is inherently a poor financial risk. But it wouldn't be if it were done right."

"That's big money you're talking." Sam sighed.

"I know." Helga smiled softly. "It's a pipe dream of mine—a country with a rangy network of high-technology trains for both freight and passengers. Super express trains between major cities, small connecting systems to outlying areas. Trains that travel three hundred miles an hour."

"Did your brothers have electric trains?" Sam looked at her with a quizzical smile.

"You think my obsession is the result of deprivation?" Helga laughed. "I think you may be right. They never let me play with their trains. Girls were supposed to watch. I adored those trains . . . I don't think I let on."

"I'm sure you didn't." Sam's searching look made her pulse race.

"You're an expert at hiding what you really feel." His voice was soft and devoid of any accusation.

"I guess I am," Helga replied softly. "But in my own defense —"

"You don't need to defend yourself, Helga," he interrupted.

"I know I don't," she persisted. She pressed the palms of her hands together and was surprised to find them damp and warm. Except for his one bitter allusion earlier, they had both been careful to avoid any reference to their night together. Oddly, their forbearance had only increased the feelings of intimacy between them. In one respect Helga felt as if they were meeting for the first time, or perhaps it was only that this encounter was different from the others. While it was not so spontaneous, there was a feeling of deep trust, unspoken as it was, that passed between them.

"But sometimes," Helga continued resolutely, "it may be better not to let on. I mean . . . sometimes, isn't it just as well to leave certain things unsaid?"

"Maybe," Sam ruminated. "Someone like me probably says too much. Someone like you . . . Well, frankly, I think you could err on the side of confession."

Helga shrugged. It was true. As close as she was to Marilyn, she had not mentioned anything about Sam. She could always find too many reasons why she should keep things to herself. And now that Lauren had declared herself out of the picture she couldn't even use that as an excuse anymore.

"Did you solve the problem that took you to New York?" Helga changed the subject.

"Solved some, created others." Sam stretched his long legs out toward the fire.

Helga looked at him a moment. She could almost feel the vitality of his lean body flowing into her. "Isn't that the way?"

Sam slouched farther down in the chair until his body was almost prone. "Yep. Solve some problems, create others seems more or less the rule. You pays your money and you takes your chances."

Helga was overpowered by a numbing sensation as their eyes locked. She knew precisely what he was saying. She had taken no chances.

"Your husband must have been quite a man," He sat up and leaned forward until his face was level with hers and very close.

She nodded. It seemed perfectly natural that he would introduce John into this particular conversation. But if he thought

134

that John, that her memories of John, were responsible for her sudden reversal he was wrong.

"He was a junior partner at Matthews, Matthews, and Stubbs." Sam was watching her closely.

"How did you know?" Helga's surprise was barely perceptible.

"I asked." Sam gave her a brief apologetic smile. "Are you upset?"

"No, no," Helga jumped in. "It's not that I have difficulty talking about John. I can see where you might have wanted to know. I . . . I should have explained . . . that morning. It was all so rushed, you were in such a hurry and I—"

She broke off suddenly nervous about exactly where this line of conversation was taking her.

"We . . . you and I didn't really have much time to talk." Sam sensed her hesitation but proceeded anyway. "Kenyon Stubbs said your husband was the sort of man that nobody could say a bad thing about. I would think it would be hard to forget someone—"

"That's not the reason," Helga interrupted passionately, then, retreating, she shook her head. "It's not a question of forgetting."

"That's not exactly what I meant." Sam lowered his voice when a couple came into the room. "I know you don't forget someone you've loved. I just meant it may be more difficult to go on . . . to let go and become involved with someone else."

Helga felt herself begin to waiver. She had been so absolutely certain that her reasons for not wanting to become seriously involved with him were logical, intellectual reasons, reasons that she was conscious of. But what if it were true that there were deeper reasons buried in a secret place where not even she dared to look? She recalled the strange almost queasy sensation she had experienced upon seeing the bronze bust of John Kennedy earlier that evening at Kennedy Center. What if her fear was of losing

135

Sam in some bizarre and bloody incident? Maybe she was afraid she would not be able to survive another senseless death.

"I shouldn't have brought this up." Sam shook his head dismally when she did not respond. "It's typical of me to barge in where I'm not wanted like an old bull. I really didn't mean to upset you . . . It's a party after all."

"It's all right." Instinctively Helga reached for his hand as he started to stand up. "What you said just started me thinking . . . But don't be sorry you spoke up. I'm not a fragile person, I don't have to be handled with kid gloves. My best friends"—a small smile played on her lips—"the people I most admire, are the ones who jolt me out of my complacency with their candor. That's one of the things I love about Marilyn."

"I don't think you're complacent." Sam moved the palm of his hand against hers, then stopped as if he were waiting to see how she would react.

"I guess I have a lot to think about," Helga acknowledged after a moment. She had reached out to him in an instinctive gesture of friendship, but now with his large hand wrapped warmly around hers she was sinking into a sea of tantalizing erotic sensations. One touch and the passion was sizzling between them. And they had not intended for that to happen. She was sure that he had been feeling every bit as circumspect and cautious as she, yet here they were, their palms sealed, their fingertips rapturously sensitized to all the glorious sensual possibilities that existed for them.

Still holding her hand, he knelt down on the floor in front of her and stared up at her. Helga shivered slightly as the hot blood surged within. She had all but forgotten her self-consciousness over the red gown, but suddenly she was aware of how it clung to her body and of the knowledge he had of each gentle curve.

"To friendship." He brushed his lips lightly against her knuckles.

"Yes . . . to friendship." Helga's eyes glistened but her face remained composed.

Sam placed her hand discreetly on the top of her thigh. "I have to admit"—he stood up slowly and sat back down—"it doesn't seem to be easy being with you. What I mean is . . . I've never been so attracted to a woman before . . ."

His confession took her by surprise. She, after all, had been the one to send out the blatant signals that had finally landed them in bed together. She wondered if he realized how exceptional that behavior had been. She drew in a slow, steady breath to try to control the rising urgency to feel his body pressing into her.

"I'm afraid I . . . there's no other way to put it . . . lost my mind the other night," she admitted faintly. "Isn't it funny . . . how accurately the most trite phrases describe feelings that are . . ."

"I know what you mean," he jumped in as if to help her over an awkward moment. "There are only so many ways to say . . . a certain thing."

Helga closed her eyes and nodded. Of course she knew what he was referring to. There was only one way to say I love you . . . and he had said it, so easily, but then it had all become confused and now it seemed as if their night together had taken place a million years ago. They had gone too fast, but then whose fault had that been? Perhaps she had just been desperate . . . starved for some physical experience. She opened her eyes and looked at him. No, there had been other men in her life since John, and not one of them had had this devastating effect on her.

"Maybe I had too much to drink that night." She amazed herself by looking directly into his eyes. "Marilyn and I had been having a big old time. I'm not used to . . ."

Sam shook his head. "No. You were sober and you know it. So was I. We were going faster than the speed of light."

"You felt it too?"

Sam laughed. "What a question!"

"Swept away . . ." She could feel the laughter welling up inside her the way it had the day they first met. What a relief to bring up their night together after avoiding the subject. It amazed her that she was sitting here with a man who had been her lover under the most dramatic of circumstances and actually discussing what had happened between them. More amazingly, she did not feel embarrassed or awkward even though her body tingled with ripe, erotic sensations.

"It would be an understatement," Sam said, "to say that we were both struck down by the forces of biology. I guess if that had been *all* . . . I mean if we hadn't been so aware of and sensitive to all the other areas of attraction, it might have been easier."

"I don't understand." Helga cocked her head to one side.

"I've been attracted to women before." Sam looked at her evenly and his hazel eyes deepened until they seemed almost black. "Physical attraction is one thing and . . . I've never been one to shortchange it. But . . . well, here's another trite but apt phrase for you. What happened between us was *mind-blowing*. I mean . . . here I am, a fairly egotistical son of a bitch when it comes right down to it. And I'm sitting on the bank of the river and all of a sudden I see this Nordic sleeping beauty. First I was amused. I wasn't just sitting there lusting after you all the time you were dozing. I'm not *that* crazy."

Helga laughed softly as he went on. "I just thought it was nice, and it gave me a warm feeling about the world to know that, as bad as things are with crime and pollution and greed and avarice, ours is still a world where a beautiful woman can fall asleep by a river. I thought to myself, a hundred years ago a woman couldn't fall asleep by a river . . . not unless the river was her own, and even then she'd be takin' a chance that a band of ruffians didn't come by and take advantage. I thought, that's progress. That's *some* progress and it's important to acknowledge progress even if it's not enough, even if there are still plenty of hard fights to be fought. So I began to see you, as you slept, as a symbol, a political symbol, if you will, of the delicate and often magical nature of progress. I was predisposed to love you even before you woke up."

"You're making this up." Helga shook her head, laughing. "This is political hokum. You're taking advantage of your poetic political license!"

"Cross my heart." Sam made an extravagant gesture across his broad chest.

"You mean you think like that?" Helga asked. "No wonder you're in politics."

"I'm a natural embellisher." Sam grinned. "My mind just does it for me. It's not lying is it, if your mind does it? I swear I didn't make it up. That's just what I thought when I first saw you."

"Never let anybody else write your speeches." Helga laughed.

"Well, I was a journalist. I do have some modest experience in putting my thoughts on paper. Do you really want to draw the line at friends?"

The smile faded from Helga's face and she looked away.

"I'll play it whatever way you want," Sam said softly.

Helga considered his offer for a moment. "I don't believe you."

"And I don't believe you." He caught her hand and tugged it. "I have tickets to a new play at the Arena Theater tomorrow night—some far-out comedy that the *Post* said was hilarious. We'll start fresh—a nice proper theatrical evening and a quiet supper afterward?"

Helga allowed him to draw her to her feet. He knew as well as she did that there would never be anything perfectly proper between them.

"You're very persuasive," she said after a moment.

"Yes." He brushed his lips lightly against her cheek, and though the gesture was chaste and discreet, she felt her entire body sizzle in anticipation. "But only because you want to be persuaded . . ."

"I'm not playing a game." Helga pulled back and looked warily over her shoulder toward the door. "Unless we want to headline the social page of tomorrow's *Post* I—"

"No one's coming," Sam reassured her. "And I know you're not playing games. Will you come to the theater with me?"

"I guess I will . . ." Helga gave him a dazed smile.

"You guess?" He tilted her chin up and gazed into her eyes.

"I know I will," Helga murmured.

He placed his hands gingerly on her bare shoulders and smiled down at her. "You won't regret it." He bent down and kissed her cautiously, then stood up to look at her. She recognized the look of desire that colored his face and the fiery sensation of what it had been like to lie naked in his arms flooded in on her.

"Thanksgiving?" he asked with the same hungry look.

The sensual giddiness that she had experienced before swept over her again and she laughed.

"I mean"—he bobbed his head—"I mean . . . won't you have Thanksgiving dinner with me? And the day after there's a football game, though something tells me football is not your cup of tea."

"You're terrible." Helga laughed as she stepped out of his arms and caught her breath. "I just agreed to go to the theater with you and you're already lining up—"

"Damn right!" Sam caught her arm and pulled her back against him with a rugged, satisfied smile.

"And you're right, I don't particularly like football . . ."

"But you'll come?" He lowered his face to hers and his warm breath increased her giddiness. She felt herself melting, yearning toward him with unabashed eagerness.

"We'll bundle up, wave banners, and drink hot tea with honey and lemon." Her voice was breathless, she had forgotten that the door to the library was ajar . . . had forgotten everything.

"Yes." He kissed her again with the same soft discretion. "Maybe we'll spike the tea with some dark rum. It won't matter who wins or who loses."

Sam glanced over her head toward the door, then with a sly, beguiling smile he planted another light kiss on her parted lips. "And what about Thanksgiving?"

Helga slipped out of his arms, laughing. It was typical of this flamboyant man to press his case, to proceed directly toward the finish line as soon as he had made the least headway. There was a tireless gusto about him, an iron determination that, even though she laughed at him now, was registered in some part of her psyche as an awesome, perhaps not altogether benign trait.

"I can't have Thanksgiving with you." She taunted him slightly, eager to see what means he would use to turn this defeat to his advantage.

He gave her a charming smile. "You're flying back to Minnesota?

She shook her head, teasing him.

"I know." He folded his arms across his broad chest and gave her a cocky smile.

Helga gave an irrepressible laugh, backing up as he made a lunge for her as if they were two children involved in a game of tag.

"I bet you're going to work. Closet yourself up in that crummy office with a ham sandwich and a Thermos of instant coffee."

Helga shook her head, her eyes bright with merriment as she darted out of his grasp for a second time. It occurred to her that she was behaving like a loony person, but the thought only made her laugh. Her laughter was apparently contagious because a great guffaw escaped from Sam, and for no reason whatsoever they stood face to face in front of Senator Wiley's smoldering fire laughing like fools.

"Oh, here you are!" Tate Brown's voice cut through their sputtering giggles.

"Sam tells a mean joke, right, Helga?" Tate stood just inside the door to the library with an edgy smile plastered on his smooth face.

"Oh, he tells a mean joke, all right." Helga caught Sam's eye as she brushed the tears of laughter from her cheeks.

"Sam, there's someone out here I want you to meet." Tate shifted his attention directly to the Texan.

"Tate has infallible timing." Sam winked at Helga and gave Tate a grin.

"Whadaya mean?" Tate adopted a jovial air that struck Helga as phony.

"I waited till after the punch line." Tate strode across the room and pounded Sam on the shoulder. "You'll excuse us won't you, Helga?"

"Of course." Helga's eyes were still dancing as she nodded at the men.

"I'll be with you in a sec." Sam gave the smaller man a playful shove.

"I'll be in the parlor off the foyer, the one with the Jackson Pollack." Tate gave a friendly wave as he left the room.

"We seem to be developing a pattern." Helga ran her hands through her blond hair. "Interruptions by Tate Brown."

"Tate's a good old guy." Sam took her hand and swung it gently. "So what about Thanksgiving?"

"Don't you ever give up?" Helga beamed up at him.

"Nope." Sam grinned.

"I'm having Thanksgiving with Marilyn and her family."

"Can I come?" Sam asked without missing a beat.

"I thought we were going to go slow this time." Helga's heart increased its already rapid tempo.

"We are going slow," Sam insisted. "Look how long we've been here in the library . . . alone." He gave her an insinuating smile.

"True." Helga matched his look with a seductive glance.

"Maybe I can wangle an invitation," Sam mused.

"I'm sure you can." Helga smiled.

"It's all right with you then . . . if I can come up with some subtle . . ."

"I'm not sure how subtle you'll be," Helga teased. "Subtlety doesn't seem to be your style."

"You'd be surprised." Sam chucked her under the chin and

his hand lingered as he regarded her tenderly. "I should go out and see what Tate has on his mind."

"Always doing business." Helga was amused.

"Not always." Sam pulled her close and their lips met with a brief burning insistency.

"I'm a well-rounded fellow." Sam gave her a long look then started for the door. "You'll see."

CHAPTER EIGHT

Helga stood for a moment feeling the warmth of the fire against her back. Hadn't she known all along that he was her sole reason for coming to the senator's party? And hadn't she known somewhere in herself that somehow they would surmount the hurdle of her reservations and continue to see each other? No, nothing was resolved. She was still uncertain about the intrigue of Washington political life. But even with all of her reservations, all of the nervous fluttering in her stomach, she was happier and more excited than she had been in years.

In an odd way the lapse of time since she had spent the night in his arms had given a sense of solidity and continuity to their relationship. It seemed to her now that even the time without him had been time with him. Although it had only been a month and a half since their first meeting, they had managed to cover a great deal of ground, and in some strange way it seemed that the time spent apart was as important as those few hours they had spent together.

She turned around and stared at the antique brass clock on the mantel. It was nearly one thirty yet sleep was the farthest thing from her mind, and she was fairly certain that if she did not slip out now Sam would return to press his luck. Her body tingled at the thought, but her mind prevailed. This time she would proceed slowly, with caution. This time she would behave like herself, like the circumspect woman she knew herself to be.

The party was beginning to thin out. Only those political

diehards were left sipping their brandies and talking in hushed, intense whispers. No doubt Willard and Mimi had taken their leave long ago. A quick look around told her that even Neal and Marilyn had gone home. Probably Marilyn would give her a scolding tomorrow morning for ducking out so early. She could just imagine Marilyn's face when she told her she'd spent the evening in Senator Wiley's library with Super Sam. Her face broke into a radiant smile and she wondered what he would say if she told him she called him that.

In a way she was glad the Sells had left. It was a good night for a walk. The Wiley mansion wasn't far from Georgetown and a breath of fresh air was probably just what she needed to calm herself down before going to bed. She paused at the sound of Sam's laughter coming from another room and then quickened her step as she went in search of the senator and his wife to pay her respects.

"I admit to browsing in your library," she told tall, distinguished Senator Wiley as he pumped her hand. "It was a wonderful party . . . truly."

And it had been. Helga felt a rare buoyancy as she turned away from Senator and Mrs. Wiley and glided across the room to retrieve her coat from the butler stationed at the cloakroom at the rear of the foyer. It occurred to her that there was a knack for being happy, and that perhaps over the years she had lost that knack. She was so in the habit of searching for the logic in situations that she instinctively perceived all possible pitfalls. But life was not some legal case to be dissected and analyzed. Perhaps the wisest course, the course she had somehow chosen, was to follow her heart. There was another one of those trite phrases, but oh, how apropos it seemed.

As Helga slipped into her coat, a warm shiver ran up her spine at the sound of his voice. Not surprisingly the "important person" Tate had been so anxious for Sam to meet was a beautiful dark-haired woman whose vivacious smile as she looked up at him reminded Helga of Lauren. She waited until he had finished telling his story—a yarn about his bronco days that had a distinctly well-rehearsed ring to it—then she started toward the door, skirting slightly out of her way so that she was visible.

"Good night Tate, Sam." She threw him a knowing smile before stepping out into the night.

She stood for a moment on the front porch pulling on her black leather gloves and smiling. Jealousy was the farthest thing from her mind and that, she thought, was amazing because the woman who was clearly deemed by Tate an eligible match for the Texan had been beautiful, with a marked air of sophistication and intelligence. The situation was simply too absurd, too ironic to warrant any feelings of jealousy. If anything she felt sorry for Sam. Being the most eligible bachelor in town might have been a treat for a while, but in the long run she suspected it must be a terrible drain.

Helga walked slowly down the front steps and cut across the yard toward the street. For the first time she realized Tate Brown's initial interest in her had not been on his own behalf. According to Marilyn, Tate was certain to be Sam's campaign manager if and when he ran for a higher political office. Was it possible that Tate had seen her as a prospective mate for Super Sam . . . and then rejected her?

The idea brought a bitter smile to her face. No, she shook her head resolutely. She was not going to become embroiled in hypothetical negative thoughts. Sam McCalahan was his own man. She knew that much about him. In the long run nobody would tell him what to do.

"Hold up there!" As if Helga had created him out of her own thoughts, Sam appeared flushed and breathless at her side, pulling on his overcoat.

"I'll be damned if I'll let another man pick my women for me!" He jerked at his overcoat.

"Oh, really?" Helga could not help smiling.

"Yes, really!" Sam thundered.

146

"You mean it's never happened before?" she asked. "Tate never introduced you to—"

"Sure as hell did!" Sam interrupted. "He sure as hell did. Only my ego was so blown out of proportion by all that female pulcritude I just never noticed. Till tonight. Till you zapped me with that wise smile. I mean, everybody knows Tate's a wheeler-dealer. A good one. He works good behind the scenes and that's important. But it never occurred to me he'd get personal about it. I mean, I just suddenly put it together that all the women Tate wants me to meet, nice and pretty as they are, have certain qualifications. Like they're all Thoroughbreds . . . they all kinda fall into a category."

"I think I was one of Tate's rejects." Helga chuckled as they turned out onto the street. Sam gave her a quizzical look.

"Let's just say"—she looked up at him—"that Tate found my reticence . . . unacceptable."

"Your reticence!" Sam hooted. "I never saw you at a loss for words."

"Well, I am . . ." Helga flushed as he slipped her arm through his and hugged her against the side of his body as they walked. "I am a . . . relatively quiet person, with most people, anyway."

"Quiet maybe." Sam grinned at her. "Your voice may be soft, but a verbal recluse you definitely are not! Whatever made you think you were reticent? Whatever gave you the idea that Tate rejected you?"

"Maybe I do talk more with you," Helga admitted.

"Funny," Sam reflected, "the way people see themselves. I see you as a person who never says anything extraneous, a thoughtful person, but most definitely a woman with strong opinions."

"With most people I keep my opinions to myself." Helga found it exhilarating to match his long, even stride. The night was cold and damp and the small misty halos around the streetlights lent a faint mysterious air to the shadowy streets.

"That's a shame," he replied in a soft voice as they rounded a corner and were suddenly enveloped in deep shadows.

Without warning he stopped walking and pulled her close as his mouth covered hers in a kiss that seemed to erupt from the depths of his being. He seemed to suck the very breath out of her as his tongue surged inside her mouth with a force that made her recall all of the intimate details of their lovemaking. She felt as if he were devouring her, and even through the heavy fabrics of their coats she felt the warm surging of his strong, eager body.

"Sam . . ." His moist, hot mouth silenced her protest and her body grew soft and pliant as his tongue stroked her dark recesses rhythmically.

When he drew back to look at her, his breath created a heady steam as it swirled into the frosty night. "Don't say anything." He nipped hungrily at her lips when she started to speak. "Don't say a word. I've been dying to do all that all evening. And that damned Tate . . ."

His mouth covered hers again, and she shuddered as the volcanic eruptions gained control over her so that she had no choice but to match his passion. For several moments she was plunged into a mindless ecstasy, experiencing only the smooth underside of his thick tongue contrasted with the sharp edges of his even front teeth. Her entire being seemed to enter the complete erotic darkness of his mouth. She was beguiled, wholly and completely fascinated, by all of the various textures, tastes, and temperatures as her tongue nimbly explored every crevice. She knew she was somersaulting deeper and deeper into a mire of erotic bliss, and only with a supreme effort was she finally able to pull herself away.

"You . . . you caught me off guard." She tried to smile offhandedly, to gain control of a night that seemed to veer off into territory she was determined to avoid for the moment.

Sam gulped for air and when he exhaled his features were briefly obscured by his steamy breath.

Helga seized the moment to explain. "I can't, Sam. I mean . . . I thought you understood."

148

"One kiss?" He started to reach for her but she held him off, shaking her head.

"One kiss on Massachusetts Avenue with Lord knows who passing by." Helga buttoned the top button of her coat and gave him a reproving smile.

"I'm sorry." Again he reached for her and again she avoided him.

"I don't think you understand." Helga's face was drawn and perplexed and for a moment she wondered if she even understood.

"I'm a very private person." She looked at him earnestly.

"I know that." He reached out and touched her cheek.

"No . . ." She shrugged him off. "You don't really understand how private. I don't want to be fodder for D.C. gossip. I know how this town is and . . . and I don't want my private life to be public."

"I kissed you at Senator Wiley's." Sam made a feeble attempt at teasing her.

"And that was ridiculous on my part." Helga shook her head. Thinking about it now, it seemed to her they had behaved like two furtive adolescents, sneaking timid kisses, casting shy glances.

"Ah, come on." Sam nudged her. "Nobody came in. Anyway all I did was give you a friendly little peck . . ."

"Well, this was hardly a friendly peck." Helga tossed her head but was unable to achieve the desired look of cool disdain.

"Would you mind if we had this discussion over a cup of tea," Sam suggested with a grin.

"You're not taking me seriously." Helga glanced at him as they proceeded down the street. "Where are we going?"

"To my car. To my apartment." Sam looked sideways at her and winked.

"You're not taking me seriously!" Helga exploded and stopped walking. She folded her arms resolutely in front of her chest.

149

"All you need to do is tap your foot impatiently," Sam suggested.

Helga narrowed her eyes, lifted the red gown slightly to reveal her shoe, and tapped her foot. "Do I have your attention?" A slight smile played on her lips.

Sam nodded. "But I still think we should talk where it's warm. You're a snow bird, these frosty nights don't bother you, but I'm just a poor Southern boy and I'll catch my death of cold if you—"

"One cup of coffee"—Helga fought back the smile—"in a public place."

"Anything your little heart desires." Sam nuzzled her neck as he hurried her down the street toward his car.

"It's absurd to be having an argument like this!" Fifteen minutes later they were seated across the table from each other at a deserted Pancake Palace off Wisconsin Avenue.

"It's not an argument," Helga protested. "Ever since I came to Washington I've been hearing about how many times a week you make the social page and with whom."

"So maybe I'm turning over a new leaf." Sam frowned and waved at the sleepy-eyed waitress for another cup of coffee.

"That's not the point." Helga leaned across the table. "Honestly, it's not. I'm just speaking about myself."

"I won't ever kiss you on Massachusetts Avenue again." Sam stared glumly into his muddy coffee.

"You're being a pain." Helga gave him a cool smile.

"You're being a prude." Sam looked at her after a moment. "You're saying we can't sleep together. I don't understand you."

"I'm not saying that . . . I'm saying exactly what you hear. That I am a very private person. That I like . . . that I *insist on* my privacy."

"Will I have to wear disguises?" Sam could not resist.

"Yes," Helga answered him with a perfectly straight face.

"You're kidding?"

150

"Yes." She nodded slightly but her expression did not change. "I don't want to be an 'item.' Why can't you understand? It's not because of any silly old conventions. I really don't care about those conventions."

"It's true. After all, you seduced me." Sam kicked her leg under the table.

"I know." Helga felt an unwanted warm tugging in her stomach. "So obviously . . . I'm not a prude."

"Point well taken." Sam assumed a stiff professional manner.

"For instance"—she tapped her forefinger on the table—"why did Tate call my apartment that morning? Did you tell him you were—"

"Of course I didn't!" Sam interrupted angrily.

"Well, I didn't think you did," Helga rushed in. "But it just seems people are always keeping tabs on you. Everyone seems to know who's in your bed and when."

"That sounds like a moral judgment." Sam grimaced.

"I swear it isn't!" Helga said sincerely. "All of those affairs were pretty public and . . . and I guess that's fine as long as nobody minds. I'm not passing judgment on the other women in your life either. Marilyn loves publicity. I can just imagine, say, if she were single and got involved with you, she'd adore all of the hoopla. But not me. That's all I'm saying. Not me. I just want you to know that."

Sam drained his coffee cup and sat back in the booth with his handsome face twisted into a pensive frown.

"Shall I just deny we're anything more than friends?" he asked after a long pause.

"Why not?" Helga answered quickly.

"You don't believe in always telling the truth?" he asked archly.

"I believe in telling the truth when it matters and to the people it matters to," Helga said calmly. "I don't believe that everyone is entitled to know all the details. A lot of people ask questions they have no right to ask and they deserve whatever answer is

151

given—whether it's the truth or not. If a small lie protects some-one's privacy, then I say it's a lie well spent."

"You really should be a lawyer." A slow smile spread over Sam's face and he reached across the table and clasped her two hands in his. "In your own *quiet*, even-keeled way you are fright-eningly convincing."

"Frightening?" Helga felt her breasts stiffen in response to his warm palm rubbing against her wrist.

"I'm scared to death." He gazed lovingly into her eyes. Ben-eath the table his knee pressed urgently against her legs until her breath quickened and a hard knot of desire made her shift in her seat.

When she was seated next to him in the front seat of his littered Oldsmobile, he drew her close and kissed her gently on the lips. Out of the corner of her eye she could just barely make out the numerals on the small clock.

"Ten after three," she murmured as his hands slipped inside her coat and covered her breasts.

"It would be a shame to go to sleep now." He pressed his hands against her full breasts, flattening them until she drew in a sharp breath as the dizzying sensations swept over her.

"Tomorrow is a day off," he crooned. "I heard your boss say so. My staff is gone for the holiday. We could have the whole day and the theater at night. Everyone is too busy making stuffing to notice."

His fingers moved enticingly over the flimsy fabric of the red dress. "I love this dress. I promise . . . you will never be an item."

Helga rubbed her cheek against the prickly stubble on his chin. "You know I want to . . ."

"I know." He flicked his tongue softly along her lips, then shot it inside for a deep, penetrating kiss. He sat up suddenly and looked down the long, deserted street.

"We may be the only people still out on the town." He hugged her against him as he switched on the ignition. "When I first came here I was shocked at how early they roll up the streets."

152

"It's not early," Helga reminded him.

"I know." He turned to her and the look in his eye made her throb with impatience. "I do understand about the privacy. And while you're absolutely right that this is a burg that loves gossip, you'd be amazed at the number of well-kept secrets. Do you trust me?"

CHAPTER NINE

The incredible thing was, she did trust him. Against all logic, all of her preconceptions, her reservations about becoming involved with a public figure, his amorous reputation . . . the bottom line was that she trusted him. He was astute. He had posed precisely the right question and he had known her well enough to know that she would answer him honestly. She trusted him . . . therefore, there was no reason not to come home with him. No reason whatsoever!

Helga stripped out of the red dress and hung it up next to his bathrobe on one of several Lucite wall hooks. She wriggled out of her pantyhose, resisted the impulse to rinse them out, and tucked them neatly inside one of her shoes, which she had placed unobtrusively in a corner of the bathroom. The low, resonant strains of a cello filtered in from the living room, where they had spent the last two hours sipping tea, listening to music, and talking.

Oh, yes . . . and several long kisses. Her stomach gave an ecstatic contraction and she snatched up the brown cotton robe he had given her and sashed it tight at the waist. She stared at her face in the medicine-chest mirror. It was after five in the morning and she looked more alert and rested than she usually did after a night's sleep. She had been up almost a full twenty-four hours. It hardly seemed possible that this time yesterday she was just getting up to get ready for the trip to New York.

Time, at least time spent in Sam's presence, was irrelevant.

Something happened to the minutes spent with him, something different, something so intense and probing that a night, one simple night, could feel like a year. She fingered the tube of oozing toothpaste with a fond smile. She might have guessed he'd be the type to squeeze from the wrong end.

"You hungry?" He tapped on the door.

Helga opened the door and smiled. "You are, I take it?"

"Only if you are." Sam's eyes traveled down the brown robe to where it hit her just above her knees. "Nice caps."

"Thank you." Helga pressed her legs tightly together and her heart pounded furiously as he gazed at her and began to remove his tie. Behind him in the modest blue and white bedroom was an old four-poster cherry bed, a traditional double bed with a worn white chenille spread.

"Maybe I'm not hungry after all." He ran his hand lovingly along the soft contour of her cheek, then turned away as he unbuttoned his shirt. "I'll bring in a glass of sherry. How does that sound?"

He crossed to the far end of the bedroom as he removed his shirt and tossed it onto the heap of clothes in the bottom of his closet.

"Sounds fine." Helga leaned against the bathroom door, staring after his broad naked shoulders as he walked into the living room. In a daze of unreality she held her position listening as he put on another Bach cello record. He loved the cello, loved Bach. Each new discovery about him fell like a blessing on her head. She felt drenched in good fortune and the wonder of it all was reflected in her face as she padded across the deep blue carpet and fell onto his bed.

She ran her hand lightly over the little tufts of the white chenille spread. She loved the fact that he had an old-fashioned double bed. He was such a giant of a man; she would have thought surely he would have had a king-size bed, something more obviously befitting a bachelor with his reputation. But no, he had added a piece of plywood to the old bed, to lengthen it just enough to accommodate his six-foot-four-inch frame. If Thomas Jefferson and James Monroe, both tall, tall men, had done without "modern monstrosities" as he referred to king-size beds, then so could he. He was a man who put stock in historical precedents.

Helga crawled to the center of the bed and propped herself up on the pillows so she could see out the door and into a portion of the living room. Everything about his small town house pleased her—the clutter of books and periodicals, the plethora of papers and yellow legals pads with his huge scrawling hand-writing angled across the pages. There was an ambiance of business, not messiness in the clutter. Even the piles of dirty clothes had a purposeful order, their placement careful as opposed to indiscriminately tossed laundry. He had been sensitive about that though. Helga smiled, recalling how he had dashed ahead of her offering a rush of explanations about his ailing housekeeper, apologizing for the few dirty dishes in the sink and the week's worth of newspapers stacked on the coffee table.

It was appropriate that he chose to live not in one of the most fashionable "in" sections of Washington, but in a mixed-income development in the southwest section of the city. Although he had not said so, Helga understood that the choice was a conscious one reflecting his own egalitarian beliefs. For all of his complexity Sam McCalahan was a simple man, a man who recognized the validity and the beauty of a life unencumbered by artifice. It was difficult to imagine him falling prey to the pomp and circumstance of Washington society. It amused, and even touched her that he had shipped his lumpy sofa all the way from Texas because "it still had another ten good years of life left in it."

The home, like the man, was comfortable and inviting yet full of surprises and fascinating little quirks. Who would have guessed Super Sam was a devoted chef? Who would have thought he owned not only a Cuisinart but one of those fancy Italian ice cream machines and a pasta machine? Helga frowned

156

suddenly. Maybe that was what had drawn him and Lauren together . . . food. Someday she would ask . . . someday.

Shrugging off thoughts of Lauren, she flexed her toes and a delicious shiver of anticipation rippled through her body. Coming home with him had been absolutely the farthest thing from her mind, yet once the decision had been made there had not been the least awkwardness. Though a thrilling and often dizzying sexuality pervaded the atmosphere, they had both felt compelled to talk, to exchange secrets and compare notes about the past. Such different lives they had lived. She could hardly imagine the warm and rangy vastness of his home state.

It was odd how at home she felt, almost as if she had been here before, almost as if this night was one of many. An eternity of nights . . . Helga opened her eyes dreamily as he entered the bedroom. Somewhere along the way he had lost his trousers and shirt and now he was clad only in a pair of beige boxer shorts.

She heard him pull the drapes, and when she felt his weight on the side of the bed, she opened her eyes.

"Life is full of interesting little twists." He smiled as he handed her a tiny stemmed glass of sherry.

"Your bed is comfortable." Helga touched her glass to his.

"Didn't you know it would be?" His eyes caressed her as he sipped the sherry. They had all the time in the world, and their eyes locked in a dreamy acknowledgment of their good fortune.

"Yes," Helga answered softly as he switched off the bedside light. In the darkness she shifted to the far side of the bed and shrugged off the robe as he pulled back the covers. Then they both slid beneath the cool sheets and sat propped up against the back of the bed sipping the sweet liquid. How different this night was from their first recklessly passionate encounter.

There was something almost spiritual in the dark silence that surrounded them, something artfully fragile and intensely personal in lying together naked without touching. Earlier in Sam's living room they had both gone on nonstop about their families, and until Sam declared five thirty as an arbitrary curfew, it

157

looked as if they might gab on until just before curtain time that night. But now the silence was binding them even closer than the details from their pasts could ever do.

As her eyes became accustomed to the darkness, Helga could clearly distinguish his noble profile. The white sheet was drawn up under his arms, and though she could not make out his expression, she knew it was pensive. When she finished the sherry she set the little goblet on the bedside table and reached for his hand beneath the sheet.

"I'm glad you're here." He gave her hand a warm squeeze and moved it close against the outside of his thigh. The soft down of hair contrasted with the steely muscles flooded her with warm, erotic sensations. She moved her hand along the tight muscular indentation, testing the hardness with a slight pressure, reveling in the fineness of soft hair against her fingertips.

"I admire you for changing your mind." He shifted his leg to accommodate her inquiring hand.

". . . and so quickly too." Helga's voice was breathless. The inside of his thigh was warm and moist. She moved closer to him, nestling into the roundness of his smooth shoulder as her hand continued the exploration.

"Most people would have pretended to need time as a way of affirming their principles. Or as a way of gaining power . . ."

"But I didn't want to wait until tomorrow night." Helga kissed his shoulder.

"Me neither." Sam rolled onto his side and gathered her full against his warm flesh. His mouth opened onto hers in a soft, coaxing kiss, deep and languorous.

A cataclysm of burning desire shot through her and she threw her arms around his neck, pulling him closer in a rapturous embrace that melded their undulating bodies together. Sam's hands skimmed the curves of her body and cupped her behind firmly, guiding her against him in a slow, sweet, swiveling movement that made her hunger for more. The glory of his hard, muscular body overwhelmed her senses. She wrapped her long legs around him, squeezing and hugging him, wanting to feel all parts of him at once, wanting all of her soft suppleness to thrill and nourish him.

She could not get enough of him. Even more than before she felt the perfect compatibility of their bodies as they sensed each other's rhythms and flowed into each other as irresistibly as the river flows to the sea. His deep moans signaled the depth of his passion, driving her to higher peaks as she thrust against him, offering him more and more with each undaunted movement. Sam gripped her hips exuberantly, and Helga cried out as his hands paved the way for that ultimate ecstasy.

Her thighs seemed to melt beneath his knowing fingers, and she twisted urgently in readiness as he caressed deeper and deeper, setting off torrents of coursing liquid fire.

"I love you." He breathed the words against her damp hair as he plunged into her. "I love you, I love you!"

Every crevice of her body glowed with the raging delicious fire he sparked through her. She was burning white and pure and her body seemed possessed by a power of such intensity that she found herself leading him, initiating new rhythms that made him gasp and cry out.

"And I love you." Helga's eyes were glazed with love as she looked down at him. She rested the palms of her hands on his shoulders and watched the expression on his face as he fondled her breasts. Even at the height of passion there was an innocence about him that moved her almost to tears. She lowered her face and tasted the damp perspiration on his forehead. How could she have thought, for even an instant, about rejecting such a man? It seemed to her now that her reasons had been absurdly superficial. He was a rare man and somehow she would find the strength and courage within herself to give their love a chance to grow and flourish.

He fingered one nipple tenderly as she moved her hips from side to side slowly, tantalizingly. Then, once again, unable to endure the near agony of such exquisite pleasure, he grasped her shoulders and began another tempestuous journey. Helga thrilled to his wild, unbridled lovemaking and, flinging her head back, cried out as the waves of passion broke and crashed inside her body. She was in a near state of frenzy as he continued the abandoned race, and when a loud, hoarse cry broke from him, her body went limp and she fell on top of him drenched.

When she awoke it was to the strains of a deep, melodious cello and to the distinct aroma of some major culinary endeavor going on in the kitchen. She smiled and stretched languidly, wondered vaguely what time it was, and finally got out of bed to open the heavy drapes. The sky was overcast, but judging from the muted halo overhead it was probably about noon. It had been, at least according to Sam's reputedly always accurate "inner clock," eight when they had finally decided to make a supreme sacrifice and fall asleep. She padded back across the room and fell into bed again, feeling not so much tired as peaceful. The five days of vacation that had yesterday loomed ahead of her now seemed like a gift of some beneficent god.

Several minutes later the bedroom door opened slowly and Sam stuck his head inside. "Good! You're awake!" He disappeared immediately, but a few minutes later he reappeared balancing a large tray laden with steaming food.

"You've been . . . busy!" Helga's stomach churned at the sight of a huge piece of steak and two omelets garnished with parsley and small cherry tomatoes.

"I hope you're ravenous." Sam, clean-shaven and wearing his plaid robe, was ebullient as he plumped up the pillows and placed the tray between them on the bed.

Helga's stomach gave a threatening lurch, and she had to force herself not to turn away from the sight of so much food. How could she tell him that she never had anything more than a cup of tea or a glass of cranberry juice until she'd been up for at least four hours?

"I'm starving." Sam smacked his lips in anticipation. He sat cross-legged next to the tray as he poured her a cup of coffee and handed it to her.

"You take cream?" he asked.

Helga shook her head and prayed the nausea would abate.

"You do take coffee?" Sam detected her discomfort.

"I usually take . . ." Helga averted her eyes from the food.

"Tea!" Sam picked up a small pot and poured her a mug of tea with a triumphant air.

"I hope you like your steak rare . . ."

Helga felt the blood drain from her face. "I've never had . . . steak for breakfast. I . . . I've heard of it . . ."

"Good Lord, woman, it's afternoon. Lunchtime!" Sam reached for her hand and patted it.

Helga pulled the sheet up around her shoulders and eyed the tray with a skeptical smile. Actually, now that the shock of confronting so much food upon first awakening was wearing off, a few pangs of hunger were beginning to stir.

"There's a first time for everything!" Sam announced as he dished up her omelet and sliced off a portion of steak. "A breakfast like this makes your mind work faster, revs up the motor and gives you sustaining power."

"You eat this every morning?" Helga accepted the plate warily.

"Yep!" Sam dug in with a grin. "Oh, not steak every morning. Sometimes I have lasagne."

"You're kidding?" Helga's eyes flew open and she dropped her fork.

"Nope." Sam was enjoying her dismay. "Usually breakfast is my main meal. Sometimes I have oysters and—"

Helga waved a restraining hand. "Don't say any more!" she cautioned. She stared at the steak a moment, sliced off a tiny portion, and popped it into her mouth like a pill. The succulent juices were redolent with garlic, and once again her eyes flew open in surprise as she chewed. The amazing thing was, it was delicious.

"Steak and garlic." She shook her head incredulously as she popped another slice into her mouth. "If anyone had told me . . . Sam, what have you done to me?"

"I've bewitched you with my panhandle ways." Sam winked. "See what you've been missing."

"I'll get fat." Helga savored the omelet with an approving nod.

"Guaranteed," Sam said, "not to get fat if you eat your main meal first thing in the morning."

"I suppose you have apple pie for desert," Helga teased.

"Nope." Sam gave her a sly smile. "Pecan."

"Now come on," Helga protested," you don't get up and cook five-course dinners for yourself every morning."

"Mrs. Magnum cooks for me most of the time. She sets things up in the evening before she goes home. If it's a steak I just throw it on . . . takes less time than you'd think. I'll tell you a secret."

Helga caught his eye and laughed at the devilish glint she read there.

"Another reason I eat my big meal first thing in the day is to throw my opponents off."

Helga chewed thoughtfully on another delicious morsel of steak.

"Imagine going to lunch with a big guy like me and seeing me piddle around with a vegetarian salad. Wouldn't that throw you off a tad? Not only that . . . it's to my advantage not to have to cut my meat and chew and all that. I can devote my full attention to the issues at hand. I don't like to mix business and food. It's one of my principles."

"You . . ." Helga shook her head and eyed him narrowly. "You're ruthless."

Sam grinned. "I know. It is underhanded, especially when the rest of the world structures its life around the business lunch."

"Better not let the word get out," Helga told him.

Sam grabbed her big toe beneath the sheet. "Is this blackmail?"

"You may have made your first big mistake." She gave him a sinister smile.

Sam leaned over the tray and moved his hand upward along the outline of her leg. He rested it on the top of her thigh and gave her an insinuating smile. "And you may have made yours!"

Helga fell back against the pillows, laughing. Perhaps, she thought, it was the garlic but she felt positively intoxicated, delirious, giddy. And she was a woman who could not only not manage to swallow solid food until she'd been up for several hours. In fact, she generally could not muster more than a few syllables of conversation either.

"Go ahead, laugh!" Sam sat back and sliced himself another portion of steak. "I suppose you've never laughed at breakfast. As I recall our last breakfast together was not terribly hilarious."

"I was only drinking tea then," she gasped. "I guess I've been needing a big breakfast all my life and didn't know it."

"No flapjacks in Minnesota?" Sam queried.

Helga shook her head. "I can't remember my family ever sitting down to a big breakfast. There were always so many chores. Everyone was eating at different times. Lunch was the big meal."

Sam polished off his omelet and steak and looked at her hungrily. "I ever tell you how I managed to get the party nomination back in Texas?"

Helga shook her head, smiling. She could already feel a yarn coming on.

"True story," he prefaced it. "All of the important party bozos were real skeptical about makin' me the nominee. I was too much of a character as far as they were concerned. Oh, they like a bit of eccentricity, but I, as my friends pointed out, went a little too far, and they weren't real sure they could keep me in line. So there was this big fancy lunch planned at the fanciest restaurant in Dallas. See, they even took me out of my own turf, invited me way up to Dallas to try to throw me off. But I outfoxed them

163

by ordering green beans and not having anything to drink . . . nothing alcoholic, that is."

"I would have thought that would have been the end of you," Helga observed dryly. "You ate only green beans at a fancy restaurant and you're telling me that cinched the nomination for you?"

"Maybe I'm just superstitious, but it always seemed that way to me."

"I think you're just superstitious." Helga considered him with a penetrating smile. "Or . . . you're making it up, which is more likely."

Sam grabbed her big toe again and pulled hard. "You're so smart. I'd like to see you trying a case before the Supreme Court."

"It doesn't take many brains," Helga remarked dryly, "to detect a born storyteller, a born exaggerator, I should say."

"I did eat green beans though." Sam removed the tray from the bed and slid under the covers next to her. He rubbed his leg seductively against hers. "Have I told you I think you're wonderful?"

Helga flushed as he moved his hands down her silky body and clasped her around the waist. "That I think you are the most perfectly formed creature one could imagine, not to mention the smartest, the most intriguing, the most mysterious . . ."

Helga placed her hand over his mouth to silence him. "Your nose is going to grow, Pinocchio."

Sam removed her hand and stared at her emphatically. "I mean it. I've been waiting thirty-eight—almost thirty-nine—years to feel this way. I'd begun to think that people, poets certainly, had made up the myth of love."

Helga's blue eyes were luminous as she gazed at him. But no words would come. All she could do was drink in the details of his handsome face and marvel at the absolute rightness of every phrase, every gesture he made. His was a face she would never tire of, a mind and intellect that would stimulate her unceasingly and a sense of humor that would jolt her out of a mode of thinking that was often far too somber for her own good.

"You don't mind if I repeat myself." Sam gathered her face in his hands and studied her. "I love you."

He shrugged off his robe and kissed her gently, lowering her back onto the pillow just as the phone rang.

"Hello!" he barked into the phone and sent Helga an exasperated grimace.

"Hey! Yeah . . . How are you Bill? No, no, you didn't interrupt." He shot Helga an apologetic glance.

"Hell no, been up for hours. What's on your mind?"

Helga turned onto her side and watched the expression on his face change from one of tolerance, to mild interest and finally to total, intense concentration. He nodded and made a few acknowledging hmms, and after several minutes he walked unabashedly naked across the room and sat down at his desk to take a few notes.

"Well, I know it's a blow, Bill. I'd counted on Symington's support as much as you but we'll just have to go a different route. I don't want to make light of the setback or sound like some ol' Pollyanna, but it may be for the best that Symington's pulling out on us even if it is at the last minute. Look, I got a couple ideas. Let me make a few phone calls."

Sam stood up, put one big bare foot on the desk chair, and hunched his huge body over the telephone as he listened. "No, no . . . not everybody's gone home to eat turkey. I think I can still dredge up some support. And if not, I'll fly to Texas and set a coupla sticks of dynamite under the local task force. Now you call Henderson, Morris, and anybody else you can think of. I'll get back to you by late afternoon."

Sam hung up, scratched his head, and sat down at the desk to finish scrawling a note on one of the ubiquitous yellow legal pads. A warm feeling flowed through Helga as she stared at his broad bare shoulders, which dwarfed the desk chair and made it look like child's furniture. After a moment she reached over

165

to the bedside table, picked up a copy of *Time* magazine, and began to read.

"Sorry," Sam called after a moment, "I'll be with you in just a minute."

"It's okay." Helga snuggled down in the bed contentedly. She liked the idea of being with him while he was at work on some problem. In a way she was flattered that he felt free enough with her to attend to what was obviously an important matter. She skimmed an article criticizing the present administration on their cursory treatment of environmental issues and looked up just as Sam wadded up a piece of yellow paper and tossed it irritably into the wastepaper basket. He rubbed the back of his neck, and as he began writing again, his left hand tugged at a lock of sandy hair.

So that was what gave him the tousled look. Helga smiled as he tugged more resolutely and hunched farther over the desk. She considered tossing him his robe, but he was so engrossed she knew he was completely unaware of his nakedness.

Odd that this morning, or rather, afternoon, she did not in the least mind that they had been interrupted. So it wasn't the business per se that gave her pause. The actual logistics of behind-the-scenes political life was something she could handle. In fact, the internal working of the political system intrigued her. But being in the public eye? Now that was another matter entirely and she could not deny feeling anxious at the prospect of being on parade.

She picked up the magazine and tried to immerse herself in another article. It was too soon to worry about any *real* future. Besides it was unfair to Sam to give in to all her fears and reservations the minute his back was . . . literally turned. The last time she had allowed her fears to come between them. This time though she was determined to fight them. There was too much of value here not to be tenacious and stubborn about it!

Still, she argued with herself, it would be foolish to give in entirely to the euphoria they both felt. She had never been the sort of person to cry full steam ahead. That might be Sam's way, but it certainly wasn't hers. No, discretion was still a consideration and for the moment, she concluded, that meant Marilyn too. But how exactly could she arrive home at three or so in the afternoon wearing the same dress she had worn last night?

While Sam made his phone calls, Helga toyed with several possible stories and finally settled on telling Marilyn that Willard Matthews had been called unexpectedly back to Minneapolis and had asked her to keep his wife Mimi, whose high blood pressure was a constant trial, company for the night.

"Well, I'm impressed with the story." Sam finally slipped into bed next to her. "Does Mrs. Matthews have high blood pressure?"

"Of course." Helga nodded smugly.

"And none of the parties know each other?" he questioned.

"Willard and Mimi know each other," Helga observed dryly.

"I know that." Sam nudged her.

"No, Marilyn doesn't know them, not really. She may have met them, but they don't travel in the same circles."

"Interesting." Sam stroked his chin ponderingly. "I wouldn't have thought you were the devious type. It only adds to your many charms. However"—he winked—"don't accuse me of mendacity, my dear. You are equally capable when the occasion arises."

He gazed at Helga a moment, then took her in his arms and gave her a long, shattering kiss, pulling her closer against his heaving chest as the kiss grew in intensity.

"Do we have a little time," he asked breathlessly, "before you go help Marilyn with tomorrow's stuffing?"

Helga molded herself against his hard, virile body, luxuriating in the wild, instantaneous sensations he unleashed in her. Before she could reply, his tongue plunged deep into her mouth and he lifted her up until she was settled firmly on top of his brawny body.

"And don't forget my invitation." He pulled away and looked at her with love-bleary eyes. "And I won't even ask you why you can't tell your best friend . . . as long as we can share turkey on the day of Thanksgiving."

"Yes . . ." Helga ran her hands lovingly through his hair as he skimmed his hands along her bare back and stroked the firm curves of her behind.

"It's going to be the first of many Thanksgivings." He moved against her until she was bursting with joyful agony. Her breasts swelled and prickled under his warm, stroking hands, their rosy nipples pulsating with life. She moved her hand along the side of his torso, wedging it between their warm, undulating bodies until she grasped all of the burgeoning power and felt him seething and eager. He moaned with pleasure at her touch. When he could endure the exquisite pain no longer, they rolled over as one and she arched up to him at the very moment that he thrust smoothly into the lavish, deep darkness.

They were both breathing heavily, gasping and clinging to each other, stimulated beyond thought into throbbing, fluttering oblivion. Helga tightened her legs as he gave an exhilarated cry and surged into her again and again, bringing them both perilously near the brink, only to retreat and surge forth once again. At times he teased her with a rhythm so elusive and tantalizing that a sort of madness seemed to take over, infusing her with a willfulness she had not known she possessed. She felt herself, in all parts, expanded—her mind as well as her body. She seemed to be learning who she was, who she might be. And for the first time in her life it occurred to her that she had no limits, no limits at all!

Later that afternoon, dressed in faded jeans and wearing a snug navy sweater, Helga sat perched on one of Marilyn's kitchen stools chopping celery for the cranberry salad that was to be her contribution to tomorrow's feast. Although she wore no makeup, her usually pale face glowed with a rosy radiance as if she had just come inside after a brisk walk. None of the Sells had been home when a taxi dropped her off at the front gate around two thirty. Actually there had been no reason to use the fabricated story about Willard and Mimi Matthews, but a new kind of excitement was driving her and she found herself telling Marilyn the contrived yarn for the sheer fun of it. Marilyn would appreciate the added touch when she finally told her about Sam. And she was going to have to tell somebody soon because she was practically bursting with happiness.

"Do we need creamed onions?" Marilyn hopped up on the stool next to Helga.

"You've already cooked enough for a small army," Helga told her.

"You can't have too much on Thanksgiving." Marilyn added some more brandy to the mincemeat and stuck her finger in to savor the results.

"Maybe the Matthewses would like to join us." She offered Helga a sample.

"Oh . . . they're busy!" Helga felt the blood rush to her cheeks. So much for her prowess as a scheming Mata Hari. "But . . ." She paused as she dumped the celery into a bowl that contained walnuts and crushed cranberries. "There is someone I was chatting with at the Wileys' last night . . ."

"I told you to ask anyone you wanted." Marilyn scurried back to one of the steaming pots on the stove.

"It's Sam McCalahan. He was going to spend Thanksgiving with his family in Texas, but apparently something came up to keep him here." Helga kept her eyes riveted to the gelatin mixture as she added it to the other ingredients.

"Sam McCalahan!" Marilyn bounded back across the kitchen. "What's going on? That's the second time . . . There's something going on, isn't there? Come on, confess. You've been seeing him on the sly."

Helga shook her head coolly. "No, I haven't. I just ran into him last night at the Wileys'." She gave Marilyn a self-contained smile.

"But you said after that night he insisted on driving us home that you found him overbearing. Isn't that what you said?" Marilyn eyed her closely.

Helga smiled easily. "That is what I said. But he was different at the Wileys'. He just happened to come into the library so he could eat in peace. I was there. We started talking and it was very pleasant."

"Well, of course he can come!" Marilyn cried. "Isn't it weird though . . . First Lauren and now you. Now listen, Helga, this is not a guy to get serious over."

"I'm not getting serious." Helga laughed as if it were the most ridiculous notion in the world.

"Oh, no!" Marilyn exclaimed with a horrified expression. "Lauren's coming."

A queasy, dark sensation threatened to overpower Helga's euphoria. "Well, that settles it. It's not that important, Marilyn. He just happened to mention that he was at loose ends . . . It was insensitive of me. I should have known Lauren would be coming for dinner. Really, it's no big deal . . ."

"Let me give Lauren a buzz." Marilyn zipped over to the phone and began to dial.

"Really, it's—"

Marilyn silenced her with a wave of her hand. "Lauren? Hi, it's me! Listen, give me a straight answer on this, okay? I know you're not seeing the Texan anymore . . ."

Helga drew in a deep breath and wandered into the dining room where she began setting the table. Lauren and her and Sam all at the same Thanksgiving table? She didn't know if she was up to such sophisticated, civilized triangles. She fingered the ornate pattern on one of Marilyn's silver knives. It was all too complicated, just as she had expected it would be. And wouldn't it always be that complicated? She could feel her resolve waning already, and she frowned, irritated with herself for lacking fortitude. After all, it was not a difficult problem unless she allowed it to become one in her mind.

"Lauren says it's fine. No problem with her." Marilyn grinned triumphantly.

"Maybe she's just saying that." Helga's eyes were pained.

"No." Marilyn was firm. "Lauren doesn't fake it. But . . . well, to be safe you could mention it to Sam. So he won't be shocked."

After helping Marilyn with the rest of the preparations, Helga returned to the stone cottage. Although she was seeing him for dinner in less than an hour, she decided it might be easier to broach the Lauren question on the phone.

"Hell no, I don't mind! She's a great gal. Wonderful woman." Helga felt the slightest twinge of suspicion at his enthusiasm. After she hung up the phone, she sat sipping a cup of tea and tried to sort out her reactions. In theory she thought it was wonderful that two people could part without awkwardness, without blame. Against her will she found herself wondering about Sam's relationship with Lauren. How long had they been lovers . . . or perhaps they hadn't been at all. It was possible that Marilyn, with her penchant for the dramatic, had blown everything out of proportion. But why did it matter so much?

Life had been so simple in Minnesota. She rinsed out her teacup, and after slipping into a black knit dress that clung to her gentle curves, she sat back down at the table and resumed the same train of thought.

It was true that the slightest obstacle, real or imagined, seemed to thwart her. There had been no obstacles in Minnesota. There had been no life. There had been no interruptions because there had been nothing to interrupt. She thought of the sense of power and promise she had felt earlier in the afternoon when they were making love, and even with the old shadows lurking in the background she knew that was the woman she wanted to be. She wanted to go forward, to do more than merely meet each new opportunity as good old reliable Helga Tarr, always dependable, always predictable. Marilyn and yes, Sam, too, were right. She had underestimated herself. She had always perceived her role with Matthews and Stubbs as her niche in life, and she had felt lucky, even grateful to have found something to devote herself to.

That a dynamic man like Sam McCalahan saw such strength and vitality in her was like rain on already fertile ground. But Sam's love for her and hers for him was only the beginning. The real core of her happiness was the result of rediscovering the irrepressible, determined person she had been before John's death. The gift Sam McCalahan had unwittingly bestowed on her, in addition to his love, was the gift of her true self. Now the long-dormant ambitions were stirring for the first time in ten years.

With her usual decisiveness Helga dialed the admissions office at George Washington University, even though the prospects of reaching anyone were dim. From early adolescence she had nourished the dream of being a lawyer, of defending people less fortunate or able than herself. She knew now that it was a romantic dream, that logistics, bureaucracy, and paperwork were the enemies of such dreams, but at least she had recaptured the spirit of those youthful goals.

Her pulse accelerated with each ring of the phone, and she experienced an excitement not unlike the heady sensations that sped through her body when she was in his arms. It didn't matter that no one answered. A decision had been made in the depths of her being and the one thing she had, the one thing time had taught her she could expect from herself, was tenacity and commitment. It was already too late to enroll in law school for the second semester, and since the entrance exams, the LSATs, were given only twice a year, she would have to wait until next June to take them and until September to be officially enrolled in George Washington University Law School. But there was much to be done in the meantime. Ten years had passed since her student days, and though she had been in constant touch with

172

the legal process, she would need to adapt herself to the rigors of academia. Given her contacts here in Washington, she was certain she would be accepted as a pre-law student and it was possible that a few strings might be pulled to allow her to audit a course or two at the law school. Then, if she devoted herself to her studies, she would be primed for the LSATs in June. Perhaps she could even win a scholarship if she did well enough.

When Sam knocked at the door, she flew into his arms and kissed him.

"You should make a habit of living on only four hours of sleep." He gazed at her serene face. "You're even more beautiful. What's new? You seem particularly excited."

"I'm happy." Her blue eyes sparkled as she wrapped her arms around his neck and looked up at him.

"Anything special?" Sam helped her into her coat and held the door open for her.

"You." Helga slipped her arm through his and leaned into him as they walked through the still, frost-covered garden. She would not tell him of her momentous decision now. For just a while longer she needed to keep the knowledge to herself, to savor it, to weave rich fantasies about her future as she had done as a girl.

CHAPTER TEN

A few snowflakes danced merrily around the windshield of Sam McCalahan's Oldsmobile. As he turned the corner at Twenty-third Street, the Lincoln Memorial appeared in all of its classical Greek profundity, glowing white and flooded with light against the dark December night.

"I love it best at night." Helga snuggled against Sam's camel's hair coat and stared out at the magnificent edifice with its peri-style porch of thirty-six columns representing the thirty-six states that existed at the time of Lincoln's death. They were on their way home from Arlington, Virginia after attending a huge reception in honor of the new Saudi ambassador. Beneath her trusty black coat with its smart classic lines Helga was wearing the red gown that she had first worn with such trepidation. What with the receptions, concerts, and formal dinner parties, the dress had practically become her uniform over the past three weeks.

"I think," Helga rhapsodized, "if I were to live in Washington the rest of my life, I'd never get over the thrill of seeing these monuments rising up in the distance. The Jefferson, the Washington, not to mention the Capitol. I never thought of myself as a flag-waving patriot. I certainly never thought of myself as sentimental, but somehow living in the midst of so many histori-cal reminders, I'm constantly aware of how really incredible and rare our system of government is."

"Shall we stop?" Sam slowed the car as he approached the turnoff to the monument.

"I shouldn't." Helga was torn. "I have an early meeting at the office tomorrow and thanks to you and Charlie Monroe in the Justice Department, I've been accepted to audit the corporate law classes that Richard Deiber is giving."

"Is that a no?" Sam nudged her.

"Who can resist the Lincoln Memorial during the first snowfall of the season?" Helga scooted over to the far side of the car and pressed her nose against the cold glass to get a better view. The weeks since Thanksgiving had been a whirlwind of activity. It seemed to her that between the concerts, football games, dinners, and receptions, not to mention her work and the two classes she was now auditing, she had crammed more into this brief span of time than into all of her thirty-three years combined. And the crazy thing was there always seemed time for more. As busy as she was now she found herself more accessible to new ventures, more receptive to last-minute contingencies, more willing than ever to take time off and break from the rigidity of her former orderly existence. She realized now that even the long daily walks she had indulged in back in Minnesota had been a militant expression of her need to operate within a closely prescribed and controlled framework. In the past she had been almost obsessed with the idea of getting enough sleep, sure that without a minimum of nine hours she would be inefficient and listless at work. Now to her constant amazement she thrived on sometimes less than six hours a night.

Though the nights spent at Sam's town house were not as numerous as either of them would have liked, what they lacked in frequency they more than made up for in passion and intensity. Quality, Sam insisted, not quantity was what really mattered. According to him the gullible American public had been duped by the slick commercial portrayal of sex as something that had to occur *all* the time with the earthshaking, mind-blowing effects *each* time. Helga smiled at his tirade (it was one of many!), but

175

she had to agree that as much as she longed to feel the warmth of his body next to her on nights when they did not share the same bed, she had never been happier or more fulfilled in her life.

Together they mounted the steps that led to Daniel Chester French's colossal figure of Abraham Lincoln, which faced out through the colonnade toward the Washington Monument. Their hands were locked as they stood in reverential silence, gazing at the soft, compassionate expression on Lincoln's face. Still it was a powerful Lincoln that French had sculpted, for while the expression was gentle, the right hand of the statue was clenched and charged with energy. Helga stole a glance at Sam's almost stern profile. Sam possessed that same humanitarian spirit, a sensitivity and gentleness that continued to astonish and surprise her. But he was no one's fool, and she saw now that he always knew just how far he could go before turning hard and truculent. The new word on Capitol Hill was that Big Sam was not the easygoing, smiling man everyone had thought. The word was that he could deceive and plot with the best of them, that the quick wit and captivating candor belied a razor-sharp intellect and cunning that most people had underestimated. One would have thought that such a reappraisal would improve his viability as a party contender, but that was not the case. Helga was quick to perceive that in government circles too much brilliance was not necessarily an asset. Sam McCalahan was unpredictable, therefore he was dangerous. He could not be contained; therefore it was possible that when it came time for the party to promote one of its younger members, grooming him for the presidency or some other high office, Sam McCalahan might well be passed over.

Such was the scuttlebutt on Capitol Hill. Undoubtedly Sam had heard the rumors, probably from Tate, who liked to keep his fingers on the pulse of political activity. Oddly that aspect of his life remained an enigma to her, for though he spoke of work and the issues he was involved in, she had yet to hear from him, instead of the rumor mongers, what precisely his ambitions were.

176

As they walked around the seated figure of Lincoln to the inscription carved in marble on the rear wall, Helga wondered if he entertained notions of the presidency. Was it something he dreamed about, a hope he nourished as she now nourished the hope of getting her law degree? She was afraid to ask.

"It's not going to stick." Sam put his arms around her waist and pulled her back against him with his chin resting on the top of her head.

Their figures were dwarfed by the mammoth marble form of the Great Emancipator. They stood like that for some time, drinking in the majestic hush while the wind made a soft purring noise and a few leaves swirled in with the dancing flakes.

"It almost makes you know for certain," Sam said lowly, "that life is eternal, that immortality is as simple, as inevitable as snow in winter, rain in spring."

Helga turned in to face him. She reached up and smoothed his cheek with the palm of her hand, and he closed his eyes, relishing her touch, relishing the unspoken love that passed between them. Lately much of the time they spent together was spent in intimate silence with Helga reading one of her law books and Sam hard at work on some congressional matter. They had fallen so easily into rhythm that in the best sense they had begun to take certain things for granted. The love that had gotten off to such a rocky, halting start had in the past weeks bloomed into something not only beautiful but sturdy and rooted deeply in respect and trust.

"I could stand here all night." Helga turned back out to look at the white flurries. It was hard to believe that he had earned such a reputation as a ladies' man. That had worried her at first. Now, even when she tried, she could not dredge up a twinge of insecurity or, God forbid, jealousy. He exuded such love for her that she felt herself enveloped in a miraculous cocoon. He had been the one to bring up the subject of Lauren after Thanksgiving dinner. His ability to articulate why things had not worked out between him and Lauren, while at the same time giving

177

Lauren full credit and respect, *and* not threatening Helga with his praise for the other woman, had won her full admiration. Perhaps he had sensed her slight reserve at dinner, though Lauren with her usual vivaciousness had made it clear that there were no hard feelings. It was more likely that he truly wanted her to understand what had happened so that she would not embroider fears of her own or allow some of the stale gossip that was still lingering around to break the bond of trust. He and Lauren had been lovers, but very briefly because, according to Sam, despite the amiability and laughter between them, they both recognized there was a certain spark missing. How amazing that his explanation had satisfied her so totally. And she had been as relieved to have everything out in the open as he was. They both liked Lauren. It would have been a shame to have her drop out of their lives for no good reason.

Oh, there were so many reasons for loving him! She turned in to him again, and this time she reached up and drew his face down. His lips parted and he drew in a little breath as she ran her tongue along his upper lip, tantalizing him and unleashing in herself a warm, luscious sensation. His eyes were closed and his lips parted farther in a slight, languid smile as she wrapped her arms around his neck and pushed her tongue very slowly deep into his mouth. She stroked long and deep and felt, even through the thick camel fabric of his coat, how his heart accelerated to match her own.

"I looked for you in the library tonight," he murmured against her mouth. "I thought we could lock ourselves in Mrs. Ardley's powder room and make love."

Helga pressed into him, knowing that beneath the layers of winter clothes his hard, muscular body was warm and ready. He thrust his hips forward as if he were having the same thoughts, and they swayed against each other until they were both intoxicated and taut with desire.

"This is not the best place to make love." Sam ran his moist tongue around her ear. "I don't believe it quite complies with your high code for discretion and privacy."

"I can't stop kissing you." Helga turned his face back to hers and captured his mouth again, drinking in his hot, fragrant breath with its faint taste of bourbon.

"And you're sure you can't spend the night with me tonight?" Sam slipped his hands inside her coat and ran them lightly over her tight stomach.

"I have to be up so early . . ." Helga felt herself grow moist with longing as his hand smoothed and stroked along the silky red fabric. Lower and lower he stroked until she could almost feel his fingers touching her bare flesh. The flames were licking and curling, urging her.

"How can I say no?" Her head fell back and her body seemed to grow limp as Sam increased the pressure of his slowly stroking hand.

"Oh, I want you now!" He growled and his mouth sought hers in an insistent kiss that left them both breathless.

"We're crazy!" Sam slipped his arm around her waist and they ran down the steps of the monument to his car.

"I hope no one but Abe was watching." He laughed as he turned the key in the ignition. "For a lady who wants to be discreet you pick some pretty public places to turn a guy on."

The only problem, thought Helga as she sat in her office the next afternoon staring at her desk calendar, was Christmas. It was December 15, and by the twenty-first practically all of the government offices would be slacking off activities and by the twenty-third the exodus would nearly be complete. Her parents just assumed she would be returning to Minnesota to spend Christmas with them. The assumption was so complete that no one had even mentioned it in letters.

She opened the bottom drawer to her desk, took out a large fat pink folder, and began sorting through the stack of letters until she had located the five letters she planned to use as the backbone for her new idea about gaining congressional support for the case. The truth was she did not want to go home for Christmas. She wanted to stay right here in Washington, read her law books, work on the case, and spend every night with Sam. That was what she wanted to do, but a nagging sense of guilt had prompted her to phone the airlines and make a reservation anyway. Besides Sam's plans were vague. He had suggested she should come to Texas with him, but then the subject had been dropped, and so far the Christmas holidays appeared as a dim vista on the horizon.

She was excited about her new idea for the case. So far she hadn't mentioned it to anyone. Both Willard and Kenyon had been back in Minneapolis for the two past weeks, and although there were daily conference calls, she was reluctant to break new ground on long distance. Her idea, though not a major one, was to put together a modest press kit, a collection of persuasive letters to be distributed among congresspeople whose districts faced the same critical questions about mass transit, the railroads in particular. Of course, everyone in Washington knew about the Northern Railway case, but everyone had their own priorities. So much of what went on in this town was a vying for attention, and essentially her gesture was no more than that. But it was a gesture that until now had been neglected. Perhaps it had even been discounted as being naive. Only now time was growing short, and she was more and more convinced that the solution was going to have to come from a conglomerate, that solving the problem on a local level was not the answer. There wasn't enough pressure at that level. But if all the small railroads joined forces, then there would be some real clout, then the White House and the National Mediation Board would have to take notice.

She gathered up the papers and went out into the hall to begin making copies on the Xerox copying machine. It had been chilly in the office recently and today she had worn gray slacks and her favorite ski sweater, a white Irish knit with a delicate gray and beige design around the neck. She had just finished sixty copies of the first letter when Kenyon Stubbs interrupted.

"When did you get here?" She gave him a surprised smile. "You didn't say anything about coming yesterday on the phone."

Kenyon slipped his hand into the pocket of his gray pinstripe suit and regarded her for a moment. "You're looking wonderful, Helga."

"Well . . . thank you." Helga felt a twinge of nervousness. Kenyon never complimented her. He never really looked at her, and now he was leaning against the wall staring at her as if he'd never seen her before. She glanced quickly at her watch. She had shed the nervous gesture weeks ago when she and Sam had begun seeing each other steadily; now it was back.

"Always changes." Kenyon watched as she gathered up her papers. "Snow is forecast for the beginning of the week. I decided to take advantage of clear skies. Maybe you'll want to fly back with me next Tuesday before the blizzard hits."

"Blizzard?" Helga managed a calm smile as she started for her office.

Kenyon followed her, too closely she thought. "Yes, they're practically guaranteeing a white Christmas for the whole country, except the South and Southwest of course."

"Of course." Helga sat down at her desk and put the stack of papers away. Something told her this was not the opportune time to bring up her idea.

"What about a drink?" Kenyon drummed his fingers on the corner of her desk and smiled casually as if he always treated her with such friendly ease.

Helga glanced at her watch again, biding time. Rather than protest by saying she had planned on working another hour, she acquiesced, smiling at him with the same friendly ease with which he was treating her.

Some game, she thought as they entered the cozy dimly lit Casper's Cafe around the corner. Helga nodded at the bartender.

Sam often met her here for a quick sandwich on nights when she audited classes at the university.

"Just tea," she told the waitress.

"Come on, Helga," Kenyon teased. "At least have a beer . . . a light beer."

A small smile played on her lips as she thought of Sam's green bean story. "I'll stick with tea," she told the waitress. "I've been feeling a cold coming on." She turned to Kenyon. "That's why I look like I'm ready for the slopes."

"You like to ski?" Kenyon inquired after their drinks were in place.

"I used to." Helga looked at him evenly. Kenyon Stubbs had never ever evidenced the slightest interest in her private life. As a matter of fact, now that she thought of it, he had always treated her with a touch of disdain. Considering that he and John were classmates, that John was taken into the firm at the same time as Kenyon, wasn't it odd that he had never, in all of these years, treated her as an equal, if not as a colleague? But no, he had treated her very much as if there was a line of demarcation, both social and intellectual, drawn between them. She had, of course, met his wife, but she had never once been invited to their home. Clearly it had never occurred to them to ask the dull, lifeless secretary home to dinner. Not that she'd ever really minded, ever really given it much thought. But ten years was a long time and one dinner, one lunch, or a birthday card would not have been exactly out of line. Well, at least he had never sent her for coffee. There was that to be thankful for!

"What's so different about you?" Kenyon asked. "Willard said the same thing, by the way. Well, you know Willard . . . *Our* Helga, he says, is blooming down there."

"Yes." Helga cupped her hands around the steaming mug. "I ran into Willard at a Thanksgiving party."

"You've been making the social scene, have you?" Kenyon flashed her one of his most charming country club smiles.

"Yes." Helga returned his smile with a mischievous twinkle.

Kenyon Stubbs's new interest in her amused her. It had not escaped her that Kenyon harbored certain political ambitions himself. Perhaps he saw the Northern case as a way of establishing a track record here in Washington.

Kenyon toyed with his dry vodka martini a moment. "I hear you've been seeing a lot of Big Sam McCalahan."

"You hear that, do you?" Helga gave him a blank look.

Kenyon gave a self-conscious chuckle. "That's why you're so damned invaluable to us, Helga. It's that impenetrable way of yours, that composure. If I hadn't known you for—how long is it now, over ten years?—I'd be stopped by it too."

Helga smiled slowly. Known her for over ten years? Why, he knew nothing. She doubted if he even knew that she'd been living on her parents' farm since her husband's death. What he knew about her could be summed up in one sentence with no clauses.

"Yes, I've been seeing Sam McCalahan," she preempted his further inquiry and waited for him to press her on the subject.

"Is it serious?" he asked after a moment.

"Not really," Helga said evenly. "Or rather yes. It's serious in that it's a friendship I hope to continue. Sam's a very good friend."

"I never would have figured you'd—"

Helga interrupted with an ambiguous smile. "Well, Kenyon, it's possible to have all sorts of friends, isn't it?"

Kenyon flashed her another smile. "I suppose so. Tate doesn't think you're just friends."

"Kenyon, did you really come here to inquire into my love life?" Helga's laugh was genuine, but underneath a quiver of doubt was threatening to cut off her amusement. She really wasn't bitter that Kenyon had drawn such firm social lines between them. Although she was perhaps seeing him for what he was for the first time, she would never be able to dislike him. He was what he was—a small-time, very smart, very ambitious lawyer who, when it came down to it, would always devote more time to his tennis game than to his case. He would always be split in his ambitions and he would always be vaguely frustrated by his lack of achievements. And he would probably never know why.

"No, no . . ." Kenyon assured her with a wave of his hand. "I didn't fly back to Washington to check up on you."

"Well, that's a relief." There was a touch of irony in Helga's smile. "I haven't seen much of Tate recently. He doesn't stop in the office the way he used to."

"He's gearing up to get things rolling for McCalahan." Kenyon swizzled his martini and signaled for a second one.

"Really?" Helga felt her stomach tense. Sam hadn't mentioned a word about it. In fact, since she had revealed her reservations about Tate, he had not even referred to him.

"Fund raising." Kenyon did not notice her wary response. "McCalahan doesn't have much financial backing at this stage, but knowing Tate he'll have the coffers filled and overflowing in plenty of time."

"Plenty of time." Helga nodded. "Plenty of time for what?"

"The presidential primaries," Kenyon clarified. "McCalahan will have just hit forty by then, and it's my opinion that his age'll work against him. But Tate says no. He thinks the country is ready to swing back to a youthful image. He thinks McCalahan will have a real shot . . . But then, as I'm sure you've noticed, Tate is a bit of a dreamer himself."

Helga finished her tea and resisted an impulse to glance at her watch again. There was still plenty of time before starting for her class. She looked up at Kenyon, folded her hands in her lap, and waited for more questions about her relationship with Sam, convinced that Tate was behind this little tête-à-tête.

"The case is going well," Kenyon announced briskly.

"Well, I don't know." Helga looked skeptical. "Nothing's come together yet . . ."

"But the groundwork has been well laid and a lot of it is thanks to you." Kenyon lifted his glass in a toast.

"There's much left to be done," Helga said. "In fact, I've been wanting to approach you and Willard about an idea I have."

"We'd love to hear it." Kenyon dismissed her with a perfunctory smile. "In fact, things around here are running so smoothly that you may not have to come back to Washington after Christmas vacation."

"What?" Helga's placidity was shattered and her face reflected all the anguish and confusion wrought by Kenyon's announcement. Conflicting thoughts collided in her mind: Tate had put him up to this; Tate wanted her out of town, out of Sam's life. Or maybe Kenyon wasn't as decent as she thought. Maybe he begrudged her the whirl of Washington's inner social circle.

". . . and we need you at home, back in Minneapolis," Kenyon continued with a bright, eager smile that told her that he expected her gratitude, that in return for his praise for a job well done he anticipated more than a blank stare.

How she managed to survive the remaining time with Kenyon and then to concentrate during the three-hour lecture on corporate law she wasn't sure. Somehow she arrived back at the stone cottage around ten, and when the paranoid thoughts would not let her rest, she decided the very least she could do was to phone Willard Matthews in Minneapolis and verify Kenyon's news.

"How nice to hear your voice." Willard, ever the benevolent father, was congenial even late at night.

"I'm sorry to phone you at home." Helga hoped she sounded calm, though the fact that she had not waited to call in the morning no doubt suggested some problem to him.

"It's just that we need you desperately back here," Willard said in answer to her questions. "There's a big conflict-of-interest case coming up, which means an enormous amount of research. Kenyon and I both thought you'd like that."

Helga felt the tears spring to her eyes. She had counted on being in Washington at least until May. Willard referred to the research on the new case as if they were doing her a favor by allowing her to put in long hours at the library. She was a workhorse and for the first time in ten years it occurred to her

185

that for all of his fatherly solicitude Willard Matthews was not above taking advantage of her.

"This may seem like a strange question." Helga pressed her lips together to compose herself. "Was this your idea?"

Willard paused. "Tell you frankly, Helga . . . I don't know if it was mine or Kenyon's. You know how these things are. Do you have a problem with it?"

"No . . ." Helga's knuckles were white as she clutched the receiver.

"Maybe you need a vacation? Does a week in the Bahamas appeal?"

"That's nice of you, Willard," Helga said faintly. "It's not that. Just . . . as soon as you know, you'll let me know."

"Of course, dear." Willard sounded concerned. "It may not be till after the first of the year. Whatever is most convenient for you. Leave your things in Washington or bring them back for the holidays."

"I was considering not coming home for the holidays." Helga felt numb.

"Whatever is best for you," Willard said.

"Thank you." Helga replaced the receiver slowly. Kenyon and Willard had no idea she was going to go to law school; they had no idea how incredibly her life had changed in the past two months.

Only . . . now what? Perhaps she should make a clean breast of it and tell them she needed to stay on in Washington to see the Northern case through to the end. She had never once asked anything of them, and it certainly wasn't as if her continued presence here would be superfluous. Maybe it was time to be assertive, to ask for what she needed.

And she needed to stay! Helga threw off her sweater and slacks, her face set in a tense, frustrated expression. She could not altogether ignore the possibility that Tate really was pulling a few strings.

Helga padded back to the phone clad only in her bra and

186

panties and looked up Tate's phone number in the directory. How the hell could she confront him without revealing her feelings for Sam? In the end it didn't matter what Tate Brown did. Oh, yes, it would be nice to know. It would be nice to have the information, but she could not let what Tate Brown did have anything to do with her life, with her decisions. If he had forced her hand then so be it. She had not reckoned on having to make a choice. Matthews, Matthews, and Stubbs had been her life, her salvation, but it just might be time to let all of that go.

But breaking with a job that had kept her afloat during those horrible months after John's death was going to be more difficult than she liked to admit. For the next three days Helga threw herself into her work, ignoring the reality of her tenuous future and telling herself that now was the time to look on the bright side of things. After all, it wasn't certain that she would be transferred back to Minneapolis. There was still some slight chance that the Northern case would demand her presence here in Washington. Although Kenyon remained in town, she did not broach the subject of her new idea, nor did she state her very strong preference for staying in Washington until the case was resolved.

On Friday evening, dressed in a new black velvet suit with a frilly white lace blouse, she and Sam attended a benefit symphony concert at Kennedy Center and later an enormous reception at the White House. Three times during the concert Sam leaned close and asked her if she was all right and three times she denied that anything was the matter.

The truth was she was exhausted. She had almost looked forward to the White House Christmas reception, but now shuffling along in a long tedious line to shake hands with the President, she felt annoyed, irritated by the pomposity of the protocol and put off and overly critical of so many backslapping compatriots. Everyone seemed to be gushing their enthusiasm to the point of absurdity. In the midst of so many glad tidings her mouth tightened, and she felt like the female incarnation of Dickens's Scrooge.

For the first time Sam's exuberance was putting her on edge. Had she been blind not to notice how obnoxiously loud he could be? And despite her requests to steer clear of the newspaper reporters with their flashing cameras when they had first entered the famous residence, she had the distinct impression that he had raised his voice in order to attract their attention. He was no different from any other ambitious bureaucrat vying for publicity. Perversely, she stared into the flashing cameras with a placid expression despite the urgings to "smile when you look up at the Congressman's face!" She was damned if she was going to be labeled as Sam McCalahan's beautiful *gay* companion.

"Hold on a minute there, Bill!" Sam darted out of the reception line to clasp some tall Western type by the shoulders and jostle him around in a friendly greeting.

Helga turned away sharply. He was behaving as if he were on a football field. If one day he were elected president, he could write a book of memoirs entitled *Roughhousing in the White House.* It was a mean thought and thinking it only made her feel worse. When Sam returned to introduce her to his good friend from Houston, Bill Smithers, she made a supreme effort to chink away some of the ice that was forming around her heart, but once they had actually shaken hands with the President and were imbibing some deliciously spiked punch, the same ambiguous anger that had hovered over her all evening swept in on her again. She excused herself from a talkative coterie of Sam's friends and found her way to the powder room.

No one would miss her anyway. She had scarcely uttered more than two dozen words all evening. And whose fault was that? She stared at her reflection in the oval mirror. Her face looked sour and drawn to her. Under any circumstances an affair of this magnitude would have been an ordeal, but tonight she was finding it intolerable. It would be childish and stupid to sneak out, but that was just what she felt like doing. Sneaking past all of the uniformed guards, slithering unseen down the long corridor and out into the cold night.

Suddenly she longed for those subzero temperatures of her home. She wanted desperately to hear the crunch of snow and look up and see the stark black limbs of trees stretching up into the velvety night. Well that was fine, wasn't it? She would be home soon enough, ensconced in her old life. Soon enough she would have all the silence she craved.

Tonight she felt painfully inept in the presence of so many vital loquacious dignitaries. The words seemed to stick in her throat, and she had the overwhelming sensation that she was under scrutiny, that she was being judged and that she was being found lacking. Any other night she might have found some humor in the observation that at the White House one could not exactly retreat into the library for a respite while nibbling on one's repast. She might have whispered this observation to Sam and they might have shared a laugh. Only tonight she was unable to share anything; tonight she wanted to shut him out, to shut the world out.

Senator Wiley's wife called to her as she left the powder room and, complimenting her on her black velvet evening suit, whisked her over to introduce her to several other senators' wives.

The women were older than Helga, and they greeted her with a warmth and graciousness that only drove her deeper into despair. She wasn't like these women. These were soft-voiced ladies who had devoted their lives to their husbands' political careers. Their charm, without exception, was genuine, and had it not been for her particular mood she would have enjoyed talking to them.

But she wasn't like them. She envied the honest joy they took from these gatherings, but it was a joy she would never feel. Her tension mounted as she tried to rise to the occasion, tried to find a way of getting outside of herself so she could have at least one exchange that would not make her feel such a failure.

189

She was letting Sam down. She was, just as she had suspected, not his equal. If the archangel Gabriel flew down and said he would grant her one wish, it would be not *ever, ever* to have to attend another enormous, handshaking, backslapping reception.

"Here she is . . ." Sam came toward her, smiling, and took her hand, drawing her into yet another circle of new acquaintances. He slipped his arm around her waist and introduced her with his usual charm.

"Norma"—Sam nodded toward a tall, stately white-haired woman—"is from St. Paul."

"Oh." Helga's smile felt lifeless and forced as she racked her brain to come up with a logical course for this opening to follow.

Somehow she managed to arrive at a topic of conversation that engaged Norma and they stood chatting for several minutes before Sam drew her away for more introductions. A dull headache was beginning to throb in the back of her head, and as the evening wore on it seemed that Sam's every glance was a criticism. By the time they left and she was seated next to him in the front seat of the Oldsmobile, she was convinced that there was no hope whatsoever for anything lasting between them. She would be a dead weight on his political future, a millstone, stubborn and unsmiling. She thought wryly that she could use a good dose of Southern belle hormones . . . some miracle drug that would allow her to exude an air of bewitching frivolity. Good heavens, if the press had criticized Jacqueline Kennedy for being shy and aloof, what would they say about her?

"Nice party." Sam pulled her close the way he always did, but her body felt stiff and awkward. She could always go to law school back in Minnesota. It wasn't as if everything was lost from her life. It was important to keep a perspective here. Many positive changes had occurred during the past months.

"Did you have a good time?" Sam hugged her. "The White House functions always turn out to be less formidable than I imagine."

"It was interesting," Helga said lowly.

"That means you had a lousy time." Sam laughed.

"You'll get used to it," he told her after a moment.

No, she thought, I won't. They were just too different. Sam might well like to eat in the library, but it was more clear than before how much he loved being in the spotlight.

"Do you want to talk about something?" he asked as he pulled into the garage next to his town house.

"I suppose we should." Helga's stomach knotted. Why hadn't she stopped him from driving her to his house?

"Hey!" Sam tapped her arm to rouse her. "What's wrong?"

"Let's go inside." Helga avoided his eyes and opened the car door.

"I don't get it." When they were inside Sam threw his overcoat on the lumpy sofa and poured himself a drink. "It's the Christmas season. Ho! Ho! Ho! We're supposed to be jolly. Come on, Helga, what's going on? I can feel you slipping away."

Helga accepted the glass of brandy and sat tentatively on the edge of the sofa.

"How long are you going to sit there?" Sam stomped across the room and stared at her.

"I don't know where to start." Helga stared at the amber liquid.

"Well, just start, damn it!" Sam swigged down his brandy and loosened his bow tie.

"Don't yell." Helga gave him an icy look. "You've been yelling all evening." She winced inwardly at the brittle critical tone in her voice. "I'm sorry . . . you haven't been yelling. I . . ."

"Well, so what if I've been yelling!" Sam roared. "Who the hell cares if I've been yelling? It has nothing to do with you if I yell and make a bloody fool of myself."

"I suppose you're right," Helga said tightly.

"Damn right, I'm right!" Sam fired.

"I asked you . . . please, not to encourage photographers . . ."

"Oh, come off it!" Sam exploded. "What is the big deal about a couple of pictures?"

His face softened and he sat down next to her and looked at her closely. "You looked beautiful tonight."

Helga swirled the brandy. She hadn't had a drink all evening and she wasn't going to start now. She shoved the glass aside.

"Sometimes"—Sam stood up impatiently—"you are just too Scandanavian."

Helga felt herself harden at his criticism. It was true. She had spent the evening withdrawing. No, actually the process had started right after the conversation with Kenyon. But what was done was done. She was stuck with it and she was resigned.

"I guess I'm exhausted from so many . . . functions," she said finally.

"I don't believe that." Sam poured himself another brandy and drank it down.

"You're drinking—"

"Don't tell me what I'm doing," he said hotly.

"Suit yourself." Helga looked at him coolly, and further enraged, he poured a third brandy, gulped it down, and poured another. Childish, thought Helga.

"Thanks, I will." Sam made a grand show of swirling the liquid and sipping it.

"We're very different, you know." Helga tried to suppress her rising fury.

"That's astute of you." Sam slammed his glass down and eyed her truculently.

"Look." Helga did not like the unwieldly anger that was boiling inside. "Look, I . . . I hate those monstrous, impersonal parties like the one tonight. There have been too many of those lately—"

"Now wait a minute," Sam interrupted, "there haven't been that many."

"Not as far as you're concerned." Helga glared at him. "You love them."

"Yeah, I do love them . . . so what?" He thrust his chin out like an adolescent aching for a fight.

"I can't deal with them. I guess it's a flaw of mine but I just can't. It's like time wasted for me. And you're wrong. We went to three last week and the week before—"

"It's the holiday season!" Sam shouted. "That's why! That's why there's so much activity. Anyway, I didn't twist your arm."

"I know you didn't." Helga's face was tense. "I'm not blaming you . . ."

"It sounds like that's just what you're doing."

"I don't mean to." Helga clenched her hands into fists. There was no easy way, no way to make it all come out right. "But your life is going to be more and more involved with this sort of thing—handshaking, picture taking. I tried to tell you once before that I'm a private—"

"And I respected what you told me. Has your name been dragged through the muck and mire of the social columns?" Sam asked.

"No, but my boss, Kenyon Stubbs, seemed to have gotten wind of—"

"You know what"—Sam stormed across the room—"you should be a hermit. Save your money, buy yourself a nice little island in the Aegean, and raise sheep."

Helga gave him a bitter smile. "That appeals to me enormously after tonight."

"And you know why?" Sam paced back and forth in front of her like a prosecuting attorney. "Because you're too self-involved to let go and enjoy yourself. You're not supposed to go to these affairs and stand around *thinking*. You're not expected to form meaningful relationships with everyone you shake hands with."

"I'm not that stupid," Helga fired.

"You're not stupid at all!" Sam fired back. "But you're stubborn as hell, and you have a knack for freezing over when the situation gets too hot. Now what in God's name is going on!"

"I told you!" Helga sprang to her feet and grabbed her coat.

"You go to these functions"—Sam stepped in front of her—"to make contact, superficial as it may be, with your fellow man, fellows, fellow people . . ." He weaved slightly and screwed up his face. "I always look on these things as a public forum . . . like the old town meetings."

"But it's not a town meeting," Helga argued. "Those aren't regular people—they're politicians, politicians' wives."

"You are very cynical at times." Sam grasped her shoulders and stared at her. "They're people and yes, some of them do get turned around and distorted by holding public office. Some of them do get off on the expense accounts and the glamour . . . but not all. Not me!"

"I'm no good at it." Helga fought back the tears.

"Oh, God!" Sam pulled her close. "I don't expect you to smile at the photographers."

"I know you don't," Helga's tears were falling freely now. "I do! I expect it of myself . . . and I can't do it! All my pictures, the ones they took in grade school even, were serious. That's the way I am."

"You don't have to change." Sam smoothed the top of her head. "As long as you smile at me. I don't want a little cutie robot. I want you."

"I'm a phony." Helga pulled away from him and collapsed back on the lumpy sofa.

"The last thing you are is phony." Sam sat down next to her and took her hand.

"I may have to leave Washington." Helga looked at him after a moment. "I'm phony because I guess that's what all the histrionics are about. Kenyon told me they're starting to wind down the work here and they need me back in Minneapolis."

"But that's not a problem." Sam pulled a handkerchief out of his pocket and dabbed carefully at her eyes.

"Of course it's a problem." Helga slumped back into the cushiony sofa.

"I think it's a bonus," Sam said.

An unexpected smile trembled on Helga's mouth. "You would. You're an optimist. You think everything is a bonus. Unless you want to get rid of me, my having to go back to Minneapolis is no bonus."

"Of course I don't want to get rid of you. All this means is now you can really concentrate on preparing for the LSATs in June. And in the fall go to law school full-time! That's what you should do anyway, and you know it."

Helga shook her head. "It's my job, Sam. My job! I have to have a job!"

"I'll stake you." Sam tilted her face toward his. "If you need help, I'll—"

"I can't accept money from you!" Helga laughed then grew wistful. She was deeply flattered and touched by his offer.

"Well, I knew you'd say that." Sam grinned. "It'll be a loan, just until you pass the bar exam and hang out your own shingle. If you like we can draw up a contract, and if you insist I'll even charge interest."

Helga's face crumpled and she turned against the sofa sobbing softly. "I'm sorry," she apologized.

"It's all right." Sam began massaging her neck.

"I don't usually cry like this . . . I don't want you to think . . ."

"It's okay." Sam's strong hands prodded gently at the constricted muscles in her shoulders. "You've been holding it all in. How many days?"

"Two . . . three . . ." Helga felt a sense of relief flood over her as the tears continued to fall.

"Let's do this right." Sam lifted her up and removed the black velvet jacket. "May I ask that you remove your blouse, mademoiselle? For professional purposes only. I want to work miracles with those poor tight muscles."

"I behaved like a bitch," Helga muttered with downcast eyes.

"Why, I've never heard you use such language." Sam chuckled as he unbuttoned her blouse. "Listen, nobody noticed your bad behavior but you. I wasn't even aware that a glacier had moved silently into place. At the concert I guess I noticed that you were preoccupied, but you're entitled to be preoccupied, and honestly later on you seemed fine. Okay, maybe I was absorbed in other things, but I can assure you if you'd been the ogre you think you were, I would have been aware of it."

"I wasn't expecting to have to make any decision so soon."

Helga's expression softened as a ripple of warm pleasure coursed through her body. She leaned back against the couch, tucking her chin under to watch his large fingers fumbling with the tiny buttons on her blouse.

"I'm grateful," she said softly as he removed the fragile covering, "that you have such confidence in me."

"Well, I do." Sam unfastened the button on her skirt and removed it with a flourish. "Now stretch out on your tummy," he ordered, but before she could follow his direction he held her at arm's length and gazed at her.

"Black becomes you." He ran one finger around the top of her lacy bra, pausing to test the softness of her breasts, which spilled appealingly just over the top of the garment. He gave her an ardent glance as his hand moved down and across the taut white abdomen, then unexpectedly he lowered his face and rubbed his cheek against it.

"I am seriously intending to give you a back rub"—he trailed kisses from one prominent hipbone to the other—"eventually. Are you warm enough?"

"I am now." Helga ran her hands through his sandy hair as his tongue made a slow, seductive circle around her navel. His mouth, as it moved and sucked against her pale skin, seemed to be drawing out the last residue of strain and tension. She could feel herself melting, then a warm churning began as his hands stroked along the silky contours of her body.

"We haven't made love enough lately," he murmured as his fingers moved enticingly under her scant black bikini panties.

196

"What happened to your theory?" Helga smiled languidly and closed her eyes as he stood up to remove his clothes. "I thought you believed in quality over quantity."

"Wisecracking broad!" When she opened her eyes he was standing naked over her. The magnificence of his huge, muscular body unleashed a torrid flood of desire, and she stretched her arms out to him.

"And how's come you're not drunk?" She writhed in anticipation, still drinking in his beauty. "You drank all that brandy and you're—"

"'Cause I'm a *real* man!" He did a comic swagger but continued to stand over her.

Helga drew in a deep breath. From this angle he seemed even more enormous, more godlike and magnificent. Everything in her body was geared to feeling the force of his hot power bursting in on her. "More likely it's because you weren't drinking the real stuff."

Helga smiled broadly. The moroseness was gone, replaced by the euphoric giddiness that was so often a part of their lovemaking. Never, she thought, had laughter seemed so sexy as it was with Big Sam.

Sam sank down beside her and drew her up to a sitting position. "You have colored water in one of those crystal decanters." She could not keep a straight face. "I checked the other day. Is that another one of your cunning tricks? You ply poor unsuspecting visitors with spirits while you sip sugar water and stay sober."

"You snoop!" Sam placed one finger over the front catch of her bra.

"I discovered it by accident . . . cross my heart!"

Helga wriggled toward his muscular chest, and when he had unhooked the bra and her breasts spilled out, she pressed into him, luxuriating in the feel of the wiry hairs that covered his skin.

"It's not polite to let people drink alone." Sam cupped one full breast in his hand and lowered his mouth to tease the rosy nipple into a tight bud. Helga stroked the thick, sinewy muscles of his upper back as he ran his tongue around the nipple, barely touching it.

The texture of his warm back had never seemed so deliciously smooth, and the sensation of his mouth opening and closing on her tight nipple was far sweeter than it had ever been. That so much pain, fear, and doubt could have been transformed into a moment as breathtakingly erotic and beautiful as this was nothing less than a miracle. She had been so angry, so fiercely angry, and her heart had been filled with such bleakness. And yet it was all dissolved, and in its place a love equally fierce . . . a love intensified and made richer by all that had preceded.

She should have gone to him at first instead of allowing all of her fears to fester. As his hands stroked her tight, narrow buttocks, she vowed that as foreign as it was to her solitary nature, the next time she would force herself to turn to him, if not to ask for his help, then to allow him to share in her distress. She would want him to do the same, wouldn't she? Yes, if there was something threatening his well-being she would want to be the first to know, and she would feel shut out if he could not share it with her.

"Why are we in the living room?" Sam pulled away from her and looked at her with drugged eyes. Before she could reply she felt his huge hands scooping under her bare behind and hoisting her up until her legs were wrapped around his waist. The sensation of his warm flesh on her inner thighs sharpened the lush, voluptuous feelings bubbling inside, and she moaned her acquiescence as he carried her into the bedroom.

Balancing her with dancerlike dexterity, Sam pulled back the covers and lowered her onto the bed. As he fell on top of her, she felt the wild erratic pounding of his heart beating into her, increasing her desire for him. He moved his body from side to side in a rolling motion as his tongue sank into her yielding mouth.

Helga moved eagerly beneath his weight, content for the moment to celebrate the matchless perfection of the way they were together by undulating against him. Sam nipped tenderly at her long, slender neck, then surprised her by changing course for the moment and sliding down her body until his head was buried in her stomach. The ecstasy of his searching mouth filled her with a sweet pain. With each flick of his tongue he neared his goal. His breathing grew louder, ragged and more uneven, and his fingers fanned in and out in a kneading motion on her inner thighs. She could not contain herself, could not resist the hot violent passion that rushed through her, and she thrashed involuntarily, almost delirious with so much pleasure. At the height of her wild delirium, when she thought she could endure no more, he plunged inside her, filling her with an all-encompassing force that left her gasping. She was gasping, crying out, weeping, and laughing all at once. It seemed as if every existing emotion had shot to the surface, as if he had dived into all of her secret corners and set free everything she had been unable to release.

And she rejoiced in the release, and the knowledge that he would go this far for her drove her to reciprocate. Now it was she who became the demanding demon lover. It was the cunning of her swiveling hips that drove him so near the edge that he pleaded with her to slow down, never to stop.

"I will try," she murmured into his open mouth, "never to turn to ice like that again."

"We mustn't let anything ruin this." Sam's eyes beamed with the innocence she most treasured.

"Nothing will." Helga gulped for air as his movements became slower and more intense, so that each stroke was like lightning, initiating a myriad of dazzling responses.

"We have so much!" And when she felt Sam's shudder, she arched into him with her entire being.

CHAPTER ELEVEN

The next day was Saturday, and as she had done every Saturday since deciding to apply to George Washington University Law School, Helga spent the day in the library. At five o'clock she shoved the sleeves of the white ski sweater up to her elbows and returned the stack of reference books to the librarian. Sam was in New York for the evening and she was meeting Marilyn for an early dinner at a nearby Italian restaurant.

As she trotted down the library steps the sense of well-being that had flourished all day during her studies seemed on the point of withering. If only there were more time. She stood for a moment scanning the sky for stars, as if that would signal something significant. It was warm for December. The weather in Washington could always be depended upon to be off the mark. In a way she wished that the blizzard Kenyon had mentioned would strike with a vengeance, leaving her no alternative about going back to Minnesota for the Christmas holidays. Time was what she needed, more time!

There were three stars in the sky and a sliver of a moon low on the horizon. Helga sat down on the bottom step and wrapped her arms around her knees. Sam's offer to loan her the money to go full-time to school had been incredibly generous, but the truth was . . . money was not what was stopping her. Sam would razz her unmercifully if he knew how much money she had saved over the past ten years. Apparently it hadn't occurred to him that for all that time she had had virtually no expenses. Of course she had contributed to the food budget and she'd had her automobile expenses, but rent, usually the primary expenditure in anyone's budget, was something she had never paid. Her father wouldn't hear of accepting money. A melancholy smile crossed her face at the thought of her parents. What would they think of Sam bursting in on their quiet, orderly, decorous life? The house in Minnesota was always cold and drafty; even in warm weather a dankness seemed to permeate it. How would Sam react to so much Scandanavian severity? He liked to tease her about her northern temperament, but she could not imagine her father or her brother taking too kindly to his sometimes raw brand of humor, his effusive physicality. She thought of the stiff formality of manly handshakes that passed for affection between her brothers and her father. If Sam, on the other hand, liked someone, he pawed at them with the playfulness of a romping bear.

She stood up slowly and began walking in the direction of Emilio's Pizzeria. No, money was not an issue. She could, with no hardship, well afford to quit working for the time it would take to complete her studies and take the bar exam. It was the notion of change that terrified her. In broad daylight, or at least when she was not wrapped in Sam McCalahan's persuasive arms, she simply could not imagine life without Matthews and Stubbs. She could feel herself gravitating toward a compromise, and not an altogether painless compromise. She could very easily return to Minnesota, continue working at her old job, and go to law school there. There was no reason to stay in Washington *just* to go to law school.

She frowned as she entered Emilio's gaily decorated red and white *taverna*. She was already breaking her vow. But Sam was in New York and she could not stop the thoughts from coming. She sipped a glass of red wine and waited for Marilyn. Staying in D.C. was tantamount to making a commitment to Sam. That frightened her too.

And had he made a commitment to her? She tried to ignore

201

the doubts. Well, he had offered her money. But what about a future? Had there ever been any mention of anything permanent? Suddenly everything between them felt vague and flimsy. Maybe this was just an affair, maybe . . .

"Hi!" Marilyn breezed in and shrugged off her down parka. "Hot. Too hot for all these clothes. The forecasters keep talking about a blizzard but I don't see any signs."

"I know." Helga signaled the waiter and Marilyn ordered a glass of wine.

"You're pensive." Marilyn eyed her.

"I guess I am," Helga admitted ruefully.

"Well, your picture's in the *Post* today. I suppose you know that." Marilyn grinned. "Good picture too. You look very regal, like you're about to make some important declaration."

"Great!" Helga winced and did not try to hide her displeasure.

"Shouldn't I be the first to know," Marilyn persisted busily, "what every columnist is hinting at?"

"You mean that Sam McCalahan and I are . . ." Helga paused and shook her head. "I don't know what Sam and I are," she said after a moment. "I'm afraid things are coming to a head rather quickly. There's a pretty good chance that they'll want me in the home office after the first of the year. I honestly hadn't given a lot of thought to . . . the future, to what it would mean for Sam and me."

"Well, I guess it would mean marriage," Marilyn said after a moment's consideration. "If you love each other . . . and I'd say that's pretty evident."

"I guess you're right." Helga nodded painfully. "And maybe I've thought of marriage in the way far back of my mind, but it was way out there, you know? Way out there in the future, months, maybe years, away. I'm in no rush. I don't think Sam is either. We've never even talked about it."

"So you feel pressured because of your job." Marilyn nodded understandingly.

"Basically." Helga took a deep breath. "I'm just getting started, Marilyn. Even if Sam was interested, am I really ready to take on a new husband *and* a new career at the same time? Not to mention the fact that Sam is not just any man, his job is not just any man's job. I'm just getting a sense of my own identity after all these years. I can't help feeling that becoming Mrs. McCalahan would be the end of all that."

"Quit your job. Stay here in Washington and see. You can have the cottage for as long as you want."

"That's sweet of you." Helga smiled wanly.

"I like having you around." Marilyn waved to the waiter and ordered a large deluxe pizza.

"I don't know." Helga squirmed in her seat and wished she were out jogging instead of about to stuff herself.

"I think I know what you're going through," Marilyn said sympathetically. "If I hadn't seen you and Sam together I wouldn't have believed it was possible. Let's face it—you are not exactly the kind of person one imagines hitting the old campaign trail."

The old campaign trail? Marilyn's words reverberated inside Helga's head for the duration of the sausage pizza, through the movie, and on into the night as full panic set in. She tried phoning Sam in New York and then at his house. Finally at ten past midnight he answered.

"I'm having another attack." Helga made an attempt at lightness.

"I'll come by and pick you up." Sam did not consider it a trivial matter.

"No, no. I just wanted to hear your voice."

"But we could talk," Sam said quickly.

"I don't know what there is to talk about." Helga flexed her foot beneath the sheet. "I keep going round and round. The minute I make my mind up one way, I make it up the other. I'm not used to this sort of indecisiveness." If only he would say something to make it . . . concrete. Was that what she wanted?

"We'll go to the Pancake House and talk."

Helga made a distasteful face at the mention of food.

"Look, I've been thinking," Sam continued, "maybe you should come home with me to Texas for Christmas. You could meet my clan and really, Helga, heat is what you need, not ice."

"I don't think so." Helga stared up at the beamed ceiling above her loft bed, feeling more confused, more ambivalent. A trip to Texas to meet his family was not enough.

"You answered that question too quickly." Sam sounded defensive.

"I'm sorry," Helga apologized.

"At least consider it," Sam said. "Come home with me to Galveston, enjoy the sun and—"

"I think I need to go back home." Helga rolled over on her side and propped herself up on her elbow. "Maybe going back will give me the perspective I need."

"Then I'll come along," Sam jumped in. "I've never been, you know, and . . . Well, I don't see this as a good time to be separated."

"I want you to come sometime," Helga interrupted, "but now doesn't feel right."

"Whatever you say." Sam sounded hurt.

"Please understand." Helga closed her eyes, feeling more miserable than before. What good was it to talk, to open up when the basic facts remained the same?

"I'll try," Sam said tightly.

"Don't you see!" She sat up suddenly. It was crucial that he understand, that this effort on her part to open up to him not be a failure. "I'll be able to sort things out. There may not be a problem. Kenyon and Willard may decide they need me here."

"I've never seen you so wishy-washy," Sam replied in a sullen, distant voice. "Helga, you're abdicating. You're not making a decision at all . . . you're waiting for it to be made for you."

"Thanks," Helga replied in a frosty voice. "I didn't need to hear that from you. Last night you encouraged me to turn to you and not always keep things to myself. And now when I try you're cynical and accusing. I don't need you to tell me I'm stuck, or that I'm wishy-washy as you so tactfully put it."

"I'm not perfect." Sam's response did nothing to reassure her.

"I'm not asking you to be . . ." Helga flung herself back on her pillow in frustration.

"Christmas is an important time to be with someone you love. We could still stay here like we'd planned."

"I know." Helga felt a stab of remorse, but that was all. None of the alternatives seemed to make a difference.

"I think you want to go back to Minnesota because you don't want to break with your old life. It's more than your anxiety about leaving the firm.

"I think," Sam added after a moment, "you want to return to your old life because it continues to tie you to your husband. I don't think you want to forget or to let him go."

Helga stared into the darkness with a stunned expression, and for several moments she could not even form the words to protest. It wasn't true! She had scarcely thought of John in the past two months.

"Helga?" Sam's voice was suddenly filled with concern. "I shouldn't have said that."

"It's ridiculous!" Helga denied it vehemently, but when she hung up there were bright tears in her eyes and for the second time in two days she was sobbing.

What sleep there was was fitful and riddled with vague, uneasy dreams in which John, for the first time in years, was present. When she finally decided it was senseless to toss and turn for another hour, the sun was already coming up. She clambered down the ladder from the loft and dressed in a gray jogging outfit. By six thirty she was puffing past the Washington Monument.

It did not take a psychiatrist to interpret the dreams. John's benign appearance, while underscoring her uncertainty about the possible changes in her life, had shed some new light on the real source of her ambivalence. In the dream she had not felt love for her husband as she had in their life together. She had felt guilt—guilt because she had turned her back on him, guilt because . . . she loved another man.

Dreams did not distinguish between life and death. It made no difference that John was dead and Sam was alive, that logically guilt was an entirely inappropriate response. Helga paused to adjust the red earmuffs Sam had bought her. The panic she felt was not exclusively at the possibility of severing her ties with Matthews, Matthews, and Stubbs. It went deeper, and Sam with his usual clarity had zeroed in on it. She was reluctant to commit herself to the future because she was still, however tenuously and unwillingly, holding on to the past.

Of course Sam felt hurt, even though he logically understood just as she did that it was absurd to allow a memory, however fond and dear, to infringe upon the present. Helga increased her gait until a stinging stab of pain in her side forced her to slow down. If Sam hadn't pointed it out to her, she wondered how long she would have managed to stifle that strange dichotomy and relegate it solely to the subconscious. But thank heavens he had been forthright enough . . . and angry and hurt enough to bring it out into the open. For already, even with a sleepless night behind her and the same uncertainties in front of her, she was beginning to see the situation more clearly. She loved John. She loved Sam. No one was asking her to make a choice . . . neither the living nor the dead.

They had planned to enjoy the day at the Smithsonian Institute, to have an early dinner and spend the night at his house. She had hoped to stop in the office briefly on Monday before catching her plane at three. Now the idea of leaving Washington, leaving Sam on such a sour, apprehensive note was even more upsetting. One night was not enough time for a reconciliation, though why she thought of it as a reconciliation she did not know. She slowed to a brisk walk up Fifteenth Street past the monument of Sherman, swinging around past the Executive

Office Building. Finally she stopped to peer through the iron fence that surrounded the White House.

Some sort of compromise was in order and she knew it. Christmas was a time to be spent with loved ones, and there was no one on this earth she loved more than Sam McCalahan. But there would be other Christmases. If only she could make him understand that she had to go home and that this was not the best time for him to come along.

The White House was still and impenetrable in the gray early-morning light. It was hard to believe that people, a family of laughing, crying, struggling, happy, and unhappy people lived inside its walls, that dogs yapped down its corridors and the aroma of coffee filled the kitchen. What would it be like to live there? The question made her shiver.

By the time she turned back to the street the ubiquitous picketers had begun to form with their various banners of protest. There was scarcely an hour of the day when the sidewalk in front of the White House was not dotted with protesters. A wizened old man carried a large hand-lettered sign board that denounced the fatal effects of acid rain. There were five women with small children gathered to protest the construction of a nuclear power plant in their vicinity. Another group was forming with the opposite message.

As she left the band of protesters behind, she wondered if, over the years, any members of the official family had ventured out to mingle with those who came to voice their opinions. Perhaps, she thought, in Jefferson's time or Lincoln's or Jackson's such mingling was possible. Now . . . there was too much fear, too many threats. The people who lived in the White House were more and more isolated. The way she had been back in Minnesota? The idea struck her hard and she started as if someone had shoved her from behind.

Oddly, when she allowed her mind to roam in the fantasy of "what it would be like," she had far greater trepidation about official receptions such as the one she and Sam had attended the other night, than she did about venturing out to exchange a few words with protesters. It would be interesting, she thought, as first lady, to sort of appear on the other side of the fence, that is, the same side as the protesters, and to make real human contact. She had never been one to defy tradition, had never thought of herself as a particularly innovative person, but maybe she had been wrong. Lately she kept surprising herself.

Well, perhaps Eleanor Roosevelt had gone outside to chat with protesters. She'd have to look into that. And of course Jackson and his wife used to invite all the home folks right in.

Helga stuck her hand in the tiny pocket of her running pants and found a dime for the phone booth. If she had had a rough time sleeping Sam probably hadn't done much better. She dialed his number. She would invite him to breakfast, someplace fancy like the Mayflower. They would drink champagne (her treat), forgo the Smithsonian, and spend the rest of the day in bed with the Sunday paper. She could delay her flight to Minnesota by one day so they could have tomorrow night together as well.

After the twentieth ring she was about to hang up when he answered with a faint gravelly hello.

"Can I make amends?" she asked softly. "Can I take you to breakfast?"

"What time is it?" Sam moaned.

"Nearly eight thirty. I've been out running since dawn. I had a bad night but I'm glad I did. I'm glad you said what you did about John. I want you to bear with me on this. I . . . I'm going to change my flight—push it back a day—so we can have tomorrow night too." Helga paused expectantly but he did not reply.

"Sam?" Her pulse quickened and a look of alarm flickered in her blue eyes. "Sam . . . you didn't fall back asleep did you?"

After a moment he answered. "No."

"Well, what do you think?"

"I'm leaving for Texas tonight," he said curtly.

"Oh." Helga was stung by the brevity of his reply.

"There's a storm on the way. I suggest you move your flight forward rather than back."

"Aren't we going to the Smithsonian?" Helga clutched at the receiver.

"I've got to pack. And I've got to clear up a few details at my office and—"

"Fine," Helga cut in. "Have a merry Christmas."

"It's probably best we don't do any more talking now," he said. "You were right. We both need time, I guess."

"Yes, I guess we do." She hung on to the receiver, feeling sick, wondering why neither of them made any move to sever the connection.

"I'll phone you in Minnesota," he said finally.

"Okay." Helga's face was drained and set.

"Good-bye . . ."

The click of the phone on his end of the line was like a silver knife ripping through her heart. For several minutes she stared at the black box of the pay phone, reading the various instructions that appeared on a small card at the bottom. How to dial the operator, how to call information, how to file for lost coins.

He had paid her back all right, and it had been mean, unfair, and totally uncalled for. She ran the rest of the way home with her hands clenched into tight fists. He talked a good game all right, but that was all it was . . . talk! He liked to believe that he wanted an open, reciprocal relationship, but in reality, when things did not run smoothly, he couldn't handle it. For more than a month they had enjoyed an idyllic time of laughter, loving, and sharing. Not once had there been a cross word or a a misunderstanding. Now, just when they needed each other most, it was as if they were both wired with high explosives.

It didn't matter, it didn't matter. Thank God she hadn't counted on him. Thank God she hadn't quit her job or made some other rash move. Her life was still intact and her heart would mend. Soon! Her heart would heal so quickly that if he knew about it he would be devastated. She thought bitterly of the leather-bound volume of Jefferson's writings that she had bought him for Christmas. She had been so excited about the gift, so eager to see his childlike enthusiasm when he unwrapped it this evening. Perhaps she would do something nasty like mail it to his home in Texas with a cryptic note. Well, she was better off without him. No one had ever inspired her to behave in such a low, belittling manner. He really did bring out the worst in her. Before she met him she had been self-contained, even-tempered, and, some people might have said, bland. Well, she preferred bland to feeling like a stick of dynamite.

As she turned the corner onto Marilyn's tree-lined street, Betsy, Marilyn's four-year-old came careening toward her on a tricycle.

"You have company!" Betsy chirped happily as she pedaled at breakneck speed with her older brother in hot pursuit.

"Mr. McCalahan," Tommy said as he raced after his little sister. "And Mama wants you to stop in this afternoon and pick up your Christmas present!"

Helga ducked her chin down and trotted on as if she were ready for round one. She clenched her jaw in an effort to subdue her precarious emotional state, but when she saw him, standing with his hands shoved into the pockets of his old trench coat, wearing the battered western hat that always struck her as incongruous, all of the venom evaporated.

"I'm sorry." he looked utterly woebegone as he leaned against the fender of his Olds.

"Me too." Helga's heart raced as her eyes met his.

"We seem to be going through a period of adjustment." Sam pressed his lips into a resigned thin line.

"I guess that's what it is." Helga looked around the deserted street. She wanted to leap into his arms and to feel herself cradled against his manly chest, but instead she stood looking up at him with a shaky half smile.

"There's no storm sweeping in on the country." He wrinkled his nose as he confessed. "There's supposed to be a low-pressure system heading this way but not till Tuesday. I figure you'll be okay if you stay tomorrow night . . . that is, if you still want to."

"I want to." She took a step toward him and her eyes caressed him.

"And we can have our own Christmas celebration." He moved forward until he was standing so close that her breasts brushed against his coat.

"Okay." She swallowed back the knot of desire that rose in her throat. There was a heightened sense of awareness between them as they stood staring at each other, as if they had never seen each other before.

"A very small party." He smiled slightly in silent acknowledgment of the highly charged sexuality that quivered in the misty air. "The sort of intimate party you can't object to."

"Am I that difficult?" Helga's eyes were moist with longing.

Sam shook his head. "No more than I am. Anyway, I want us to have Christmas together, and the day on which we celebrate isn't so important. We'll share with a few friends and then . . . just the two of us?"

"It sounds nice." Helga detected the faint aroma of his spicy after-shave and her stomach did a crazy flop.

"Maybe you'll invite Neal and Marilyn." Sam reached for her middle finger and held it.

Helga nodded, unable to speak for wanting him. It seemed like an eternity since she had been in his arms. He caught her eye in a mischievous, knowing look. "Shall we go to my place and make up for last night's lack of sleep?"

"Or we could stay here," she suggested with a raised eyebrow.

"And confirm those terrible rumors." Sam pressed in closer.

"Why not?" Helga closed her eyes and raised her chin, waiting to be kissed.

"In broad daylight?" Sam brushed his lips to hers. "In a perfectly decent Georgetown family neighborhood?"

"Bring on the photographers!" Helga opened one eye and looked at him as their lips met.

* * *

Sam's intimate Christmas dinner party was marked by all of the rich, unbridled flair that was his trademark. An enormous Norwegian spruce traditionally hung with multicolored lights, candy canes, and strings of popcorn dominated the living room. Next to the tree, in lieu of presents or, as Sam laughingly pointed out, a gift for everyone—a quartet of university musicians who favored the guests with chamber music throughout the evening. It was a touch, Helga knew, meant expressly to please her.

In addition to Marilyn and Neal, Sam had invited two other couples, all close friends dating back to his university days in Texas. The extravagance of the cuisine, which was served by his housekeeper but mostly prepared by Sam himself, was another matter entirely. The first course, which was served with a fine dry champagne, was avocados in aspic flavored with tarragon and port. The group was far from decorous and there was much high-spirited teasing when Sam, in a flurry of culinary nerves, disappeared into the kitchen to return moments later with what he rightfully claimed was his specialty, roast duck in whiskey sauce. As Marilyn laughingly put it, the sauce alone was enough to make everyone pie-eyed. The duck was served with fluffy potatoes and crisp green beans, followed by an endive salad in a delicate vinaigrette dressing. As the dinner dishes were being cleared in preparation for dessert, Marilyn raised her wine goblet in a toast to the chef. "If you ever lose your seat in Congress, Sam, you can always work for me. What a fabulous meal! Where did you learn all this? At the Cordon Bleu?"

Sam moved easily around the table, pouring more of the delicious red Burgundy into the long-stemmed crystal goblets. "Do you want the truth?"

"Yeah . . ." Bill Smithers, a fellow Texan with something of Sam's burly rowdiness, spoke up. "We want the truth but we sure aren't likely to get it from you."

Helga laughed along with the others, noting that Sam rather enjoyed his reputation as a prevaricator of sorts.

"Honest injun." Sam adopted his homespun storytelling personality. "It's true. Therefore not much of a story . . . or maybe it is much of a story. Depends on how you look at it."

"Get on with it McCalahan!" Merv Goldman interjected laughingly.

"I learned to cook because of an old girl friend. I mean she wasn't too old"—Sam grinned at Helga—"at the time."

"Not me!" Helga was wearing a plain white cashmere sweater, and with it a gold locket that had been her grandmother's. "I certainly didn't teach him to cook."

"I'll back her on that," Marilyn piped up. "This one"—she nodded at Helga—"has made *not* cooking part of her life's work!"

"No, this goes back a ways to before I was a big-deal congressman." Sam sat back down at his place at the head of the table, which was set with heavy gray ceramic dishes. "I learned to cook because of a woman named Jane Labinski who was the first gal to point out to me that I was so hopelessly dependent that if I ever lost my can opener I'd starve to death. I got so sick and tired of her attacks that I decided to really outfox her. I wasn't going to be a meatloaf man and risk further derision. No, sir! I wanted to shame her, outcook her, make her grovel and bow down before my culinary prowess. When I started cookin' stuff like this, the fanciest I'd ever eaten was maybe a little bèarnaise sauce on a piece of steak. And I didn't speak French so I had to learn a little of that too, to really lay it on thick. I cooked Jane Labinski a meal she will remember till her dying day. It was a meal that Nero himself would have died for and . . . I say that in all modesty."

"I'm sure you do." Helga gave him a sly look and everyone laughed.

Later, as everyone was leaving, Marilyn pulled Helga into Sam's bedroom and fixed her with an authoritative expression. "If I didn't love Neal, or if I could arrange some amicable bigamy, I'd give you a run for your money. It's not just the way he cooks. Helga, you've got to marry this man!"

Helga covered her mouth as she laughed. "You and your advice. We're not at that point yet."

"I think you should go with him to Texas. Can't you change your plans? He wants you to go . . . go!" Marilyn scanned Sam's bedroom as she talked. "He hired a quartet for you, for heaven sake! I think I'm in love with him. I really do. I just ate that duck and whiskey sauce and fell madly in love with him."

"Oh, Marilyn!" Helga hugged her dark-haired friend impulsively.

"I'll tell you what I notice." Marilyn's eyes danced. "I notice that since he's been going with you he's even yummier. He's always had that swaggering charisma, but there's an expression on his face when he looks at you that makes me want to cry."

Helga felt the tears spring to her eyes. The past few days had been so tense and now this evening, their special Christmas evening, was a rich, wonderful dream. If anyone had asked her to plan the perfect evening for herself, she would not have planned it as flawlessly as he. It was a balance, that balance he seemed to achieve so effortlessly, of elegance and informality, of culture and backslapping, raucous laughter.

"This is a lecture!" Marilyn tugged at her arm. "Don't you dare go back to Minnesota and turn all morose and start brooding over all the reasons why you shouldn't come back. I swear, if you're not here by January second, I will fly out and bring you back myself."

After everyone had left and they had finished the last of the cleanup, they sat on the floor beneath the colorfully ornamented tree sipping brandy and listening to Christmas music on the radio.

"I love your friends."

"And they reciprocate." Sam picked up the leather-bound volume she had given him and caressed it. "This is my first leather book. I don't think they have them in Texas, at least not in my neck of the woods. I never saw a leather-bound book till I came north, and I remember wonderin' who the heck buys those. I figured just the English—you know, cause they were always talking about leather-bound books in English novels. But this . . . this is . . ." He turned the book over in his hands gingerly as if it were spun glass.

"It's the nicest present I ever had." He smiled softly.

"And this was the best Christmas I've ever had." Helga moved closer and leaned up against him as the strains of "Silent Night" filled the room. Never had the meaning of Christmas been more clear to her. She reached for his hand and moved it to her mouth, kissing his knuckles, closing her eyes to savor the richness of the moment.

"I have a present for you." Sam whispered when the strains of the lovely old carol faded.

"A duck in whiskey sauce to take back to Minnesota?" Helga teased.

"An inducement," he said softly.

"I don't need any inducements." Helga climbed to her knees and put her arms around his neck. "I'm not going to waiver anymore. I think I've purged all of that wishy-washiness out of me."

"Just in case." Sam's mouth was warm and dry as he leaned in to kiss her.

"Now . . . close your eyes."

Helga obeyed. Her body was quivering from the kiss. Already she was wondering how she would endure the next ten days without him. He placed his hands on her shoulders and propelled her across the room, cautioning her to keep her eyes closed. When she was seated, he lifted her hands and placed them side by side. He lowered them slowly until they rested on the piano keys.

"You didn't!" Helga's eyes flew open and she turned to stare at him.

"You've never played for me." Sam gazed down at her. "You must miss your piano terribly. I know you occasionally play Marilyn's, but let's face it, you're here more than you're there and—"

"But a piano!" Helga gasped.

"Your Washington piano. Now you'll have to come back"— Sam knelt down beside her—"if only to play me some Chopin." He moved over to the radio and switched it off.

"I can't believe this." Helga turned to him with adoring eyes, then, too overcome to articulate how deeply his gift had moved her, she placed her pale hands on the keys and began a haunting Chopin nocturne. Although it had been months since she had practiced the piece, she played it perfectly, as if the rarity of the moment had infused her with a superhuman memory and sensitivity. She had never played with so much feeling, never felt so clearly the fine spiritual connection between the sound of the notes and the sensation of her fingers moving smoothly over the keys. Her face relaxed into a beatific expression of intense absorption as she approached the concluding bars of the music, a difficult crescendo that demanded intricate rapid fingering.

When she finished she bowed her head and stared at her hands. She had never executed that last phrase with such passionate abandon. Her playing had always been admirable; she was an accomplished musician insofar as technique was concerned, but she had known she lacked something. Now, after months of scarcely touching a keyboard, she experienced the joy of giving herself over to the music. And she had been playing for him.

When she turned around he was staring at her with a rapt expression. They smiled at each other, shyly almost, as if they were again meeting for the first time; then they stood up, as if by mutual agreement, and still in silence, with their arms wrapped around each other's waist, moved through the living room switching off the lights.

Sam's dark bedroom seemed to reverberate with a holy silence, the silence of Christmas after the bells have ceased and the snow has begun to fall outside. Helga raised her arms as he skimmed the white cashmere over her head. She could imagine the snow falling, although she knew that with temperatures in the fifties that was impossible. Yet the feeling was there and the magic too.

Her hands moved to his belt buckle, and he drew in a deep breath as she slid her hands inside his trousers, tugging gently at his shorts and falling to her knees as she removed both garments at one time. His fingers sifted through the golden strands of her hair as she nudged him toward the edge of the bed. Once he was sitting down she removed his shoes and socks. Then, as if her fingers were memorizing every detail, she stroked the top of his feet, pausing to experience the hard, round anklebone, the tapered ankle, the rocklike calf with the deep indentation, and the large bony knee. Still kneeling, she ran her hands lightly over his thighs; then pressing them apart, she placed her head into the damp, musky warmth, kissing the sensitive skin as the power began to throb around her and his hands grew more forceful as he ran them through her hair.

While her mouth was still nuzzling against him, he reached across her back and unfastened her lacy white bra. She shrugged it off and pressed her full breasts in against his hair-roughened legs. His hands were on her back now, urging her and pressing her in more tightly. Suddenly a cataclysmic tremor shook him and she felt him tearing off his shirt, and the next moment he had lifted her up on the bed next to him, impatient to feel her smooth, warm flesh against his eager, ardent body. His hands were voracious as they freed her of the black velvet skirt and stripped away her pantyhose. Helga was filled with wild, tumultuous currents as she wound her legs around him and finally felt the blessedness of his weight fall upon her. They moved against each other, still in silence, trembling and straining toward each other with a subtle desperation.

"I don't like saying good-bye," Sam groaned as his tongue swirled around one stiff rosy nipple.

"It seems absurd." Helga sighed. "I know I've made the right decision, but at this moment leaving you seems like the most idiotic thing I've ever done."

"Well"—Sam was panting—"I'm glad you feel that way." He teased and taunted her breast until she groaned and closed her eyes against the waves of tingling sensations. She ran her hands through his hair and caressed his damp forehead.

His eyes were closed and she touched the fragile lids lightly, storing that delicate sensation deep within. His hand moved tenderly down the side of her naked body, then up again to her breast. He, too, was memorizing; he, too, was storing up images to gird him during the separation.

How could they part? How could they possibly part even for a day, even for an hour? Helga felt her desire whipped and bubbling beyond endurance. She clasped his firm behind and arched up to him with a burning sense of urgency, feeling herself ripe to the point of bursting. He responded with a thrust that made her cry out in ecstasy, and as he moved above her she felt his need and his hunger in every impact of their bodies. He slowed then and indulged in deep, languid strokes that set her spinning off and made her feel light-headed. The ceiling above his bed was whirling, so she closed her eyes and opened herself farther to his power.

"I could go on forever," he groaned, and Helga turned her head on the pillow, smiling because she knew it was true. Each time they seemed on the point of exploding they would pull back, again as if by mutual consent, and each postponement drove them higher, into new and vast uncharted territory. She was surrendering to him more competely than she had ever surrendered before, and with his heaving, trembling body moving against her she felt a lasting, insatiable hunger. He cupped her buttocks and directed her in a slow, erotic circular pattern, first

218

one way and then the other. He was finding new spaces, new mysteries to explore in that unfathomable darkness.

His hands were intent on eliciting the last shred of pleasure from her as he propelled her into a shuddering, mindless bliss that only seemed to nourish and to feed her so that each convulsive climax drove her to demand more from him.

"Helga!" He roared her name from the depths of his passion, clasping her closer and closer still.

Just at the peak of their ecstasy he rolled off her drenched, trembling body, panting and repeating her name in a hoarse voice. "You're killing me . . ." He lavished the accusation on her breast with his moist mouth; then turning her sideways toward him, he showered kisses from nipple to nipple.

"I love you so . . . You are so . . . so beautiful!" His hands moved down her slim torso, and with his eyes fastened on hers he began to caress her with his muscular hands. His loving fingers, plunging so delicately into the darkness, ignited her again until the flames licked and leaped with joyous agony and she cried out, her body quivering with pleasure.

Helga felt herself overflowing yet still they continued gorging themselves. Sometimes they pulled away smiling, saturated with the delicious nectar in which they seemed to swim. Each new bout stirred old embers, and time and again they reached out to each other. Just as she was about to drift off to sleep, Helga felt his warm hand inching down the soft skin of her stomach.

"You'll have to carry me onto the plane," she sighed as she opened herself and gave in to the exquisite fiery tremors.

"It's only five." Sam teased her with a feather-light touch until she craved more.

"I'll fly back in time for New Year's Eve," she murmured, "if you will."

"I thought you'd never ask." Sam smiled gently as her body shook with desire.

"I love making love to you." Some time later Sam collapsed onto the pillow and framed her face in his hands.

Helga gave him a lazy smile. "I should be tired."

"But you're not." He wrinkled his brow as if he were scolding her. "You should be asleep."

"I'll catch up when I get back to Minnesota." She wriggled her naked body against him and they both laughed at the speed with which she ignited him. "I'll sleep later," she murmured. "I'll come back to you . . . all rested. I promise."

CHAPTER TWELVE

"So how's business in Washington?" Helga's older brother Olie had driven the sixty-three miles to meet her at the airport. As might have been expected, there was over a foot of snow on the ground and more was expected beginning Christmas Eve, which was tomorrow night. The temperature, even at four in the afternoon, was already hovering around zero, and Helga had to remind herself that that was nothing.

"Well, the case is going as well as could be expected." Helga looked out the window at the flat snow-covered fields.

"Something about the railroads, right?" Olie, at forty-five, had very little interest outside the confines of the farm where he and his wife and three children resided and which he would one day inherit from his father.

"That's right." Helga smiled at the large, bony man. Olie was her favorite brother, really. Although he was the oldest Bergson, the one she ostensibly should have the least in common with, she had always been partial to him.

"Folks are anxious to see you." Olie drove cautiously with both of his large-knuckled red hands on the steering wheel. Probably he hadn't been this far away from Norge, the village closest to the Bergson farm, since he had driven Helga to the airport last fall.

"Bob'll be down from Duluth with his family, but just for Christmas day, and Steve and his brood may arrive late tomorrow night unless the snow turns into a problem. Should be a full house."

Olie took his eyes off the road briefly and gave Helga a look that passed for a smile. They drove for several miles in silence, the heavy, cold silence that Helga remembered so well. Sometimes the entire family would be sitting around the living room after a wonderful Christmas dinner and nobody would say a word. There would be the racket of children coming from the other room—the Bergson children laughed and talked like any other children—but somehow once they officially entered the adult world they fell silent. Helga remembered one Christmas when her father's brother's family had driven all the way from North Dakota, and after they'd arrived and exchanged a few proper kisses and notes about how the traffic and weather had been, they had all fallen silent.

"So how's business in Washington?" Olie repeated the question, having forgotten he'd already asked her once.

"I'm enjoying it." Helga glanced at him to see his reaction. He nodded impassively.

"Pa bought a great new Hereford bull out at a sale in Nebraska. Paid a lot for him but I think he's what we need to strengthen the line we got going."

"Good." Helga gave her brother an amused smile, and they drove in silence for another several miles before he began to give her a rundown of his children's activities during her absence.

"They'll be glad to have you back." He cast her a shy glance, which was as close as he would probably ever come to saying he had missed her. "Karen's been circling the dates on her calendar waiting for Aunt Helga to come home."

"Well . . ." Helga felt more hesitant than she would have liked. "I don't know how long I'll be here. No longer than till just before the first."

"You can't leave before New Year's." Olie was adamant, as if the Bergsons always ushered in the New Year with some great flourish.

"Well, I have to get back," Helga told him. She was oddly reluctant to mention Sam, even to hint at the seriousness of her feelings. Suddenly she felt a panic, as if the past were about to devour her. She could almost feel the cold pine floor of her bedroom under her bare feet, feel the icy smooth sheets as she slid into bed at . . . Yes, she really had gone to bed every night at eight thirty. As she drove along next to her taciturn older brother, she recalled the effort of trying not to feel lonely on those long walks through the woods, the monotony of the daily commute into Minneapolis, the desolation of the past ten years of her life.

Later that night she sat around the large oak kitchen table sipping thick coffee with her parents and Olie and his wife, Donna. The children had been ecstatic to see her and that had warmed her immensely. Especially Tommy, the youngest, who had thrown his arms around her neck and hugged her for dear life. She had been certain he would have forgotten the hours spent reading to him, the Saturday afternoons when she had introduced him to her favorite records and given him a few preliminaries at the piano.

Nobody asked her very much about her work or about how she liked Washington. The conversation at dinner was pretty much as she remembered it. There was talk of neighbors, and about all of the family who would be arriving during the next day. As Helga stared into her empty coffee cup, she had the eerie sensation that she was being absorbed back into that old routine.

"Oh"—Mrs. Bergson turned to her daughter with a raised forefinger—"John's mother called earlier today."

Helga felt the apprehension rise in her throat. She hadn't seen John's parents since they had moved to Florida six years ago.

"They want to see you. Myra suggested you might drive into Minneapolis to have lunch with them. I said I didn't see why not since your office is there."

"Thanks, Mama," Helga stood up and began clearing the rest

of the dishes. A sense of foreboding swept over her at the thought of having lunch with John's parents, discussing the past.

Later that evening, at nine o'clock to be precise, when the rest of the family had retired and the only light burning in the house was the small night-light in Helga's third-floor room, she bundled up in her old blue parka and tramped around in the snow. There was no moon, but even so the glow from the snow illuminated the white frame house and the two large white barns. The temperature had dipped as it always did at night, and whenever she took a deep breath the frigid air made her nose tingle.

She walked a ways from the house and leaned up against the fence that Olie and her father had worked so hard to build. They were so proud of that fence, so proud that it enclosed all the land that fronted on the main road. Her mother had cooked her favorite meatloaf and Donna had made loaves of rye bread in addition to the traditional Yule bread. They were glad to see her. She knew that. Only they didn't see her, and for the first time in her life she was acutely aware of it.

Several times she had tried to tell them about her life in Washington—about how she felt when seeing all of the famous monuments, about actually going to the White House for a buffet supper. In a way she admired them for being nonplussed. The one thing you could say about the Bergsons was they would never gush or be impressed by superficial accomplishments. But a little enthusiasm would not have been remiss.

Helga squeezed her eyes shut. No, she was not going to be bitter. They were her family. She loved them and they her. Only she was beginning to see that she had acquired a different way of expressing love. She preferred something more tangible and . . . yes, more unwieldly and rambunctious. She could feel Sam's big arms clutching her close in one of his robust bear hugs. There was a tenderness in his roughness, an animallike sensuosity to the way he dealt with not only her, but everyone. He would want to sweep up her mother in his arms and kiss her. Helga couldn't even begin to imagine how her mother would react. And Olie?

Sam would backslap and shove at big Olie as if they were friendly sparring partners. He would be a bit more circumspect with her father, but his handshake alone would be enough to set the old man's teeth on edge.

Suddenly the idea of Sam meeting her family amused her. Of course he would win them over. Helga stuck her mittened hands into the pockets of her parka and cut down through the north pasture toward the pine grove. This time last night she had been in the midst of a congenial group, drinking wine and listening to Mozart. Certainly not a racy evening, she thought, smiling to herself. But a vital evening, with stimulating conversation and so much laughter. And later . . . her body flushed at the recollection of the long night of lovemaking. She had been away from Washington less than twenty-four hours and already she could think of little else but getting back. Getting back to Sam, to Marilyn and her effervescent nosy good nature, to Neal and the children, the stone cottage, yes, and even the nutty hectic social whirl, the backslapping and political intrigue.

And her new piano! She broke into a trot, entered the house with a broad smile, and stomped her boots on the wide mat next to the back door. She cocked her head to the side, straining hard, praying to hear the phone ring. Sam would be in Texas by now. He had described his homecoming as a disorganized cyclone where brothers and sisters, nieces and nephews, all stopped by unannounced after phoning his mother all day to say they wouldn't be able to come by. Then, after consuming cases of beer in celebration of their most famous son's homecoming, someone would send out for a dozen pepperoni pizzas. There would be much laughter and everyone, even the children, would be gabbing away until after midnight.

Helga crept upstairs to her bedroom in her stockinged feet. Somehow thinking of Sam's family, the way he had painted his homecoming, made the silence of the Bergson house all the more dear to her. She no longer wanted so much silence, but she did treasure it and she did very much love them for all of their unspoken words.

The next day passed in a blur of last minute Christmas preparations. She had been positive he would phone her on Christmas Eve, and when he didn't she found a tight smile forming on her lips and a kernel of doubt forming inside. By ten Christmas morning the entire Bergson family was gathered under one roof, and by nine that night the house was once again silent and immaculate. Helga sat under the six-foot tree organizing the boxes after everyone else had gone to bed. How thoughtless of him not to have phoned.

She stood up abruptly, went into the kitchen, and poured herself a small glass of her father's whiskey. She was wearing her old red flannel robe and a pair of gray fake-fur slippers. Tomorrow was Friday and she was going to drive into Minneapolis to see Willard and Kenyon before having lunch with John's parents. She wanted to make a final decision quickly, before she lost her momentum. But the ordeal would be so much easier if he would only call. It was Christmas. Surely he would call her on Christmas!

She sipped the whiskey impatiently. It was ten o'clock and sleep was the farthest thing from her mind. Even though she had spent the afternoon frolicking in the snow with her nieces and nephews, she was not in the least exhausted. But she was beginning to get irritable, or perhaps, she thought, frustrated was a more accurate description of her feelings. Each thought of Sam brought a wave of desire rushing through her body. Maybe the telephone wires were all jammed up. Maybe he'd tried and couldn't get through.

She stood up and poured herself an inch more of the whiskey. Why hadn't she thought to bring more books home with her? At least she could spend all night reading law books. Maybe tomorrow she'd stop by the university library and load up. Or maybe she would fly back to Washington sooner.

She watched the large minute hand of her mother's yellow and red kitchen clock travel from twelve till six, her face set in its usual serene expression. Suddenly she frowned, slammed her glass down on the table, and marched over to the phone, which was located in a small cubbyhole off the kitchen.

"McCalahan," she told the long-distance information operator, then frowned harder because she had no idea what Sam's father's first name was and there were five McCalahans listed.

She folded her arms resolutely, crossed her legs, and pondered the list of first names the operator had mentioned. Finally she tried a Michael, but nobody answered and she nearly slammed down the receiver in irritation. One more attempt netted her the same result, but now her determination soared. She would reach him if she had to call every McCalahan in Galveston.

On the third try a woman with a thick, sugary Texas accent answered, and Helga held her breath when the woman said she would call Sam to the phone.

"Merry Christmas!" Sam's voice rang over the wires, bringing a flush of color to her cheeks. "Who is this?" he asked when she did not identify herself immediately.

"Your snow queen," Helga replied, trying not to let any uncertainty creep into her voice.

"I love you." Sam lowered his voice to a deep growl. "What took you so long to call?"

Helga's mouth flew open, but before she could speak he went on in a jubilant voice. "I'm mighty glad to see you took the bull by the horns. I was beginning to wonder. Figured I might have to break down and make the call myself."

"You've been waiting for . . . !" Helga's face flooded with relief, and she sank onto the rickety wood chair next to the phone laughing. "You reprobate, you conniving scoundrel. You were outwaiting me!"

"I wanted to make sure"—Sam lowered his voice again—"that you were *really* missing me."

"I'm missing you all right." Helga felt a warm current swoosh through her body down to her toes.

227

"Not as much as I'm missing you," Sam teased, and then they were both laughing.

Helga wiped the tears out of her eyes. Just the sound of his voice made her feel giddy, made her feel like laughing and jumping around like one of her nieces.

"How many McCalahans did you wake up before you reached me?" he asked with a chuckle.

"How did you know?" Helga's eyes were bright.

"Well, you didn't bother to take my phone number. How do you think that makes a guy feel?"

"I never thought of it." Helga let out a loud laugh, which rang sharply through the quiet house.

"I took yours," Sam said smugly.

"You think of everything." Helga's heart quickened and a seductive tone crept into her voice.

"And I've thought of a few new things," Sam replied suggestively. "You can think about what they are when you slide under those frigid Minnesota sheets."

"I will." Helga laughed.

When she hung up she sat with her hands folded in her lap. The sound of their laughter was ringing in her ears. He had taught her to laugh like that and the laughter had healed her.

She walked slowly through the dark house, but there was a broad smile on her face. There was no question now. She was going to return to Washington . . . even if it meant giving up her job, even if it meant giving up every shred of what she had come to think of as security. It was something that had to be done and she was primed and ready to do it.

The next morning Helga bolted upright in her bed with a wild, frightened expression on her face. Another six inches of snow had fallen during the night, and outside her bedroom window she could see Olie shoveling a path to the barn. Well, it would take more than six inches to close down the roads in this part of the country, and snow or no snow she was driving into the city to talk to Willard and Kenyon today. She knew they would both be in the office because Kenyon had subtly disclosed that nugget of information should Helga feel the impulse to come in to work, as she usually did, even though it was technically still a Christmas holiday for most businesses.

She admonished herself for her queasy nervous feeling and noted wryly that she was dressing in her best new blue dress, as if she were applying for a job rather than giving notice. The phrase "giving notice" stopped her cold, and she looked around the small sparsely furnished room that had been her haven for the past ten years and before that had been her childhood refuge. Going off to Washington in the fall had been one thing. The step she was about to take was an enormous change. In the fall she had merely gone off for a short while. Now she was breaking ties, from this point on she would be a visitor in this room.

Downstairs her mother was already beginning preparations for the noon meal which, except on certain rare occasions, was the main meal. Mrs. Bergson turned away from the stove to cast an approving smile at her daughter.

"You sure you want to drive into the city today?" She poured Helga a cup of coffee and handed it to her.

"I've got to." Helga felt a twinge of guilt. Whatever was unspoken between her and her mother, Helga was her only daughter. Helga reflected for a moment on her mother's quiet strength. Perhaps in some inconspicuous way her mother had, more than she suspected, contributed to the determinism she now felt.

"Mama . . ." Helga stared at Mrs. Bergson's frail back. "Mama, I'm thinking of moving to Washington . . . permanently."

Helga waited for a response, and when there was none she continued. "I like it there and I've been studying to get into law school."

"It's not too late for that?" Mrs. Bergson's face was drawn and worried as she sat down at the table across from her daughter.

229

"You're thirty-three, Helga. Are you sure that makes good sense?"

"I'm not absolutely sure." Helga met her mother's eyes evenly. "But it's what I want. It's what I always wanted . . . even when John was alive."

"You never said much about it." Mrs. Bergson pressed her lips together.

"After John died it seemed impossible. Just lately I've started thinking about it again."

"You could go to the university here." Her mother looked at her sharply. "What about your job?"

"I've saved money, thanks to you and Papa. I don't want to sound immodest, Mama, but . . . I think I'll do well in my classes. I have the kind of mind that stores away all of those details which are essential in the law."

"Your father was looking forward to having you back here." Mrs. Bergson wiped her hands on her apron. It was a gesture, like Helga's habitual glances at her watch, which covered a multitude of feelings. What she meant, and Helga knew it, was *she* had been looking forward to Helga's return.

"You never know." Helga feigned a brightness she did not feel. "I might come back after I get my degree. Who knows maybe someday I'll be a partner at Matthews, Matthews, and Stubbs."

The drive into Minneapolis was interminable and not because of the snowy roads. She had known her mother would not say anything to stop her, but that stoic acceptance was worse than any confrontation. Of course she knew that thirty-three wasn't old. Women all over were beginning new lives not only in their thirties but in their forties and fifties. Still, she felt her mother's apprehension for her and it only increased her nervousness. She tried to imagine Sam sitting in the seat beside her, joking about her future life as a full-time student. Nothing seemed to help and nothing, she knew, would help, until she had closed the door and severed her tie with Matthews, Matthews, and Stubbs.

No, she did not want to return to Minneapolis after she got her degree. Her mother had seen right through that line. What she wanted was *everything*—Sam, her own law practice, and maybe . . . yes, even children. Her heart accelerated as if she were jogging instead of bumping along in her old Volkswagen. But maybe a life with Sam would exclude everything else . . . everything, that is, except the children. Could a senator or, heaven forbid, a president have a wife who had a full-time law practice?

Helga swung the VW into the parking lot next to the sleek modern building where the law offices were located. This was no time to look for loopholes in her decision. She paid the parking attendant and entered the lobby just as she had done for so many years. The elevator that took her to the ninth floor was filled with familiar faces. Several people greeted her and inquired as to her whereabouts over the past few months. Well, she had been something of a fixture in the building.

An eerie sensation swept over her as she stepped inside the plush wall-to-wall-carpeted law offices and greeted Margaret Phillips, the sixty-two-year-old receptionist who had worked for Willard since he was a young man.

"Washington life agrees with you." Margaret smiled.

"I didn't think I'd see you here today." Helga shook hands with the older woman and kissed her lightly on the cheek.

Margaret rolled her eyes coyly. "Mr. Matthews has some visitors here from Washington. I couldn't very well let him answer his own phone, could I? Besides, I had two days off before Christmas, and if you want to know the truth staying home bores me. Well, we're alike in that respect. I could ask you what you're doing here."

Helga laughed as she removed her coat. Margaret was a wonder—as cheerful and talkative as Helga was reserved. They had made a good combination and, she thought with a stab, she would miss Margaret.

"How long do you think the meeting will last?" Helga walked toward the closed conference room door.

"Well"—Margaret consulted her desk calendar—"I know Mr. Brown, the gentleman from Washington, has a luncheon engagement, so I shouldn't imagine they'll be too much longer."

Helga blanched. What on earth was Tate Brown doing in Minneapolis on the day after Christmas? Didn't he ever stop? She picked up a copy of *Time* magazine and leafed through it in a vain effort to find something that would distract her. It was an unfortunate coincidence and that was all. Tate Brown had nothing whatsoever to do with her.

After twenty minutes the conference room door opened and Tate, together with several unfamiliar men, emerged followed by Willard and Kenyon. Willard seemed surprised to find Helga seated in the reception area instead of ensconced behind her desk.

After brief introductions and some meaningless chatter about the weather Helga found herself seated on the leather couch in Willard Matthews's office with Kenyon hovering impatiently near the door.

"You look fabulous." Willard nodded approvingly. "New dress from Santa?"

"New dress from Woodward and Lothrop." Helga smiled, referring to the famous Washington department store.

"There's no easy way to begin." Helga took a deep breath and jumped in. "This has been my home for so many years. I'm not even sure I'm doing the right thing, but it's something I have to do."

"What the hell are you talking about?" Kenyon was suddenly interested. He sat down on the leather sofa next to her and gaped.

"I've decided to go to law school." Helga looked from one shocked face to the other. "I've arranged to take two pre-law courses next semester, and thanks to a friend, I have permission to audit some lectures at the law school. I'll take the LSATs in June and full steam ahead."

Willard shook his head. "Well, for heaven's sake."

A tight smile formed on Helga's lips. That her decision came as such a total shock was absolute proof that they had placed her in a niche. A spark of resentment flickered as she met Kenyon Stubbs's puzzled expression. Considering her devotion, the amount of legal research she had contributed above and beyond the call of duty, not to mention her obvious aptitude for legal detail, wasn't it odd that they themselves hadn't suggested such a move? Suddenly all of those instances when her quick thinking had rescued them came to mind. They had taken all of that for granted and she . . . she had never asked for more.

"Have you thought about this clearly?" Willard frowned across his desk.

"I've been auditing courses in Washington," Helga told him.

"I had no idea you were even interested . . ." Willard stared at her as if he were seeing her for the first time.

"Helga"—Kenyon smiled broadly to cover his uneasiness— "this is all because of your having to leave Washington so soon, isn't it?"

"Not completely," Helga told him. "Although I would have continued working on the case and cut back on my studies until it was finished."

"But we need you here!" Willard stood up suddenly. "It's been a long time since you've had a decent raise. I'm remiss in that. Maybe we can work something out."

"That's nice of you, Willard." Helga smiled graciously. "But I didn't come here to angle for a raise. Like I said, I'd be happy to continue working for you in Washington—"

"That's out of the question." Kenyon intervened with a touch of hostility.

"Kenyon is going to be taking over the Northern case full-time," Willard offered after a moment.

Helga lowered her eyes and nodded. So that was it. Kenyon wanted to be in Washington so she was being sent home. Maybe her original suspicions were right. Maybe he was trying to build a power base in Washington for his own political aggrandizement. Maybe that was why he seemed to be courting Tate Brown. In any case she now saw the situation clearly. She had no clout with Matthews, Matthews, and Stubbs. She was, and always would be, a functionary who could be moved hither and yon as required by circumstances. She had been treated fairly. Only she was tired of that role. It really was time to move on.

"Why not work on your degree here?" Willard inquired after a moment. "That way you could keep on working."

Helga smiled. She could just imagine what that would entail. Being a perfectionist by nature, she would continue putting in long hours at the office in addition to trying to excel at school.

Kenyon eyed her with a supercilious smile. "Does this have something to do with the congressman from Texas?"

His question rankled her, but she merely shook her head. "Nothing at all."

"It just seems to me this is pretty sudden." Willard shook his head sourly. "After such a long time I think we're entitled to a bit more consideration, wouldn't you say so, Kenyon?"

"It's very short notice, Helga." Kenyon narrowed his blue eyes and stared at her.

"I'm perfectly willing," Helga said after a moment's consideration, "to stay until I've trained a replacement. I would think two weeks would be enough time. I know it's sudden . . . but so was your decision"—she looked evenly from Kenyon to Willard —"to have me leave Washington. Initially you'd said I'd be there till March at least. I'd based my life around that. I'd already . . . made plans. As I said, I'm still willing to carry the full load of the Northern Railway—"

"But we've said," Willard interrupted with an edge in his voice, "that we don't need you there. We need you here. It could take months to find a replacement."

Helga drew in a steadying breath. Even in better times than these it would not take months to replace her. But with the unemployment rate as high as it was they would have no difficulty whatsoever. They were making it as hard as possible for her; they had not evidenced a shred of enthusiasm for what this move might mean to her.

"I'll be happy to stay until mid-January." She made the offer coldly. "I'll do everything I can to make it a smooth transition."

"Well then." Willard shrugged as if her offer were utterly meaningless.

"You might have at least mentioned something about this." Kenyon smacked his lips irritably.

"I suppose you're right," Helga replied in a dignified voice despite the overwhelming urge she felt to remind them again that they had never shown her the same courtesy.

"Look, I'm not really leaving you in the lurch," she said pointedly. "I'm sorry you feel I am, but I've said I'll do all—"

"Never mind, never mind." Willard silenced her with a wave of his hand, and a slow, well-rehearsed benign smile replaced his annoyed expression. "We'll survive." He nodded as he crossed to the door of his office. "You'll want to clean out your desk."

"I'm meeting someone for lunch." Helga stood up, feeling drained. "Could I stop by after lunch? I haven't left much . . ."

"Whatever you like." Willard smiled. He was once again his good-humored grandfatherly self.

"Good luck." Kenyon stood up and extended his hand begrudgingly.

"Thank you." Helga felt immensely sad as she shook his hand.

"Don't lose touch." Willard shook her hand and saw her to the front door.

"I'll try not to." Helga felt a quiver of emotion as the door finally closed behind her. Perhaps she was wrong, but she doubted that either Willard or Kenyon would make any effort to "keep in touch." They would expect her to make any overtures. Well, she hoped she was wrong on that count.

As she stepped out of the elevator in the downstairs lobby,

Tate Brown intercepted her with a casual grin as if he had just "happened" to be passing through.

"Coffee?" He grinned amicably.

"I'm meeting someone for lunch." Helga put on her most cordial face.

"I'll walk with you." Tate fell into stride as they walked out into the cold, gloomy day. "What's new? Having a good vacation?"

"I just quit my job." Helga decided to go for broke.

"You what?" Tate stopped walking.

"Yes." Helga could not suppress a wry smile. "I'm going to be a lawyer like everyone else."

"Oh." Tate seemed relieved that was all. "Well, the University of Minnesota has a fine law school."

"Tate"—Helga stopped walking and faced him—"I'm going back to Washington. You may as well be among the first to know. I'm not going back *just* because of Sam McCalahan, but that is certainly a strong consideration."

Tate nodded tightly. "Well, good luck," he said after a moment. "Sam's a hell of a man."

They walked a few steps to the next intersection near where Helga was meeting her in-laws at a small French restaurant.

"I hope you know what you're doing," Tate said, looking worried. "I mean with Sam. A lot of women have changed their lives for him and—"

"I'm not changing my life for him," Helga broke in gently. "I'm doing it for myself. Even without Sam, it's what I want."

"Well so long as you know that," Tate replied ambiguously. "I know you two have been seeing a lot of each other but . . . I wouldn't count on anything."

Helga stiffened at his innuendo. She was fairly sure he was playing a game and she wondered how far he would go, wondered if he would actually lie in order to shake her confidence.

"I am counting on things." Her eyes were moist with emotion.

236

"You're that sure of yourself?" Tate gave her a hard, scrutinizing look.

Helga waivered. "Not of myself entirely . . . but I'm sure of Sam." She extended her hand to Tate. "I want us to be friends, Tate. I think it's important."

"Of course we're friends." Tate gave a hollow laugh. "See you back in Washington . . . no doubt."

By the time Helga arrived back at the farm it was after dark and she was numb with emotional fatigue. First the ordeal of confronting Willard and Kenyon, then the bizarre encounter with Tate followed by a grueling lunch with her in-laws, which, as she had anticipated, consisted of story after story about John, and then a final trip back to the office to clear out her desk. The only thing she could think of was a scalding bath and nine hours of uninterrupted sleep to restore her waning spirits, but when she entered the back door Olie was sitting at the kitchen table waiting for her. Although his face was impassive, something in the way his large head jutted forward suggested that their mother had mentioned Helga's decision.

"You think it's a bad idea?" Helga hung up her coat and sat down across from him to unzip her boots.

Olie studied her with his pale blue eyes, which were identical to Helga's. When her brother did not reply, Helga shrugged and moved to the large wood-burning stove and put on the kettle for some tea. She found Olie's taciturnity exasperating, especially after her long, arduous day. She knew from experience that the longer he remained silent, the more he had to say. It was the same with her, or had been until Sam had teased and goaded her into articulating her feelings instead of sitting on them as if they would either hatch into something else or go away. Her Scandanavian silence, he called it. Now she understood how infuriating it could be.

She poured some hot water into a chipped pale yellow mug and sat across from Olie dunking the tea bag.

"Don't you think you oughta have talked to your family about this?" Olie did not look up.

"Honestly, Olie, I wasn't sure myself until last night. I've been thinking about it so much, about how I always wanted to go to law school . . . and much to my surprise I like Washington. I want to get involved in some kind of legal work that will benefit people."

"You could do that here," Olie said flatly. "There's people who need help everywhere."

"But I want to live in Washington," Helga said gently. The only other member of her family to have moved out of the state was her brother Ellis, and he had spent one year in North Dakota with her father's brother before moving back.

"I love it here." Helga spoke in a soft, urgent voice. "I'll always come back to the farm."

"Ma and Pa are getting on in years . . ."

"Don't make me feel guilty." Helga stiffened.

"It's the truth. Has nothing to do with guilt." Olie met her eyes finally. "Be honest."

"I am honest," Helga replied.

"It's because of a man," Olie said. "You're going back because of a man."

"I'm not." Helga denied it emphatically.

"Sam McCalahan." Olie's blue eyes deepened in their intensity.

"How did you know about Sam?" Helga asked quickly.

"Your boss asked me to talk some sense into you."

"What?" Helga was completely taken off guard. "What are you talking about, Olie? Who? Willard? Kenyon? How could they do a thing like that?"

"Because they care." Olie folded his large hands. He was doing his duty, as painful as it was for him to carry on a lengthy conversation on such a personal level. He was being a good brother.

"Kenyon Stubbs called. He thinks you've gone overboard for

a man. I never heard of him, but Mr. Stubbs says he's important and likely to be more so."

"And Kenyon asked you to interfere . . ." Helga bounded out of her chair. She looked around the familiar kitchen with her eyes flashing.

"It's not like you to act like this," Olie went on. "You're not a rash person. You love living out here like this. Before you went off this fall you were dreading going away. Remember how you kept hoping they'd change their minds and send somebody else? You're not cut out for that life, Helga. Do you really want to go back there and live on your own? According to Mr. Stubbs, this McCalahan is a man who goes through girls pretty fast. You going to give up a perfectly good job here and hang around some guy who has no intention of marrying you?"

No intention of marrying her? Helga fought back the tears as she sat down and picked up the steaming cup of tea. It was true Sam had never mentioned marriage, but was that really going to be the factor that determined the rest of her life? Objectivity was hard to come by often enough, but in this instance, with her brother in the role of protector playing upon her deepest fears, it was almost impossible.

"Olie," she said in a low, halting voice, "I appreciate your concern. I'm a grown woman. I know nobody here has ever thought of me in that way, and I'm as much to blame as anyone for that. After all, I did move back home after John died. I lived in my old room and behaved pretty much the same as before my marriage."

"But that's what you should have done," Olie insisted. "Look, I know all about women's freedom and I'm for it . . . only not for somebody as delicate as you, Helga. You always have been. Maybe you were stuck way out here too long, maybe that's why you let this Texan guy turn you around so."

"Maybe." Helga felt something freeze over. Olie had no idea whom he was talking to. For all of his well-meaning advice it would never occur to him that someone as famous as a United

239

States congressman would fall in love with her. John Tarr had been a local boy, his quietness had been compatible with the Bergsons, and to their knowledge the engagement had been proper. Her father had given her away in a white dress, and they had all felt safe and secure that she would be protected for life. Now she was making a choice that did not include protection. She was disturbing the image of benign, reliable "Aunt Helga."

"Look, I certainly helped perpetuate the image of a helpless, fragile creature." She looked earnestly at her brother. "But I'm not that way, and since I've lived in Washington I've begun to realize that I don't want to spend the rest of my life typing other lawyers' briefs and doing some occasional research. I want to use my mind. I've just learned I have one."

"You've always been smart, Helga, that's not the question. We've always been proud of you for that."

"I know." Helga put her hand over her mouth and tried not to dissolve into tears. The family had been proud of her good marks, but as far as they were concerned graduating first in her class from high school had been icing on the cake. It had marked the end and not the beginning. Her decision to attend college had been something of a threat to them, since no other Bergson had ever done such a thing.

"I think you need to settle in here," Olie advised, "and get a hold of who you are. If this man cares about you he'll come and see you."

"He's a congressman!" Helga exploded. "He has business . . . he's always on the run."

"And you want that sort of life?" Olie asked in the same low, monotonous voice. "Maybe you have changed after all." He pronounced the word changed as if it were the most odious judgment he could pass on her.

"I wish you could be happy for me." Helga's eyes were sad when she turned back to him.

"I'm worried about you." Olie shook his head. "You've had enough sorrow in your life."

"But that doesn't mean I should stop living just to avoid the possibility of unhappiness. That's what I did for ten years!"

Before Olie could reply the phone rang sharply, and they both turned to stare at it. Nobody called this late. It could only be one person and they both seemed to know who that was.

"Hello," Helga answered breathlessly.

"I've stocked up on Bach preludes, Schubert, and every nocturne Chopin ever wrote. I flew back from Texas this morning, and if you don't say you'll be on the way soon I may have to fly out and get you."

"Sam . . ." Helga felt the excitement surging through her tired body. The vivacity in his voice was a tonic. She glanced over her shoulder at Olie, who was staring at her with an almost contemptible smile that stung her to the quick. Was he so narrow-minded and puritanical that he actually believed she had gone bad . . . his little sister gone bad?

"Yes . . . okay. I'll be there Sunday." Her eyes were filled with tears as she whispered into the receiver.

"The day after tomorrow!" Sam was jubilant, he let out a loud yahoo. "If I had a limo I'd send it." He laughed. They were always joking about the accoutrements of power—limos and private planes. Sam maintained he was above all that.

"I can't wait to be home," Helga said.

"Are you all right?" He asked quickly.

"I'll tell you about it tomorrow." Helga thrust her shoulders back. "I'll be there in time for dinner."

"I love you." Sam's voice was hushed with concern but he did not press her.

"I love you . . ." Helga experienced a moment's hesitation before uttering the words. She was acutely aware that Olie was listening. She wondered if he had ever spoken those words out loud before . . . or even heard them spoken.

CHAPTER THIRTEEN

The reunion with Sam was everything she had dreamed it would be and more—a leisurely dinner at the elegant Chez Bosc followed by a brisk walk all the way back to Sam's town house in the southwestern part of town. As usual he had planned an evening that suited her perfectly. The long walk, more than anything else, had both a soothing and an invigorating effect on her spirits. With the lighted dome of the Capitol off to the left it seemed to her that she had truly come home.

"It was strange being back in Minnesota," she told him as they walked arm in arm down the deserted street. "I wish I could have left on better terms."

"That will come," Sam reassured her. "You've had time to get used to the idea, they haven't. We'll make a visit in the spring."

"We will?" She looked at him, smiling, and he stopped walking long enough to lean down and kiss her.

"By the way," she said after they had walked for several blocks in silence, "what was Tate Brown doing in Minneapolis?"

"Who knows?" Sam chuckled. "I think he has a lot of airline stock. He's always in the air."

Helga considered pursuing the subject but rejected the idea. She would wait. But soon, very soon she wanted to find out just how much Sam relied on Tate, just how much influence Tate wielded.

"Marilyn wants me to stay on at the cottage." Helga chose a safer subject.

"That's great!" Sam hugged her against his side as they crossed a street.

"But I think I'm going to look for a place of my own."

"Maybe you should hold off," Sam suggested. "You'll have enough to do when you start classes. Can you do me a favor?"

Helga gave him a quizzical look.

"Forget the logistics for now. Let's talk about what we're going to do New Year's Eve."

"Okay!" Helga laughed. "I can see you already have something up your sleeve."

"Only if you approve." Sam grinned.

"And I can see you've figured out a way to get my approval." Helga's eyes twinkled as she gazed up into his eyes, which were sparkling with mischief.

"San Juan," Sam announced, and waited for her reaction.

"Puerto Rico?" Helga was flabbergasted.

"The woman knows her geography," Sam bellowed to the bare trees and the deserted office buildings. "That's right, Puerto Rico. It's a fringe benefit in a way. I did a favor for one of the representatives and he's insisting I— and whoever I chose as a companion—take advantage of a weekend at the El San Juan, a very posh hotel, smack on the blue sea. If you say no I'm going to have you committed to the loony bin. Nobody turns down Puerto Rico this time of year."

"I guess I should get some studying done. Everyone else is so much younger, so used to school. I have a reading list a mile long . . ."

"Take your books, read on the beach while you eat fresh pineapple. It's only for three days. The year doesn't officially begin till January third." Sam paused outside the door to his town house. Suddenly he pinned her against the door and drew his brows together in a menacing expression. "Say yes, Helga Tarr! An unqualified yes is what I want to hear."

"Yes . . ." Helga felt the familiar wooziness sweeping over her as he pressed against her.

"That's what I need to hear." Sam shoved against the door and they fell, rather than moved, inside, locked in a ravenous embrace.

"God, I missed you!" Sam's hands burned through her clothing as they caressed first her breasts, then moved hungrily down the sides of her body and back to grip her tight, rounded buttocks.

This time there was no languorous prelude to their lovemaking. They moved through his house, ignoring the piano, unmindful of the two champagne glasses that he had readied in advance, oblivious to everything except their desire, which over the evening had reached dizzying heights. They undressed in the soft hue of the two bedside lamps and their eyes were fixed on each other, unwavering and moist with passion. Each garment removed was a new, exotic titillation. They both seemed mesmerized, as if they were partaking in some wondrous, erotic ritual. Sam paused to savor the lush beauty of her breasts as she released them from the flimsy pink bra. Her nipples were hard, poised and ready, and she faced him across the bed with her chin tilted upward at an inviting angle. Each movement was etched with an almost unendurable tension, and when they finally stood facing each other in total nakedness, they were both attuned to that heightened sense of awareness that exists between lovers who have never touched.

It seemed to Helga that she had long since ceased breathing and that she was living now on some aphrodisiac or on the electrical sensations that were shooting off from that magically lighted center, her core. As if by mutual agreement they moved onto the bed, their eyes still locked as their mouths finally made a shattering connection.

That touch was like an explosion, and as Sam's heavy tongue sought the innermost recesses of her mouth, she gasped in recognition of his penetrating rhythm, which was so like that all-consuming tempo that would follow. Their lips met with an insistency that sent the fire spinning lower and lower until she reached for his hand and guided it to the center of her desire. Each delicious curl of his searching tongue propelled her along the torrid journey, and when his fingers dipped and teased, she writhed in blissful agony.

Instinctively she thrust her body forward, every nerve straining to connect with him and with the sizzling sensations he aroused in her. She ran her tongue across his lips, wanting to taste all of him, recognizing the distinctive essence that was uniquely his. How she had missed him!

The magnitude of his large form was a constant wonder, a renewed, scintillating wonder.

As he taunted and titillated the tiny hot kernel of sensation with one hand, his other hand stroked her breast and his mouth began traveling from her long neck to her shoulder. He seemed to be everywhere at once. With a low moan she gave herself over completely to the myriad pleasures, knowing that her surrender was what drove him to an even higher pitch, that her primitive acquiescence was far more eloquent than words could ever be.

"You made the right choice, Helga Tarr." His voice was hoarse and almost inaudible. "You came back!" His hand sought the fine silky skin of her inner thigh, smoothing and coaxing her legs farther apart.

"You won't regret it!" The tension that coiled inside his huge body shot forth, and she cried out in joyous relief, clasping her legs around his muscular back as he plunged deeper. She hung on to his shoulders, gasping as he drove them both onto a higher plateau of pleasure than anything she had ever known.

"I don't regret it," she moaned. "I never will." She gulped and gritted her teeth as cataclysmic convulsions shook them both and rendered them motionless.

The next morning Helga awoke with a little smile and reached out languorously for him. He was gone. She opened her eyes drowsily and turned her head on the pillow to be sure. Ten o'clock! Of course he was gone. He was usually in his office by seven thirty.

Ten o'clock. She couldn't even remember the last time she had slept till ten o'clock. Oh, yes, the second night she and Sam had made love, the first time she had come home with him. She stared resentfully at the clock for a moment, then padded into the bathroom, showered, and dressed in a pair of jeans and a navy blue George Washington University sweat shirt Sam had given her. She stared at herself in the steamy bathroom mirror. Today was the beginning of a new life. Regardless of what Sam was saying about the New Year beginning on January 3, there was much to be done immediately.

She folded up the clothes she had worn last night and slipped them into her leather carryall together with shoes and makeup kit while her mind shot ahead to the day's agenda, which included finding an apartment and spending four hours at the library. She smiled as she walked into the sunny white and red kitchen. He had left the kettle on simmer, laid out a selection of teas, and a glass of cranberry juice was sitting in the front of the refrigerator next to two hard-boiled eggs and a note ordering her to eat some protein before she left the house.

She picked up *The Washington Post* and scanned the front page as she waited for the tea to steep. He had thoughtfully left his copy of the paper behind. Suddenly she felt a breathless panicky sensation in the pit of her stomach. It was Monday. There was no office to go to, no one depending on her, no pressure, no meetings . . . Her hands tensed and she put the paper aside before she had even located the classified section to begin her search for an apartment. The reality of her new life was hard upon her, and she felt like a spaceman floating free in the galaxy, cut off, severed from everything safe and familiar.

Never in her life had she had to deal with the logistics of finding her own apartment. Despite Marilyn's generous offer and her own anxious feelings now, she felt it was important to have her own place. If she continued staying at Marilyn's, she would still feel temporary, she would be inclined to spend more nights at Sam's; her life would be split and she would be rootless.

She ruffled through the paper with a determined expression, found the classified section, and began circling possibilities. The prices were higher than she had expected. Her funds were substantial, but she could already see them dwindling with the cost of living as high as it was. Still, there would be something, even if it were only a room . . . something to call her own. She wondered what Sam would say if she moved her piano out. He had given it to her, hadn't he? They weren't living together and as far as she was concerned they weren't going to. Even were she to agree to live with him, which she wouldn't, it would be fatal to Sam's political career. Anyway, she preferred not to think of that aspect of the future. She told herself that she was glad he had never brought the subject up, relieved that he did not find it necessary to "legitimize" their love with, say, an engagement. No, she wanted her own quarters. All she needed was a room, a bed, and a piano.

She smiled suddenly as she visualized her new abode. She could just imagine Olie's face if she described such an unconventional living arrangement. Well, one room would be enough for the time. For the moment she would direct all of her energies to her studies. It would not be enough simply to pass the LSAT and get accepted to George Washington University Law School. She wanted to excel, to exert herself to her full capacity instead of lingering nicely in the shadows, which was how she had lived her life so far.

Just as she was about to leave for the library, Sam's phone rang and she paused to make certain he had left the answering machine on.

"Helga . . . you there?" Sam's voice came through loud and clear. "Pick up. Helga! Oh, Helga, are you there? Hello . . . hello . . . hello! I know you haven't left the house because my spies have not reported in. Don't play games, Helga . . . pick up the phone!"

Helga ran across the room, chuckling at his antics. "What do you want?" she asked after switching off the machine.

"Lunch," he said, "what else?"

"I thought you ate a big breakfast. Was that another yarn?"

"Didn't have time this morning," Sam said. "I meant to mention it last night, but I got involved in something else, though for the life of me I can't remember what."

"Very funny." Helga smiled. "I can't have lunch."

"Can't?" Sam exclaimed. "We have early theater tickets tonight. You've got to eat your lunch."

"You're obsessed with nutrition," Helga said dryly. "I'd forgotten that about you."

"I don't want you to forget anything about me," Sam admonished her. "Lunch at one at Teddy's. That'll give you time to do whatever you're doing this morning."

Helga tensed. The last thing she wanted to do was to get into the habit of lazy mornings and long lunches, of being available whenever he called. "Sam, I've got tons of things to do. I just made a list and—"

"There'll be time for that, Helga." He sounded slightly irritated. "You just got back last night. Give yourself a break. It's not going to happen all the time, you know. I really do eat a big breakfast most mornings. Just this once."

Helga paused, considering. She didn't want to be too rigid, after all, and maybe tomorrow was soon enough to begin her new highly disciplined schedule.

"All right," she said, "just this once."

By the middle of March it was clear to Helga that her decision to go to school full-time had been not only the bravest decision in her life, but the wisest. Leaving George Washington University Law Library late on a Friday evening with the wind whipping through her blond hair, she felt more confident, more vibrant than she could have dreamed. The tight, retiring woman who had come to the nation's capital nearly half a year ago was as

248

articulate as any of the younger members in her pre-law classes. This was a bonus she had not expected. Somehow it goaded her on, made her prospects greater and more vivid.

She waved at Sam, who was parked at the corner waiting for her. Unfortunately, she had not been able to drag herself away from the library earlier to go home and change for tonight's function.

"Hi!" She slid into the Oldsmobile and leaned over to kiss him. "I just have to stop at home to change. I've laid everything out and it will only take four minutes."

Sam looked dubious and Helga leaned over and kissed him again. For the first time lately he had begun to voice his displeasure at the increasing number of hours she spent in the library. Why, he had wondered, if she was doing so well with her studies did she find it necessary to push even harder?

"Don't be angry." Helga gave him an imploring look when he pulled up in front of the charming little gray house in Foggy Bottom where she had been fortunate enough to find one small room to rent. "I really will be back in four minutes." She threw him a kiss and ran inside.

"Five minutes." He gave her a dour look when she returned wearing one of his favorite outfits, the black velvet suit with the white lacy high-collared blouse.

"Grump." Helga dangled her leather carryall in front of his face as he turned the key in the ignition. "We have all tomorrow morning together."

But not the afternoon. Later that night after they returned from a party fund-raising function at the Mayflower, she could not ignore the uncharacteristic sullenness that had come over him. She sat down at the piano, her piano, which she had not had the heart to remove to her own tiny quarters, and played the haunting Chopin nocturne which was his favorite.

"Can't I do anything to make you feel better?" She curled up on the sofa next to him when she finished.

249

"I think we need some time off." He shook his head. "Both of our schedules are so hectic . . ."

His voice trailed off and he wrinkled his brow as if he were concentrating deeply on something. Helga ran her hand across his forehead, caressing and soothing the deep vertical thinking lines that had formed. She climbed to her knees and began massaging his broad, muscular shoulders.

"Spring vacation isn't that far off." She nuzzled against his neck.

"Too far," he objected.

"I'm sorry I couldn't go to Boston with you last weekend for that fund raising." Helga moved her hands down his arms then placed them palm down on his chest. Beneath her right hand she felt his heart quicken.

"I was thinking we could fly to St. Thomas just for a long weekend—next week. Tate knows a guy with a boat—we could sail around."

"I can't, Sam." Helga felt vaguely annoyed that he would suggest it. After all, they had flown to San Juan over New Year's.

"You can read just as well on a boat, can't you? What does it matter where you are?" There was a guarded expression in his eyes that she had never seen before.

"I can't study just as well on a boat or in the sun."

"I forgot"—he grimaced—"how you burn."

"It's not a question of my burning." Helga struggled to retain her composure. She knew it was hard for him, but it was just as hard on her, maybe even harder, because she was always the one who was making the adjustment, carting around a change of clothes for the next day. Since she had taken the room he had spent only one night there. But she understood that . . . and in a way she felt easier coming to his house, especially after some quasi-sleazy gossipy magazine had gotten wind of their trip to Puerto Rico. She was still adamant about keeping her name out of the papers, about not confirming the rumors that continued to abound about her and the Texan. She had no way of proving

250

it, of course, but it had always seemed that someone had alerted the media about the trip to Puerto Rico, and naturally enough that "someone," in her estimation, was Tate Brown.

"Let's go to bed," she urged softly as she began unbuttoning his shirt. "I love you, Sam. You know I do. This is the hardest time right now, I'm sure of it. Maybe I am a bit obsessed with school and the LSAT. I was the same with my job. You know that about me. I'll try to be more moderate."

Sam gave her a long look as her hands moved lovingly over his hairy chest. "What do you think of when you think of the future . . . for us?"

Helga was taken aback. He had such a knack for attacking unlikely subjects head-on. She shrugged. What did he want her to say? Marriage? Was he waiting for her to broach the subject? Lately she had experienced some disquieting twinges about the vagueness of their future. Only last week Marilyn had brought up the subject, wondering if she and Sam weren't planning to spring a June wedding on Washington. Helga had laughed her off, saying a wedding was the last thing she needed now with so much studying to do. With her customary efficiency she had filed the subject in a secure compartment.

"Honey . . ." She caressed his cheek. "Let's go to bed. We're both exhausted and—"

"Don't you want to talk about the future," Sam persisted, a bit belligerently it seemed to her.

"I don't think you do, Sam," she said evenly.

He looked down chagrined and her heart went out to him. Something was troubling him and deeply. She scanned his face, waiting for him to unburden himself with his usual candor, but he remained silent.

"Come . . ." Helga took his hand and drew him to his feet. She switched off the living room lights on the way to the bedroom, and when they were in bed she nestled against him, rubbing her silky stomach against his until he took her in his arms.

But the next afternoon as she was dressing to leave after a

251

leisurely morning of lovemaking and steak and eggs, the same troubled expression returned to his face.

"Sam, what is it?" She tossed her books on the lumpy living room sofa and faced him. "You act like you have a case of the Scandanavian silents . . . Something's on your mind."

"All this fund raising," he began, "for my campaign. I wonder where it's all going to lead. Somehow I don't like collecting money from strangers."

"It takes money to run a campaign," Helga said prudently. "You trust Tate, don't you?"

"Hell yes, I trust him!" Sam gave her an agitated look. "You never liked Tate. I know that. I've tried to keep him out of our life."

"I know." Helga's eyes clouded. "I know you have. And it's not just that I don't like him. I think the reason I don't is that he doesn't approve of me."

"You're always saying that." Sam turned away and shoved his hands deep into the pockets of his tweed trousers. "I'm sorry . . . I guess something is on my mind."

"It's okay." Helga touched his shoulder gently. "You've waited patiently for my halting confessions. I can wait as long as you want." She sat down on the sofa and folded her hands in her lap.

Sam turned and shook his head with an incredulous smile. "You're magnificent," he said.

"Why?" Helga smiled. "Because I'm willing to wait to hear what's on your mind? How often have you done it for me?"

"You know I might want to run for president someday. What do you think about that?"

"You don't need my permission." Helga felt the palms of her hands break out into a warm sweat.

"I'm not saying it would happen." He sat down next to her and looked at her closely. "Well, probably this next election we'd be aiming for a vice-presidential deal. To tell you the truth, I'm

252

not sure I'd buy that. Too easy to get stuck there doin' nothing. Unless I believed in the ticket I couldn't go for it."

Helga nodded. Why was he bringing this up now?

"The thing is," he said hesitantly, "it would make sense for me to be married. I've been pressured that way for some time now."

"I'm sure you have," Helga replied with thick sarcasm.

"I'm sorry." He looked around, flustered. It was immediately clear to him that he had blundered. "I guess this is no way to propose."

"You could have fooled me." Helga met his eyes with a withering look.

"Look, you know I love you . . ."

"It's no proposal," Helga said icily. "It's an arrangement, a deal."

"Of course it isn't." Sam flushed. "Christ, you know how much I love you . . . I do want to marry you!"

"Though perhaps," snapped Helga as she moved to the door, "not before the next election."

Sam caught her elbow and pulled her back gently. "It was just a suggestion. Tate and some of the other—"

"Tate? Tate suggested you propose to me?" Helga felt a trap forming around her, around them.

"No, of course not," Sam said. "We were speaking generally. You wanted our affair kept quiet. People know we see each other, but I think, except for that one slipup when we went to Puerto Rico, we've been pretty discreet."

"I won't have my life dictated by your political advisers." Helga could not stifle her fury. "If we get married will they then dictate the birth of our first child? I'm thirty-three, they'll probably demand I have a child immediately before my ovaries shrivel up."

Sam looked horrified. "Of course not. Look, this is all my fault. I mucked it up, said it all wrong."

"Sam"—Helga's voice was deathly calm—"you are a man

253

who is a master of articulating his feelings, of rhetoric, of swinging the situation to get what he wants. Why couldn't you do it this time? If you want to marry me, before the next election, why didn't you plan things so I would say yes?"

CHAPTER FOURTEEN

Things were not the same between them. Although spring was in the air and the cherry blossoms were almost ready to pop out, there was an uneasy truce between them and no further mention of marriage. There were, of course, moments when the spontaneity returned, and then they were as stunned and speechless as before, as awed by their love as they had been in the autumn when it had struck so suddenly with such ferocity. But now there was a stumbling block that presented itself, oddly enough, in the guise of marriage. Somehow Helga wasn't sure it was that simple. The pattern of their love had grown so steadily since its rocky beginning, there was such trust and mutual respect that marriage had seemed an unspoken fait accompli, something preordained that would inevitably happen.

Dressed in a yellow slicker with volumes of heavy legal books wrapped in plastic bags to protect them from the spring deluge, Helga sloshed through the rain on the way back to her room. Three days ago Sam had announced that he was spending next week in his Texas office. Lately his congressional obligations had prompted a number of trips to his home state, but usually only for the day or at most for a night. At the time she had been relieved, thinking an entire week apart would afford her the opportunity to think things out. Only thinking was more or less stewing . . . stewing around in the same ambiguities, and so far it was no antidote for the creeping sensation that they were on very fragile ground.

Helga's tiny room was cheerful enough with its lacy white curtains, white wrought-iron double bed covered with a blue and white spread, a bright blue rocking chair, and a card table that passed as a desk. She hung her dripping slicker in the minuscule bathroom and before she could take off her boots ran to answer the phone.

"Don't read the *Post.*" It was Marilyn and there was a note of panic in her voice that made Helga freeze.

"Of course I'm going to read the *Post,*" Helga replied after a moment. She shoved her hand into one of the plastic bags and removed a slightly damp copy of the newspaper.

"Well, don't take it seriously," Marilyn rushed on. "Some idiotic gossip monger thinks he's got a hold of a juicy tidbit. Helga, I've been calling you all day."

"I've had classes," Helga said absently as she ruffled through the paper.

"Well, I'm glad I caught you in time," Marilyn said. "There's a picture of Sam with some Texas orange festival beauty queen who speaks seven languages and just came back from some semiofficial diplomatic mission to Russia."

Helga stared at the picture Marilyn was referring to.

"Helga . . . I'm coming right over!" Marilyn said after a lengthy pause. "Don't you buy into this now. So what if Sam was talking to a beautiful woman and somebody snapped a picture. It doesn't mean anything."

Several minutes later Helga sat on the edge of her bed staring at Sam's smiling face and the face of the young woman whom the columnist had alluded to in glowing terms. According to the piece, Sara Danford, a graduate of Smith at age nineteen, was at twenty-seven in line for a powerful position in the diplomatic service. The columnist hinted that Ms. Danford might well be the youngest ambassador in history. Her grandfather had been governor of Texas; in fact, her entire resume read like a press release for the ideal unattached woman of the year.

Twenty minutes later when Marilyn rang the doorbell downstairs Helga was still sitting on the edge of her bed lethargically beginning to remove her boots.

"Since you wouldn't meet for dinner or come over I brought some goodies from the store." Marilyn's dark hair was soaked. She had apparently left on the run and neglected to put on a rain hat.

"You and Sam." Helga cleared a space on the card table. "You think food is the answer to everything."

"It sometimes helps. Helga, I'd be feeling the same as you if I looked in the paper and saw my . . . fiancé with a woman who's being touted as superwoman. Well, you and Sam are the same as engaged . . . don't let's get bogged down in trivial details."

"It's his third trip to Texas since February," Helga observed stonily.

"So what? That doesn't mean he's been seeing miss what's-her-name. Sam isn't that kind of man and you know it. He plays it straight. He even played it straight with Lauren, and when I look back on that I see there was nothing between them, certainly nothing to compare to what you and Sam have going."

Helga stared at the delicacies Marilyn unwrapped and nibbled tentatively at one as Marilyn opened a bottle of wine. She accepted a tumbler with a pensive expression and sat in the straight-back chair while Marilyn eased her plump body into the rocker.

"When's he coming back?" Marilyn asked.

"Tomorrow." Helga's face was drawn and tightly concentrated. She sipped the red wine slowly, but the knot of apprehension that had formed in her stomach seemed to grow.

"I think," she said after several moments, "that . . . I've been set up."

"How do you mean?" Marilyn leaned forward, intrigued.

"I'll never be able to prove it." Helga stared straight ahead and after a moment she continued. "I think you're right. There's probably no connection, at the moment anyway, between . . . Sara Danford and Sam. But I don't think it's an accident that picture made the *Post.* Why not just the Houston paper? Is it

257

really such a hot social item that it would make the lead piece in Thursday's *Post*?"

Marilyn was silent for an unusually long time. "It wouldn't be the first time that someone tried to manipulate somebody's life."

"I never was an ideal candidate for . . . president's wife, even for senator's wife for that matter. I'm even less so now." Helga's mouth was drawn, her lips barely moved as she spoke. "I've never had many friends, but the friends I do make . . . I keep. I don't think it's a crime not to be outgoing, effervescent, and . . . bubbly. Sam doesn't think so either. But somebody does. Why do you suppose people trust a bubbly person more than a contemplative person? Oh, maybe I'm wrong about that, Marilyn. Actually people will tolerate a serious man, a man who doesn't flash a smile for every photographer. But a woman?"

"Is smiling really the issue?" asked Marilyn.

Helga drained the rest of the red wine from her glass and poured them each a refill. She picked up the newspaper and studied it, holding it at different angles and cocking her head from side to side as if she could read the entire solution if she studied it long enough. Of course smiling per se wasn't the issue. She shook her head. She seemed to be losing track.

"Bit by bit"—she tossed the paper aside—"the trust that's between Sam and me is going to be chipped away. It's already started . . . before this."

"You've been having problems?" Marilyn asked. "You didn't say anything."

"It's all so nebulous." Helga frowned. "I can't accuse Tate Brown of arranging for this picture to appear in the *Post*. But I'd be willing to stake my life on it."

"Then fight it." Marilyn bolted angrily out of the rocker.

Helga nodded firmly and her face was set. "Don't worry. I will."

But it was hard to fight when deep down she believed that Tate

258

Brown was right about her capacity, her aptitude, and, yes . . . even her desire to be the wife of a prominent figure.

To marry a man as powerful and dynamic as Sam would under any circumstances challenge one's autonomy. It would be easy enough to slip into the shadows even if he were the editor of a newspaper or a lawyer. He didn't have to do anything to project such a forceful image—he simply was that way and he would be the same regardless of the profession. And now that she was finally getting her life together, focusing on a profession that stimulated and satisfied her, did she really want to take the chance of being so fragmented by stretching herself between Sam and her own work that everything fell apart?

That night she lay awake tossing. What if she fought Tate, married Sam, and then hurt his political opportunities? Maybe the public would perceive her as cold and uncaring. Maybe they would only see a woman with erect carriage, few smiles, and a career she insisted on making a stab for?

Then again maybe she was underestimating the public. Maybe Tate Brown was underestimating the public. Maybe people were capable of understanding that a person could be shy and still be possessed of warmth and a deep humanitarian spirit. Maybe Tate Brown, who was known as one of the best troubleshooters in town, was shooting down trouble that didn't exist.

The next morning before classes Helga called Sam's office in Texas to find out what time his plane would be arriving so she could throw together one of her hodgepodge dinners that always amused him. Just to hear the sound of his voice, she thought, would buoy her. Unfortunately he was in a meeting and his secretary laughingly admitted that she was usually the last person to know what his plans were. However, she chatted familiarly with Helga and that bolstered her confidence. At least she was not an unknown quantity in his native state. After her last class Helga phoned Sam's Washington office but again received no satisfaction, only an amused chuckle about how impossible it was to pin the Texan down. It wasn't like Sam not to keep her informed. As a matter of fact, it was not like him not to have phoned for the past two nights. She struggled desperately not to attribute this lapse in consideration to Sara of the Seven Languages, but it was not easy. It would almost have been a relief to slip into something as blindly absorbing as jealousy. Only that was too simple and she knew it. What really sickened her was the realization that as much as she and Sam loved each other, something unseen could gnaw at the love until all trust was broken and neither of them understood or knew where to pick up the pieces.

All evening she made intermittent phone calls to his town house, and finally she fell into bed around midnight, having resisted the temptation to try to reach him at his parents' home in Galveston.

The next morning she awoke feeling sick and defeated. The week's separation, topped by the suggestive picture in the *Post*, had worn her down. Her bones ached as she dragged about getting dressed for class. She felt a sort of hysterical desperation to talk to him, to feel his arms around her, reassuring and strong. Had he really proposed, however haltingly? Had she really refused with such sarcasm?

Somehow she made it through the day, and when she arrived back at her room around eight that evening, the phone was ringing.

"Where have you been?" It was Sam, sounding very annoyed.

"Where have you been?" Helga could have cried with relief, but his tone put her off and she responded in kind.

"We were supposed to have dinner at Senator Freebold's tonight . . ."

"Oh, my God!" Helga shook her head in disbelief. She had been so rattled by everything she had neglected to check her date book.

"Sam, I'm sorry . . . So much has been happening."

"Can you be dressed in twenty minutes?" Sam asked severely.

"I'll try." Helga hung up, placed her hand over her mouth, and began to sob.

They managed to put on a convincing show for the Freebolds and their ten other dinner guests. Luckily Matilda Freebold was one of Helga's favorites, so that helped relieve some of the strain between her and Sam and made the evening more pleasant than she had anticipated. But the strain was there. There were no warm, loving looks, only bright, congenial smiles for the benefit of others. For three hours they managed a charade, but by the time they were alone in Sam's car, the silence between them was tense and ugly.

"How could you have forgotten?" Sam looked at her accusingly.

"How could you not have phoned me to say you'd be a day late coming home from Texas?" Helga clung to her side of the car, and the panic escalated when she realized he was not driving toward his house at all, but toward Foggy Bottom. He had decided they would not be spending the night together and after more than a week's separation. She felt her anger settle in and an icy resolve begin to form.

"I tried to let you know." Sam sounded tired. "You're never home. I should have tried the library."

"Don't be sarcastic." Helga glared at him.

"Look who's talking!" Sam snapped.

"Why can't you understand that the closer I get to the entrance exam the more nervous I am. Everything's on the line."

"You'll pass the LSATs with your eyes closed. Why are you driving yourself?"

"Because I want to. Because I never have before. You do it all the time . . . yes, you do! I want to absorb everything. I want to be . . . the best . . . for a change."

"Well, this obsession of yours is making me . . ." He broke off with a shrug.

"This isn't a good time to talk . . ." Helga had the strangest

261

sensation that she was a puppet, that this particular scene had been ordered in advance and they were simply playing it out. If only they could break free of it, wait and talk later. If only they could not be hurt and just stop things now!

"That's always your answer," Sam chided her. "I was on the run constantly in Texas."

"I saw the picture in the paper." The words burst out of her and immediately she regretted them.

"Well, I hope you'll see a lot more pictures of me." Sam stared straight ahead, unfeelingly. "It's called publicity, Helga. It's what I need to get elected, or have you forgotten that I am in the business of collecting votes."

"How could I forget that," Helga said sharply.

"Since you're so averse to having your picture taken with me, I don't see how you can object to—"

"Sorry," Helga interrupted sharply. "You're right! You're perfectly entitled to all the pictures you can get."

They drove for ten minutes in silence, and when he pulled up in front of her house, he sat staring straight ahead, almost daring her, she thought, to get out of the car without a word. Her hand itched to open the door and slam it shut, but there was too much at stake. Tonight was crucial and she knew it. She closed her eyes, trying to gather strength to overcome the hurt and anger. She reminded herself how much they loved each other and that love like theirs did not evaporate in a week or even in a month or a year.

Finally he switched off the ignition and turned to her with an impassive expression. "I can't believe you'd be upset just because of a silly picture in the paper. It's not like you. You're above that sort of petty—"

"I'm sorry I forgot the Freebolds' party. It was because I was upset . . . and not just about the picture." Helga looked around hopelessly.

"I told you I tried to call you!" Sam exploded and shook his

262

head as if she were a totally irrational creature. "I even asked Tate to call you."

"Well, no wonder no one reached me," Helga snapped bitterly.

"Okay, Helga . . . stop with the innuendos about Tate. It's getting to be a crazy obsession with you—"

"Don't tell me I'm crazy," Helga interrupted in a hushed livid voice. "He doesn't like me. Be honest, Sam, hasn't Tate inferred that I might not be the best choice for your wife?"

"Tate doesn't run my life." Sam did not deny it.

"But he's shaken your confidence," Helga cried. "Who else knew we were going to Puerto Rico? Why did that picture happen to get in yesterday's *Post*? Tate knows you and he knows me. He knows how to manipulate, you said so yourself, that's why he's a good campaign manager."

"I'll tell you what's blowing my confidence." Sam faced her. "You . . . you've put yourself under so much pressure with law school that you're not yourself."

"I am myself." Helga felt the tears spring to her eyes. "I am more myself than I've ever been."

"Tate is not a villain," Sam insisted. "I wish you'd get that out of your head."

"Look, I'm willing to admit he's not a villain. He's probably convinced himself that he's doing this for you. That's loyalty. I would respect him for it if I wasn't caught in the middle. I would be willing to stake my life . . . that he never tried to call me."

Sam slumped down in his seat. "That's something we'll never know, will we? Unless we've tapped all the phones we will never for sure know the answer to that question, will we?"

"No," Helga whispered. "No, *we* won't . . . but I will and Tate, though he'll never admit it, will know it too."

"Then what's the answer?" Sam asked rigidly. "Do you want me to dump Tate? Do you need to approve of everyone on my staff, is that it?"

Helga was stung by his sarcasm. Of course that wasn't what

she wanted. She wanted to love him, to cut through all of the messy complexity and just to be his friend and hold him.

But she was too hurt to let it go. With her hand on the door handle she turned to him. "Now I know how ambitious you are. I'd always wondered about it. You disguise it quite effectively."

There was a flicker of apprehension in Sam's face when he turned to her.

"Maybe Tate's right," Helga continued. "Maybe I would be something of a risk. No, risk is too harsh a word, too powerful a word to use where I'm concerned. Maybe I'm not dynamic enough. Certainly I can't claim any political forefathers like Sara of the Seven Languages. I've nothing against her, that's not what this is about. But maybe Tate is absolutely right that I would not add enough to your image. And . . . maybe that's why you, the artful, the convincing speech master, were unable to put your whole heart and head into a proposal of marriage. Maybe you were torn. You say you don't want private planes and all of the fuss that goes with being famous, but maybe you want it more than you're able to admit. Maybe it's easier to let me go than to risk losing the other."

CHAPTER FIFTEEN

It was torture to sit in her room and wait for the phone to ring, but it was a torture she elected to endure because it eliminated the possibility that he was trying to reach her without her knowledge. It, in effect, eliminated hope.

Since it was spring vacation and there were no classes for the days preceding Easter, she went out only to renew her stack of library books. The rest of the time she waited. She told herself it was the logical approach, that she was getting proof and the proof was that he had not called.

As the days went by she felt a detachment growing over the wound. She told herself how much easier it was to get over the loss of a living person as opposed to a dead one. When John had died she had wept for months before the numbness had set in. Now, with her books and the possibility of a scholarship for next fall if she did well on the LSAT, she threw all of her energy into studying. She had wept for the dead but not for the living.

Marilyn stopped by regularly. "You've turned off," she said. "Call him, Helga. The longer it goes on the more difficult it is. I've been married for thirteen years. You've got to nip these things in the bud."

But she didn't and she couldn't, and when she answered the phone on Good Friday and it was Sam wanting to meet her for a pizza after he finished working late, she answered coolly that she was busy.

After that she no longer waited. She took her books outside

into the April sunshine, and her ability to absorb facts seemed nothing short of miraculous. It was as if misery and pain had sharpened her intellect to a fine brilliance. She knew Marilyn was right, she was closing off. Emotionally she was behaving just as she had back in Minnesota, only this time it was school that was absorbing her instead of a job. She viewed herself with cool detachment and a certain amount of awe. She was an expert at closing off. She told herself it was a convenient attribute.

Her detachment was so complete that when Kenyon Stubbs, who had recently moved to Washington, phoned to invite her and Sam to a dinner party he and his wife were having, she was actually able to laugh about it with Marilyn.

"He called too late," she observed wrily. "Imagine, Marilyn, he waited for nearly eleven years to invite me to dinner and then his timing was off by a little over a week. I was tempted to tell him I'd come alone. Probably I should have just appeared by myself and witnessed his crushed expression at not having nabbed Super Sam as a dinner guest."

Sometimes the bitterness helped. Most of the time it did not. What helped most was submerging herself in facts, in legal facts, and by June she had advanced to the top of her two classes. Most of the men she encountered in school were a good many years younger than she, but on those nights when it did not interfere with studying she accepted dates. In a way she felt safe with these younger men; they viewed her as someone special, and even when they grew amorous as several did on more than one occasion, she felt protected from any involvement because of the age difference.

But there was always loneliness, a dull ache that by now seemed a part of her existence, a necessity perhaps to her survival. There was a deep familiarity with the emptiness. She had, when she thought about it, felt that same dull ache most of her life. Daily she could feel herself developing the sort of stoicism her mother had, and she knew that what was now rigor and prudence would one day, not so far off, turn to stringency. She was becoming Aunt Helga again.

Still, she argued with herself on one particularly glorious June afternoon, she was light-years ahead of the Helga who had come to Washington last October. The LSATs were behind her and thanks to her diligence over the past months she felt she'd done well and might even be awarded a stipend for her studies in the fall. There was much to be thankful for, and in bright moments, like these, she could even entertain the possibility of forming some sensible liaison with a man. But he would be a man more suited to her temperament. Perhaps he would be a professor, established and devoted to some academic pursuit. Perhaps another lawyer whose interests coincided with her own. It was now entirely possible that she would move back to Minneapolis when she got her degree.

The Potomac was a muddy gray from all the rains that had fallen on and off for the past six weeks. As Helga meandered along its banks and settled onto a damp grassy knoll to read her paper, it did not even occur to her that this was almost the precise spot where she had first encountered Sam McCalahan. The ground was far too moist to be comfortable but the sun felt good, and rather than retreat farther up in the mall to sit on a bench, Helga sat cross-legged in jeans and a plaid shirt with the paper spread in front of her.

As she usually did she skimmed the paper quickly, first deciding which pieces interested her and in what order she would read them. Her heart leaped at the sight of Sam's face staring out at her from the social page. She turned the page quickly so as not to have a good look at the smiling woman next to him. But then her curiosity got the better of her and she turned the page back surreptitiously, as if she were afraid of being caught.

The beautiful woman was not Ms. Sara Somebody, the Texan beauty destined to be the youngest ambassador on record. Helga stared at the picture with an uncanny expression, and suddenly she was beset with an onslaught of emotion, something far more profound than jealousy or even regret. As she continued to stare, it seemed as if some deadly poison were being painfully pumped out of her. She crumpled forward slightly and wrapped her arms around her thin body, rocking ever so slightly back and forth in a slow, soothing motion.

Suddenly, before she could censor herself, she was on her feet racing up the lawn toward the nearest pay phone with tears in her eyes. She had given up too much! They had had too much together and Tate or whatever unseen obstacles they had encountered paled beside the wealth of love and goodness they were capable of giving to each other. No one was the winner now, they were both losers. They had both lashed out, both played the power game because of being hurt. But blame was irrelevant. Love was not. What they had shared was too rare.

Her hands shook as she searched for a dime and twice it flew out of her hand before she could slip it into the slot. Although she had not phoned his office in over a month the number was emblazoned in her mind. She girded herself as the secretary said she would buzz him. It could be too late.

"Yes?" He answered in a brusque businesslike voice.

"I was wondering . . . if we could see each other." Helga's low voice trembled despite her efforts to keep it even.

He paused. "Fine." He was guarded but she felt like leaping for joy anyway. "Teddy's all right?"

"Sure," Helga said breathlessly. "Fine. When?"

Another interminable pause. She was positive he was going to say next month or next week.

"Tonight." The terseness of his reply was like music.

Tonight! She was meeting him tonight. She replaced the receiver and slumped against the transparent phone booth. Her body seemed already melting, thawing; and the pain, long buried, surfaced now with a force so overwhelming that she leaned her blond head against the telephone and shook with silent sobs.

Never had she experienced such terror, such an all-consuming

268

attack of nerves as when she tried to prepare for the meeting. She had never before pondered over what to wear, never tried on and rejected so many different outfits. She had never been so feebleminded in her life!

He had probably agreed to see her because he was a decent person, a person who would not want to bear a grudge. She rummaged in her tiny closet and withdrew a blue print peasant skirt, but after staring at it for several minutes she tossed it aside.

With a degree of humility she recalled once telling him that she wanted them to be friends, that that was all they could be, but it was very important for her not to lose him as a friend. She blushed at the memory. She had meant it then. And yes, she meant it now too . . . if that were all, if there were no way.

Her usually fluid movements were distracted, almost jerky as she continued to rummage through her closet. Nothing was appropriate. She took in a deep breath and sat down in the rocker to try to compose herself. She had never before thought in terms of images—of what image she wanted to project. Before coming to D.C. she had projected, she knew, a very definite image with her subdued wardrobe of blacks, browns, and navies, but quite unwittingly. Now what she wore seemed of the utmost importance, and at the moment she could not see the least humor in her almost maniacal dashing about as she tried to put together . . . What? How should she appear?

Teddy's was small but with an elegant leathery ambiance. How did one dress for such a restaurant? She had been to Teddy's dozens of times and never had it occurred to her to coordinate her ensemble with the decor.

She smiled, finally having reached, she thought, the limits of absurdity. She imagined that the zany, fragmented sensations, half-finished thoughts, and hot flashes were what people who were on amphetamines experienced. She never wanted to feel this way again!

Finally she chose what she must have known she would seek solace in all along, a plain black linen sheath. Her hands shook as she put on earrings and a slender gold bracelet. The dress had a matching boxy jacket, black trimmed in white . . . very chic, far too dressy for Teddy's probably, but it gave her a sense of confidence.

She walked through the twilight and arrived at Teddy's forty minutes early. After circling the block three times she decided to go inside. Maybe Sal, the bartender, had a newspaper she could read while she waited. The moment she stepped inside she saw him, seated at the bar, his broad shoulders hunched over the paper, his large hand turning a glass of bourbon in a small, slow circle on the bar. He was wearing a light beige and white checked summer jacket, plain beige trousers, and of all things, white shoes. She stared at his large feet as he balanced them on the brass foot rod. She never would have guessed him for the white-shoe type. He looked rather spiffy actually, very sporty as if he had spent a day at the racetrack.

She smiled at the idea, and despite her churning stomach that smile managed to stay on her face as she greeted him.

By the time they moved to the rear of Teddy's and were seated in one of the small circular red leather banquettes, Helga's smile had faded and she could not think of a single safe topic of conversation. She almost never did things on impulse, and that she had actually phoned him and suggested this meeting now seemed like part of a fantasy. There was a bewildered expression on her face as she looked around the familiar spot, and when the waiter appeared to take their order she flashed an unlikely smile, as if the real assignation was with him and not with the man seated across from her. After she ordered a white wine there was another empty pause.

"How have you been?" Sam asked politely.

"Busy." Helga looked at him briefly. She longed to stare at him, to take in all the well-remembered details of his handsome face.

"I'm taking off for the summer." She managed a subdued smile. "I . . . I was lucky. I think I did well on the LSATs."

"I'm glad you're doing well." The soft note of sincerity in Sam's voice triggered a rush of emotion, and there was an awkward pause as she searched for the next topic of conversation.

"What about you?" she asked finally. "You look all brown. Did you spend time on Tate's boat?"

Sam shook his head. "Public service." A glint of the old humor twinkled in his eyes. "I'm trying to get some special funding for a food project, really it's in the realm of the Department of Agriculture, which is usually the last department to get any money. I went down to Colombia with a group of Texas farmers to investigate what some eccentric American entrepreneur is doing down there with soybeans and a new kind of fertilizer."

Helga felt the tension begin to ease as he continued explaining his latest involvement. As always his own interest was compelling, and by the time they were eating dinner, between her questions and his enthusiasm for the new project, the atmosphere had eased tremendously.

"The thing is," Sam went on after they had ordered coffee, "feeding the poor, oddly enough, is not a spectacular issue. Farmers, in all their gentleness, are not the stuff that headlines are made of. Most of us take food for granted. It's my belief we've ignored our agricultural heritage long enough . . . maybe too long."

"So you're commuting to Colombia." Helga finally gathered up the courage to give him a long look. The effect was dizzying. For an instant everything seemed to stop . . . the low jazz music filtering over the stereo system, the hum of conversation, Teddy's itself seemed to vanish as they stared across the white clothed table into each other's eyes.

Helga's breathing accelerated dangerously, and every spark, denied, repressed, and sometimes even forgotten over the past two months, burst into uncontrollable flames.

"So it's been a productive move after all," Sam said as they strolled toward his car, which was parked several blocks away.

"Oh, yes!" Helga responded enthusiastically. "I have no regrets at all about—" She broke off suddenly. Except one regret and now that she was with him, feeling the easy swing of his arm brushing casually against her jacket, she knew how much she had forfeited.

"And your campaign?" she questioned once she was settled in the car, which was as jumbled and littered as ever with pamphlets, books, and tennis gear.

"I decided I was jumping the gun." Sam shifted the car into gear, and once they had turned the corner onto Pennsylvania Avenue he glanced at her. "Are you up to a pilgrimage?"

Helga's heart seemed to stop as the familiar teasing warmth crept into his voice. "The Lincoln or the Jefferson?" she asked tremulously.

"The Lincoln first," Sam said, "and then we'll see."

It was the first inkling she'd had that there might still be a chance. Even the torrid interlocking of eyes back at Teddy's might have been all on her part, but this suggestion to extend their evening, to turn it into more than just an amicable reconciliation . . . The fires that flamed in her now were more than a need to satisfy and quell the unruly sexual hunger he always aroused in her. She wanted to reach out to him; she ached with every nerve in her body to communicate her love. He intrigued her as no man could. For all of the awkwardness of this first meeting he had engaged her sensibilities and her intellect as he spoke of his new agricultural project. It was a project that she could be profoundly interested in too. It was something else they could share.

As they stood staring up at the mammoth sculpture of the Great Emancipator, she recalled the passion of their other visit to the monument. How the leaves had swirled then, how they had clung to each other, so in tune both spiritually and physically that nothing, it seemed, would ever part them.

Tonight it was warm with a hint of summer humidity that would soon make the city unbearable. For the moment, though, it only added to the rich fecundity—the sense that life was stirring beneath the grass, that the shimmering stars in galaxies millions of light-years away were waiting to be tapped. Helga smiled softly at all of these bittersweet feelings. She was not going to be Aunt Helga, after all, and whatever happened after tonight she would never be as closed again.

"I never mind the humidity," Sam said as they moved to sit at the bottom of the broad steps so they could stare back up at the majestic Doric columns. "I like the way it smells. A southern smell."

"It's true." Helga sniffed the fertile air, which was redolent with the fragrance of peony, iris, and magnolia. "There is a southern smell. I know what you mean."

They fell silent staring up at the stars, not touching but sitting side by side with their arms wrapped loosely around their knees.

"Why did you decide you were jumping the gun?" Helga asked, referring to her earlier question about his campaign.

"I don't think I know enough," Sam said flatly. "Another term in Congress started sounding pretty good to me. I'm just getting the knack. It seemed pretty unfair to my constituents to pull out and move on just as I was beginning to know who to flatter and who to ignore."

He laughed suddenly, the old boisterous laugh that brought a smile to her lips. He stopped laughing abruptly and stared at her with an incredulous expression, then he cocked his head to one side and stared harder.

"What's the matter?" Helga was alarmed, until a strange smile spread onto his face and he looked at her with eyes that were definitely teasing. She held her breath as he stretched out his hand and very gently touched her ear.

"What is it?" She could scarcely utter the words the blood was pounding so fiercely inside her head. Her tiny earlobe seemed to reverberate as his finger made a slow, delicate circle.

His eyes scanned her face and this time there was no mistaking the look she read there. He loved her! He still did!

"Your earrings," he said tenderly. "They don't match!" He touched her other earlobe as if the discovery had earthshaking connotations for him, as if mismatched earrings in one so dedicated to perfection as she, was irrefutable proof of her love, of how much she needed him and how deeply she longed for reconciliation.

"Maybe my shoes don't either!" Suddenly Helga was in his arms, laughing and crying, feeling his sturdy arms around her, hugging her so close that she gasped at the glorious June air.

"Oh, I wouldn't be surprised if nothing matched," she murmured against his hungry mouth. "I almost fainted from nervousness . . . Sam, I didn't want to say all those things I said before."

"I know." His tongue slid slowly into her mouth, and she grew supple and pliant, filled with all the warm juices that are life's most eloquent blessing.

"I didn't want to either." Sam framed her face with his hands. "I knew you needed room . . . time . . . I just didn't know how to give it to you. And it was true, Tate wasn't in your corner but hell, woman, what kind of a man do you take me for?"

His recrimination was a gentle bellow into the starry night, but his kiss was searing and it left no doubt that their long separation had left him ravenous. Still, it was the tenderness of his touch as he tentatively fondled her breast that aroused her most, and she pressed against his hand, telling him yes, yes, she wanted him and in every way!

"For all of your legal prowess, your instinctive gift for logic, didn't it ever occur to you that once we were married, Tate would find every reason to adore you? That once the knot was tied, he would sure as hell want us to stay married. What good is a divorced candidate? Didn't that ever occur to you, Helga Whiz?"

"No." Helga savored the delectable flavor of his mouth, which was tinged with the salt of her tears. "No, it never occurred to me."

"Well"—Sam gazed lovingly into her glistening blue eyes—"it never occurred to me till this minute. I'm best when I extemporize. But it's a good point, isn't it?"

"Yes." Helga caressed his cheek. "I was dying inside. I was living just fine . . . but inside I was dying."

"I tried to fall in love with the woman who spoke seven languages." Sam traced his finger around her face with a mesmerized expression. "I couldn't. I couldn't even think of anything to say to her in one language. I kept thinking of all the things I wanted to say to you and how you'd be able to shed light on some of the problems we were having with the soybeans and how you would have loved the workers in the fields in Colombia . . ." Sam shook his head and the pain of the past month and a half was clearly etched in his face as he remembered.

Suddenly Helga clasped his hands in hers and looked at him urgently. "Marry me, Sam!"

"What?" Sam looked as if he'd been thrown from a horse.

Helga burst out in a giddy laugh. "Marry me!" she shouted. "Marry me in Washington, in Minnesota and Texas!"

"Oh, good Lord!" Sam gathered her up in his arms and kissed her. When they pulled apart there were tears in his eyes. "Of course I will."

Later as Helga stretched, purring and catlike next to Sam's softly vibrating body, she ran her hand playfully around his taut nipples and down to the soft sandy fuzz on his moist thighs. Hours had passed since they had sat beneath the somber figure of Abraham Lincoln, but the wakefulness persisted as if neither of them could bear to see the night end.

"You're thinner." Sam turned onto his side and began stroking her pale flat stomach. He wriggled closer and with his ear against her navel gazed up at her. She met his gaze with a drowsy, languid smile, but suddenly the teasing was transformed and the licking flames began to taunt her. She watched the dark pupils of his eyes expand as he studied her and felt the arousal intensify. His hand roamed leisurely up to her breast, which in this prone position was nicely flattened so that the nipple dominated, pink and hard like a beacon. He fingered it gently and her breasts began to rise and fall more rapidly as he titillated the tight knot. He took in a deep breath and smiled lazily, rubbing his cheek against her stomach and rolling his head slightly lower.

Helga closed her eyes, feeling the warm waves begin to erupt as he buried his head and his tongue slid forth to make subtle, fine slippery forays.

"Oh, yes!" She arched against him, feeling the flames burning higher as he satisfied his taste for her. He burrowed more deeply, and she stroked his shoulders, writhing against him in a slow, hypnotic rhythm as unhurried and erotic as any they had ever known before.

He placed his hands fanlike over her and raised himself up to look at her face, knowing that the meeting of their eyes was the key that would unleash all their desires. Helga extended her arms out to him, and he leaned on his elbows over her, staring into her luminous blue eyes.

"The announcement goes in tomorrow." He gave her a moist, deep kiss. "No backing out."

"No." Helga shook her head. "I never wanted to back out . . . only not to be afraid. And I'm not."

He ran his hands outward along her delicate shoulder bones and sighed. "You're going to make a hellofa lawyer."

She smiled, feeling him stir rigidly against her. "Why?" Her question was a moan, she was wild to feel him bursting inside her again.

Sam laughed. The mixture of sensuality and humor always amazed and enthralled her. With Sam there were no rules for lovemaking—it seemed to encompass everything.

"You'll have to be a trial lawyer. Catching people off guard, the way you did me tonight with your proposal. You didn't give me a chance."

"I learned that from you." Helga ran her hands lightly over

his strong buttocks, urging him gently, swiveling easily beneath him. "You're the master of the unexpected."

"Well, your timing was perfect." Sam rubbed his nose against hers and began to move slowly in response to her undulating rhythm. "There's just one more thing . . ." He paused, teasing her.

Helga drew in a deep breath as the throbbing grew more insistent. "What's that?"

"If you'll only agree to a wedding in time to get the romantic vote in Texas, I'll be——"

"You devil!" Helga locked her arms around him and with all her strength began to rock his huge body back and forth on top of her until the movement ignited him and he plunged inside her, clasping her behind and driving her against him with an ecstatic recklessness that made her cry out.

How they lasted as long as they did was something they would laugh about in years to come. When they were finally satiated and lying drenched and warm in each others arms, Sam whispered, "Is tomorrow too soon? On the banks of the Potomac . . . just the two of us and some reputable official, of course . . . and perhaps that oriole who brought us together? You've never seen her, have you? She's still there. Babies just hatched. Wouldn't it be fantastic if——"

"*Tomorrow?*" Helga rolled over on her side to look at him. Surely he was teasing again. There were forms, licenses, blood tests. This was the real world not the movies.

Sam smiled enigmatically as if he had read her thoughts. "I'll pull a few strings. After all, there are some benefits a congressman can arrange without being corrupt. And wouldn't you say a private June wedding on the banks of the Potomac sounds pretty aboveboard. What constituent could object to bending a few rules to that end?"

"You've got it all figured out." Helga smiled.

"A nice quiet wedding." Sam ran his forefinger lightly around

277

her parted lips. "What do you say? Just Neal and Marilyn and the kids for witnesses . . . and the oriole, of course."

"How do you know Marilyn and Neal and the kids are free? Don't tell me you slipped out when I wasn't looking and made a convincing phone call?" Helga chuckled as his eyes danced mischievously. "I wouldn't put anything past you."

"It's true"—Sam smiled—"where you are concerned I am unscrupulous. Shall we call them and find out?"

"Sam, it's two thirty in the morning!"

"So . . ." Sam reached for the phone. "They're sure to be home."

"Sam!" Helga reached out a restraining arm.

"Only once in a lifetime can you wake your friends up with news like this!" he bellowed.

"Sam!" Helga collapsed back onto the pillow, laughing.

"I love you." Sam turned and winked at her as he finished dialing. "I love you, I love you . . . Oh, hello, Marilyn. Sorry to wake you at this ungodly hour but Helga insisted I call you right away so you can juggle your schedule to help celebrate our wedding tomorrow . . . down by the river."

Sam paused and turned to Helga. His face was flushed and he drew his mouth into a tight line to keep from laughing. Helga looked at him questioningly as he listened with the same frisky expression. Helga leaned closer, pressing her ear against the receiver. It would be just like him to dial the weather report and pretend to have reached Marilyn and Neal. But no, she could just barely discern Marilyn's voice yammering away as if she received phone calls in the middle of the night every night.

"I don't believe this!" Helga bounced up on her knees and her face glowed as she watched Sam's expression turn serious, then him nodding as Marilyn rattled on.

"Whatever you say," Sam interjected with a smile, then after another lengthy pause, "Sounds great, Marilyn. Talk to you around ten this morning."

He replaced the receiver and turned to Helga with a satisfied grin. "You've got one hell of a good friend."

"Oh, I know . . . but . . . what's going on?" Helga tugged the sheet up around her breasts and sat cross-legged, waiting for an explanation.

"The Sell family will arrive on the banks of Potomac at four thirty with a clergy friend of Marilyn's, flowers, and a Japanese oboist that Marilyn says the two of you went to hear and loved. She'll talk to you in a few hours about your attire. Now"—Sam lowered her gently back onto the pillow—"go to sleep. Tomorrow's our wedding day."

Helga stretched her arms out to him and encircled them lovingly around his neck. "It takes most people months to plan a wedding."

"I've been planning this wedding since the moment I laid eyes on you." Sam stroked her cheek.

"Political hokum," Helga teased.

"Truc," Sam said softly.

"You just phoned Marilyn. One perfectly placed phone call. That's why you're good in Congress."

Sam shook his head. "Not entirely. I mean we are blessed to have Marilyn, who is the world's most efficient and generous social creature. But I did plan it . . . in my heart. I saw us standing side by side on the riverbank . . . about four thirty which was, I believe, about the hour of our original meeting. I swear."

"I believe everything you say." Helga smiled. "Every yarn is from the heart. But what about the Japanese oboist. Did you plan him too?"

Sam's eyes twinkled as he lowered his face and brushed his lips lightly against hers. "There have to be some surprises, don't there?"

"The more the merrier," Helga murmured. "Bring on the surprises!"

Desert Hostage

Diane Dunaway

Behind her is England and her first innocent encounter
with love. Before her is a mysterious land of forbidding
majesty. Kidnapped, swept across the deserts of
Araby, Juliette Barclay sees her past vanish in the
endless, shifting sands. Desperate and defiant, she
seeks escape only to find harrowing danger, to
discover her one hope in the arms of her captor, the
Shiek of El Abadan. Fearless and proud, he alone can
tame her. She alone can possess his soul. Between
them lies the secret that will bind her to him forever, a
woman possessed, a slave of love. **$3.95**

Come Faith, Come Fire

Vanessa Royall

Proud as her aristocratic upbringing, bold as the ancient gypsy blood that ran in her veins, the beautiful golden-haired Maria saw her family burned at the stake and watched her young love, forced into the priesthood. Desperate and bound by a forbidden love, Maria defies the Grand Inquisitor himself and flees across Spain to a burning love that was destined to be free! $2.95

There are strong women. And then there are legends. Knowing one could change your life.

The Enduring Years

Claire Rayner

Hannah Lazar triumphs over grinding poverty, personal tragedy, and two devastating wars to see the children of her shattered family finally re-united. Making her own fortune in a world that tried to break her heart, she endures to become a legend. $3.95

THE WILD ONE

by
MARIANNE HARVEY

bestselling author of *The Dark Horseman*
and *The Proud Hunter*

Proud, beautiful Judith—raised by her stern grandmother on the savage Cornish coast—boldly abandoned herself to one man and sought solace in the arms of another. But only one man could tame her, could match her fiery spirit, could fulfill the passionate promise of rapturous, timeless love.

A Dell Book $2.95   (19207-2)